The Dragon Boy

For Casey and Jack,
We Be Of One Heart!
Donald Samson

The Dragon Boy

Book One

of

The Star Trilogy

by

Donald Samson

Illustrated by

Adam Agee

Dedication

For Caroline, Chris, Daniel, David, Eli, Hannah, Jacob, Jaimen, Jathan, Julia, Julian, Kiefer, Madison, Tasha, Nicholas, Rex, Robin, Sarah, Sonora, Thomas, and Wren. You called the story down so that I might tell it to you.

And for Claudia, the Sunshine in my life.

Printed with support from the Waldorf Curriculum Fund

Published by:
The Association of Waldorf Schools
of North America
Publications Office
38 Main Street
Chatham, NY 12037

Title: *The Dragon Boy*
Author: Donald Samson
Illustrator: Adam Agee
Proofreader: Ann Erwin
Layout: David Mitchell
Cover: Adam Agee

ISBN # 978-1-888365-84-9

Contents

Part I The Orphan

Part II The Dragon's Many Secrets

Part III The Making of a Knight

Part I

The Orphan

Galifalia

Galifalia sat on the worn wooden bench along the outside wall of her small cottage. She was tired and her back was stiff from bending over her rows of cabbages, beans and carrots. She leaned back and let the thick autumn rays of the setting sun warm her. A dangling wisp of graying hair tickled her right cheek. With a reflex repeated countless times, she wiped the dry dirt off on her apron and tucked the hair back underneath her scarf. It was an unusual scarf. It was dyed dark blue and embroidered with golden stars. It looked like something that might appear as part of the crest of a noble house.

She sighed and settled her hands on her lap. She looked at them and smiled quietly. Old and gnarled, covered with dirt from the day's work in the garden, they still served her well. A bit of washing would clean them up. And she sighed again.

She was happy with her simple life. She had her cottage, and although it was hardly more than a hut, it suited her needs. It kept her warm at night, the wind off her back and the rain off her head. She had her garden, and she was content to spend her time tilling the soil and bringing forth abundant vegetables and flowers. It gave her more than she could eat, so she traded her surplus for the grain she could not grow. She knew her health was not to be taken for granted. The day she could not rise to tend her garden was the day to stay in bed and welcome the long sleep. But on such an afternoon as this, with the autumn setting sun warming her cheeks and the garden looking vibrant and green, the end of her life felt too far away to consider for more than a fleeting moment.

And there was peace in the land. She knew this would last long past her death. She felt deep contentment with the role she had played. That memory prompted her to bless each morning and give thanks each evening. At the request of King Pell, she had recently completed an account of her adventure. It had been difficult to pull together all of the jumbled memories. At times she was uplifted by joy and at other moments overcome with grief at the remembering. Now that this last task was done, she looked forward to peaceful days in her old age.

And, of course, she had her geese. She looked out over the garden at their white, feathery forms as they rummaged for snails among the rows of vegetables. When her great adventure had begun, she could only dream of one day having her own flock. Now here they were in her own garden. They were good companions, faithful and alert.

"Good evening, Galifalia."

She looked up, shaken out of her reverie. How had someone walked up to her gate without her geese objecting? This was quite peculiar. They were very protective of their garden. She saw they were all on high alert, necks craning, red beaks jutting upwards. But they did not make any noise louder than meek, hoarse squawks. This was very odd, indeed.

Whoever had spoken was standing at her gate with the setting sun behind him. She shielded her eyes to see the visitor. She did not recognize the voice, yet something in it had been oddly familiar.

"Good evening to you," she responded, squinting into the bright light.

There stood a man, cloaked and hooded, though he wore his hood back on his head, revealing his face. She could make out a shaggy mane of grizzled hair, a large gray beard, a beak of a nose, a jutting brow and two eyes as fierce as sparks flying out of a fire.

"Good evening," she repeated. Strangers were common enough in her life. Even the occasional dwarf or elf dropped by to pay his respects. Most folk, though, stopped at her gate and gawked at her as if she were some rare specimen in the king's zoo. Rarely did any of them ever speak to her, let alone address her by name.

"A pleasant evening it is," the stranger said with a mysterious smile. He seemed to realize the effect he had on her and was enjoying it.

"Are you new in these parts?" She did not think she knew him, yet his voice and his looks reminded her of someone from long ago. An uncomfortable memory stirred in her heart and sent a sudden thrill through her whole body.

"I've been here before, yet it was when you only dreamed of having your own garden and a fine flock of geese. Do you remember?"

What a strange comment. How could he know so much about her without her remembering him? She studied his jutting nose and those eyes, so calm and at the same time full of mischief. Uncommonly black eyes, like the opening of a deep well. And now she noticed his lips, unusually full and red for an old man. A strange memory was welling up in her breast. Galifalia sat up straighter.

"Come inside the gate," she said. "You obviously know me better than I know you. You've come looking for me, it seems."

"My Lady," he began, "I have always appreciated how you don't beat around the bush." He stepped smoothly inside the gate. *Pretty limber for an old fellow,* she thought to herself. From the way he held his body, he looked like he was carrying something underneath his cloak. What did he want to keep hidden? Her gaggle of geese flowed towards the gate, beaks still raised threateningly. As he entered, they made way for him, something she had never seen them do before. They made soft peeping sounds, as if they knew him. "The years have been kind to you," the stranger continued.

She nodded in appreciation, but said nothing. What was he up to? And how many years ago had he known her?

"Are you still eager for an adventure?" he asked suddenly.

When the stranger spoke these words, recognition jolted her. Indeed, had she not lived for years certain that the man standing before her was no longer among the living, she would have known him the moment he first spoke.

"You're alive." Her voice was hoarse and choked. She was nearly panting with shock.

"And why shouldn't I be? Life is much too interesting to let go of that easily or quickly."

"But back then…" her voice faded away and she shook her head in disbelief.

"Back then," the stranger continued for her, "I was already an old man. Is that it?" He smiled broadly.

"Aye," she said, looking at him with awe. "I was a young, wild filly ready to take on the world and you were an old man. An old man with a young man's lips. You said you would take the adventure on yourself, if it were not for your age. I thought certainly… " and again her voice trailed off.

"That I was long dead."

She shook her head in agreement.

"Well, let's just say that in my profession, one can age younger, so to speak. You know yourself that not everything on the inside appears as it is on the outside."

Indeed, she had learned the truth of that. She had met things within her own self that she did not know were there until they were called upon.

"How long has it been, Aga?" she asked warily.

"By my reckoning, Thursday next will be exactly forty-two years since your last great adventure began."

The way he said that troubled her. There was something in his voice that hinted it had been only her most recent adventure, but not her final one.

"Aga, what brings you back to me after so long?"

"Well," he began, stepping lightly up the path to stand before her. The geese followed behind him, nipping gently at his trailing cloak. "That all depends on whether you welcome into your life again what I bring with me. Do you?"

The last time he had asked her something similar. She had said yes, and very soon afterwards, and for a long time after that, she had regretted her answer. Yet, in the end, all had worked out remarkably well. She was glad for what had happened, as frightening, strange and overwhelming as it had been.

"Aga, I am no longer young. I have enough energy to tend my garden and look after my geese."

"Oh, I am well aware of the limitations age lays upon us," he sighed with a great grin. His brown face wrinkled up like a shriveled apple, and his chuckling shook his whole body. "But is that really all the strength you have? Are you sure there isn't a bit more than for weeding a garden and chasing vagrant geese?"

"That depends what it is," she answered quickly. This Aga was a tricky one, yet she was tickled by the game he was playing with her.

"You never married again, Galifalia." He said it so bluntly. It struck like an icy wind killing the blossom on the stalk.

She was silent for a moment. This touched a sensitive, painful scar. The old, deep wounded sadness began to rise up in her heart and she paused a moment to push it back down before answering.

"I couldn't, not after…" but she was not able to continue.

"I understand," Aga said soothingly, laying a comforting hand on her shoulder. "I heard about it. Although I was far away, I heard all about it. I only wish I had been close enough to help."

"There was little you could have done, unless you know remedies against death." She glanced at Aga and grunted. "And perhaps you do. Anyway, for awhile, I blamed you that I lost him. After all, it was your adventure." She paused to see what the effect of her words on him would be. He stood there, impassive, waiting for her to continue. "The more time I had to think about it, though, and I've had over thirty years to think about it, I realized that I would have likely never seen him again after the market place if it hadn't been for you. It was for his sake, not yours, that I continued in the adventure after I saw where it was leading."

"So you were able to forgive me?"

"I became thankful to you," she sighed.

"And you never remarried."

"How could I? You knew him; it was you who brought us together."

"I knew him well, very well. And I depended on him. No one, not even I, expected you would play such a role. It was his skill and competence I was relying on. I had trained him myself, you know. You were there to fill out the company, to fulfill the prophecy. I tell you, my Lady, I never guessed the adventure to go the way it did. But then, adventures rarely do."

They both grew silent, lost in memories. For Galifalia, the memory of the man she had loved was so vivid that she half expected him to walk up to the gate any moment and greet them. More than once she had waited for that to happen, so powerfully did his memory live within her.

Aga shifted what he was carrying beneath his cloak. This caught Galifalia's eye and she looked at him suspiciously."Aga, did you want to bring me another husband?" And she laughed at her own jest.

"No," he responded, unable to totally repress a smile. "Not a husband. I will not try to do that a second time. No, not that. But since in your grief you missed the chance to raise a family..."

Galifalia interrupted him, "He died of a fever, you know. My son."

"Is that what they told you?"

"They swore to me he died of a fever," she insisted. "I was in mourning for my husband and beside myself. Then the fever came. Many died. That is why I had to leave. I couldn't bear to stay in that land after the death of the two people I most loved."

"Well, well," Aga said. "I have a better understanding now why I find you here."

Galifalia eyed him suspiciously. "What are you keeping from me?"

"You know, Gali, since you never remarried, you missed one of the great joys of life. I just thought you would like a second chance."

Galifalia opened her eyes wide at the implications of Aga's words. Suddenly, she was certain she knew what Aga was carrying concealed underneath his cloak.

"You can't be serious," she shrieked and then began laughing. "Aga, what are you doing, walking around the countryside with a babe on your arm? Do you have no better place to land this orphan than on my doorstep?"

Aga's face broadened into a big smile and his eyes sparkled.

"As a matter of fact," he said, "I do *not* know of any better place for this orphan of mine. And my circle of friends and acquaintances is great indeed. This is a special orphan, and I have always insisted that you are a special woman, my Lady. The two of you will fit very well together."

"Aga, I'm an old woman," Galifalia protested.

"Can't be helped," Aga said. "If I were looking for youth, I would go elsewhere. I'm looking for a home. I am looking for a particular home. Are you interested?"

Galifalia looked at him sharply and frowned. Here she had been counting her blessings, content with her quiet, predictable life. Suddenly she was being offered quite a different future. The more she thought about it, the warmer she grew. Perhaps a child was the very thing she needed to give her life more meaning. A familiar and rebellious voice within her protested that predictability is boring and lacking all the spirit of a life well lived. It was remarkably easy to forget that she had not been looking for more meaning and had been until now very satisfied.

"Let me see the waif," she finally said in a gruff voice.

Aga slowly and carefully opened his cloak and exposed a tiny child asleep in the crook of his arm. It was warmly wrapped in brightly woven shawls so that only its ruddy cheeks and button nose were visible.

"It's small," she whispered. She studied the child; its lips were like a puckered cherry and there was a dimple in its chin. She knew that she could argue all she wanted. Her heart had already spoken yea.

"It's a boy, isn't it?"

"Aye, my Lady, 'tis a manchild."

"I would have preferred you had brought me a daughter," she said grumpily. "I'm not sure I know much about raising a boy. At least a girl I could, I could…" she was at a loss for words.

"A girl you could raise to become a wild, rebellious filly like you were yourself, peddling garlic and onions in the marketplace, and pinching what you couldn't afford or didn't care to buy," Aga finished for her. She snuffed at his teasing, and he continued. "I have no concerns you will know what to do with a boy."

"I shall not see him to manhood," she protested with a sigh. "I'm old, and I have not learned your art of growing old younger."

Aga studied her for a moment and then said in a flat tone, "What he has of you will be enough."

"Where is he from?" She looked at Aga sharply. She suddenly remembered with whom she was dealing. Everything from Aga carried untold mysteries and secrets that were only revealed when it was too late to back out.

As if reading her thoughts and sensing her hesitation, Aga said quickly, "I assure you that the child will bring you nothing but joy and pleasure. I have only one request to make."

"Ah, here it comes," she said knowingly.

"It's harmless, Galifalia, I assure you. You would do it without my asking. I want you to make sure that as the boy grows up, Star gets to know his smell."

"Star? I should have known it would have something to do with him. Why Star?"

"Do you really want to know more? If you know less, it will stay simple."

"For me simple," she grunted. "But not for the child, right?"

"This child's fate is already far from simple, as you could guess by the fact that he's an orphan. Let his raising at least be simple. I fear the rest of his life will not be."

"Always full of secrets," she grumbled.

"I will tell you if you really insist, but I would rather not. For your own peace of mind."

"My own peace of mind," she snorted. "When were you ever so considerate of my peace of mind?"

"Then let me say that it's better for the boy if you don't have any secrets to keep from him," the wizard said with mysterious finality.

Galifalia reached out and took the babe from Aga's arm. He was so small and light. A bunch of carrots pulled from her garden would weigh more. He stirred a bit but remained asleep. She studied the tiny sleeping figure as if she would be able to read the answer to her many questions in his small angel-face.

"Where is he from, Aga?" she asked again. "If he comes with you, I can be assured that this is no ordinary orphan."

"What orphan is ordinary?" he replied lightly. "Let's just say that there is a remote valley far to the north and it is better for him to be here than to remain there."

"Why do you take such a special interest in him?"

"Let that be my business. Look, if it will put you any more at ease, I will come on occasion to visit him. The day you complain it has been enough, I'll take him off your hands again. Will that help?"

She sighed and then she scowled at him, "What difference would it make anyway? The day I cry I've had enough, Aga will be nowhere to be seen and nowhere to be found." The child stirred and she looked at him. "Oh, bless the babe," she muttered gazing at his tiny face. He was so small, helpless and innocent. Yet knowing Aga, his story held many mysteries.

"Me with a child!" she suddenly burst out at the thought of it. "Aga, people will talk."

"When did they ever stop talking about you, my Lady? It will be one more mystery that shrouds your life. If you like, I'll make sure the town gossip catches sight of me before I leave. Then concoct whatever story you like to tickle their wagging tongues. I figured you would like that part of it."

A child. An hour before she would have sworn that nothing was missing from her life. Yet she knew if she let Aga wander forth with this boy, she would feel as if a part of herself had been ripped away. She turned to gaze a moment out over her garden.

"Stay for supper," she said at last. "Stay and gossip with me. I have a dozen questions to ask you."

"I would be delighted," he said. "I can help you set up a little nest for your new guest."

"Guest, indeed," she sniffed and looked at him reprovingly. She handed him back the baby. Aga raised his bushy eyebrows in question. "Take the waif. I've got to wash," she said simply. "Go on inside. This time of year it grows cold quickly once the sun is down. Stir the fire, warm up the soup. Make yourself useful and mind the pot doesn't boil over."

In this simple and sudden way, Galifalia's life changed remarkably for a second time. The first time had been in her youth, and now again in her old age. By morning, Aga had gone his solitary way and left behind what she at first thought was nothing but a bundle of responsibility. Before the week was over, though, she had rearranged her life so completely that she knew that Aga had brought her a blessing in disguise.

The boy turned out to be very content and happy with whatever the old woman offered him of love, food and comfort. Love she lavished him with, and comfort was in accordance with her own sparse lifestyle. She made sure he had enough to eat and was kept warm and dry. The boy was very satisfied. He had a warm glow about him that brightened up the old woman's heart. Her joints seemed to ache less, and his presence gave her back some of her youthful joy and vitality.

People did talk, of course, as she had expected. But it never turned malicious. At least, nothing ever reached her ears. Respect for her age and the deeds of her youth still trailed behind her. She carried such an aura of mystery that folk were ready to believe that this was some fairy child entrusted to her in the same way the Great Task had been entrusted to her when she was young. After all, had she not traveled in the company of elves and dwarfs on that journey? If they now chose to entrust a child to her care, who were they to get involved?

The boy grew and thrived under her caring hands and watchful eyes. Aga was true to his word and would appear at the most unexpected moments to remain a day or two to check whether Galifalia had had enough.

"I thought I might take the boy back," he suggested during one visit. "Would that suit you, my Lady?" The boy, a toddler by now, was banging a wooden spoon noisily against the seat of a chair, while chanting some sort of gibberish with full-lunged enthusiasm.

The old woman turned on Aga with a ferocious, protective fire in her eyes. "You just keep your hands off the boy. He's mine; he stays here. You gave him and you do not get him back again. Understand?"

Aga smiled and winked at her. "Hey, no need to breathe fire at me. I was just wondering if he had become too much of a burden for you."

At that moment they both gave a start as the chair the boy had been banging toppled over, and he let out a little roar of victory and continued banging at the legs.

"Already fighting dragons, I see," muttered Aga, watching the boy intently. Galifalia laughed and with her skirts flying swooped him up. She buried her face in his tender belly, and he dissolved in a flood of giggles.

"He's a spirited boy," she sighed happily, holding him tightly to her breast. "And he is mine," she concluded, staring at Aga defiantly, as if daring him to challenge her.

Aga just chuckled. "Well, I am glad to see that the two of you have taken to one another so well. Soup ready yet? I'm famished."

Another time, about a year later, as they sat on the worn wooden bench that ran along the side of the cottage, watching the boy splashing in puddles and chasing grasshoppers in the garden, Aga had another question. "He's growing well, my Lady."

"Did you expect different?" she glared at him.

"Now don't take offense at my compliment. Are you growing cranky in your old age?"

"Sorry. I thought I heard something else in that statement. A question."

"So, then, tell me what the question is, and you will save me having to ask it."

"You want to know if I have let Star see him."

"And have you?"

"I haven't gone out of my way to do it," she answered, looking at him sharply. "I never said I would go to the compound. It's not easy for me, you know, seeing him all cooped up like that."

Aga looked out over the garden, trying not to react to her challenge. He so enjoyed how she went about things in her own way. It irritated him and thrilled him all in one. He took a deep breath before asking, "So what have you done?"

"Well, I haven't missed any opportunity to show him at the official processions. There are several every year, you know, and I attend them all, of course. I figure that should be enough to please you."

Aga studied the old woman sitting beside him. Still doing things her own way. But that, after all, was why she was best suited to take care of the boy. "So, what is Star's reaction?"

"Not much. I don't know what you expected. I hold him up and Star smells him. Each time, he comes over and greets me," she paused briefly, her eyes downcast, reliving the moment. "He is still magnificent, you know. That has never changed. Never will. Anyway, after greeting me, he smells the boy."

Aga nodded slowly and tugged at his long gray beard. "That's enough for me. It will have to be enough for Star."

"What's the mystery all about, Aga?" she asked in a low voice. "Don't you think I have a right to know? What does this boy have to do with Star?"

The old man sat there, silent a moment, considering his choices.

"Well," he answered slowly, "you do have a right to know. You actually said it yourself when first I brought the boy to you. Tell me, how well is the boy received by your neighbors, by your friends?"

Galifalia laughed openly at the question. Aga looked at her with raised eyebrows, but he had to feign surprise at her guffaw because he knew her answer already.

"The neighbors treat him courteously, yet they have their own to care for and worry about. I'm called to help with a fever or a woman in childbed. They ask me to bless their children, so I do it and they seem satisfied. For the rest, they keep their distance and leave us both alone. They are too narrow-minded to ever forget that the boy just showed up one day. As for my friends...well, they are all dead, except for you, and Star, if you can count him. There's still Garth, but he rarely leaves the compound and less often visits me. I've outlived most all the others. We keep to ourselves, the boy and I. It's better that way."

"So there's your answer," said Aga nodding his head. "You said you would never see him to manhood. We will have to rely on Star to do it for you."

"I'll never understand the way of wizards," she said shaking her head.

"And it's a good thing, too," replied Aga laughing in his beard as the boy came beaming over to him and placed in his hands a large, wet, messy mud-pie.

Chapter Two

The Compound

The boy stood before the great wooden gates and waited. They towered immensely high above his head. They had been crafted from sawn planks as thick as a warrior's fist and sanded smooth. He was fascinated by the intricate designs the uneven rings made in the grain of the wood. Every morning the height of the gates awoke awe in his soul. Their very size spoke silently about the creature that was kept safely behind them.

The sun was just rising at his back and he could feel it breaking the chill of the early dawn hours. He continued to study the gates to distract himself from the cold which penetrated his thin, frayed tunic.

Soon I'll stop shivering, and this thought comforted him. He played restlessly with the ragged edge of his sleeve and continued to admire the irregular concentric circles in the wooden planks. His eyes fell upon the small door that was cut into the gate and served as an informal entry. He was puzzled by that door. Its bottom edge was cut at a height level with a man's knee, rather than flush with the ground. It was also not very high. In order to pass through, a grown man would have to step up and bend down at the same time. He wondered why it had been made so difficult to pass through. He had pondered this every day as he stood waiting. He wondered if today would be different than all of the previous days, than all of the previous weeks. He wondered if that door would open a second time.

Today, though, he felt the thrill of a small triumph. He had finally solved the riddle of the door. If the compound should ever be attacked, he reasoned, and the door forced open, the defenders on the inside could easily behead the soldiers trying to enter through the narrow door in single file. By virtue of the low lintel, the invaders' heads would be already bowed and necks exposed. The reasoning was great, he knew, except for one essential point. No king, prince or great warrior hero would ever attack the dragon compound. In the grand city of Nogardia, the standing joke in every tavern was that Nogardia needed no guarding. The rough men of the streets sniggered at this and, at the same time, derived a certain pride from it. He pondered this to pass the time while waiting.

Suddenly, with the dull thunk of a bolt being drawn, the door opened. Although it was what he had been waiting for, it took him completely by surprise, and his heart nearly leapt up into his mouth. Two men, one following the other, stepped awkwardly through the narrow opening. The first was a lanky, loose-limbed fellow whose curly brown hair fell about an equally brown face. He came out smiling and looking hopeful. He wore a brown tunic with a dragon emblazoned in red on his breast. This was the guard; the boy had come to know him well by now.

"There he is, sir," the guard said, gesturing at the boy. "Still comes every day, asks for you every day, two moons now. You told me, when it's been two moons to tell you."

The other man had pulled himself through the small opening of the door and was staring keenly at the boy. He was short and squarely built. He looked immensely strong and he inspected the boy with piercing, dark eyes. He had bushy eyebrows, a shaggy head of hair and a beard that looked like a hedge in which birds would be likely to take refuge. He was no longer young, gray streaking both his hair and beard. He was casually dressed in a rough tunic tied at the waist that looked like it was made for equally rough work. His dirty boots looked sturdy and well-worn.

"So this is the lad," he grunted. The man studied the boy steadily, looking him up and down. The boy stood his ground silently, patiently waiting to be addressed. He wanted to return the man look for look, but the stare was too intense, and after only a moment or two he had to avert his eyes. He felt suddenly awkward and shy in his frayed, torn tunic. He squared his shoulders and forced himself to look the man in the eyes again.

"He could use a washing. And a brushing. Hasn't seen a new tunic in awhile," the man commented at last. "D'ye think he knows any bed better than the straw behind a farmer's barn?" The boy self-consciously brushed his matted, tangled hair out of his face with the back of his hand. He pulled at the strands of hay he could feel sticking out. He held his torn sleeve behind his back.

"There's not much of him," the man muttered at last to the guard. He sounded disappointed.

"No, sir, he is slight of build, that's sure. I told you that from the outset. But he has a stubborn spirit within him. Every morning just before daybreak, he knocks and asks for you. Every morning without fail, two moons now." The guard stood up his straightest, as if finally freeing himself of a duty, saying, "So now I've told you, just as you asked."

"Well, let's see what he's made of." Then, turning his full attention to the boy, as if they had been speaking a language the boy did not know, he asked, "Well, lad, what did you want to see me about?"

"Sir," the boy began, clearing his throat, trying his best to look calmly into those fierce eyes. "Sir, are you the Dragon Master?"

"Aye," returned the man with a gruff laugh. "That I am. Garth, the Dragon Master. Been so these past twenty-three years."

"Sir, if you be the Dragon Master, I've come to ask you to take me on as a stall boy."

Garth's wide mouth broke into a broad, toothy grin and he laughed outright.

"Boy," he said loudly, as if the street urchin in front of him would not understand if he spoke quietly. "If it's just a close look at him you're after, just say so and no hard feelings. You're not the first boy come hungry for a closer look at him. I understand that hunger. It ate at me, too, boy and man. I tend to him daily and I still haven't had my fill. You've stood here every day, it seems, two moons. That persistence earns a closer look. You can even touch him, if you dare. I promise," he ended in a low growl, "I won't let him eat you." And his grin was about as wide as his face.

"That's not what I'm after," said the boy quietly, looking down and studying his dirty hands and broken fingernails. Then looking up he added quickly, "I've come asking to be a stall boy. I want to come every morning and work within the compound." Then he looked down again at his hands, fearful of being denied even a closer look.

Garth's face grew serious again and his smile faded. "Aren't you afraid of Star?" He asked in a low, threatening grumble.

"No, sir." The boy looked up quickly but stopped there. He wanted to tell him that he was in love with Star, from the very first time he had seen him, which, in fact, was one of his earliest memories. But he was not sure Garth would understand that, so he kept silent. He merely mumbled again, "No, sir."

Garth studied this snip of a boy, standing shyly, yet unflinchingly before him. "He's big, boy," he said at last in a harsh whisper, his eyes flashing. He bent over and put his face right into the boy's to give more emphasis to his words. "You think you know what big is until you stand before him. Then you realize your idea of big was too small. He can flick you across the river with his toenail without even knowing you were there. He's a mountain on the move."

"I know that, sir." The boy said, taking half a step backwards; Garth had bent so near that his beard tickled the boy's face. He could think of nothing better to say. He had no clue what the Dragon Master was talking about. He figured he was just trying to scare him away, and he was not going to be scared away. He had lived too long on the streets and been teased, bullied and chased by worse than the man before him, fierce eyes or not. He took a deep breath and said firmly and simply, "Sir, I want to serve in the compound as a stall boy. It's really important."

His voice sounded so small to him, in front of those immense gates. He reckoned this was it, that he had given the wrong answer and he would be sent away now. It didn't matter, though; he would be back again the next day. The call of the dragon was too strong for him to give up. He vowed inwardly to stand there every morning until they let him in on his terms.

Garth continued to study him. As if those fierce eyes could read the boy's soul, he said suddenly, "Won't do any good to send him away. He'll just be back tomorrow. Let's get it over with. I have a long list of things to get done today."

Without another word, Garth turned and disappeared through the small door in the gate. His shoulders were wider than the opening, so he turned slightly sideways before slipping through. As Garth turned away, the boy saw that his lips were pressed together and he seemed to be frowning.

The boy could scarcely believe what he had just heard and stood there staring after Garth's retreating figure with wide eyes. The guard regarded him with a friendly smile. "Go on, boy. This is what you've waited for." And he motioned with a nick of his head that the boy should follow the Dragon Master. "I'm glad for you, boy. But if you don't get moving, that door will be shut in your face again."

The boy quickly shook off the shock. He just about flew headfirst through the opening. He saw Garth's receding figure striding across the hardened ground away from the gate. The Dragon Master was muttering in his beard as he walked. The boy ran to catch up with him and heard the last few words as he neared him. "…the length of three breaths, *at most*, before he runs screaming to be let out." As the boy trotted along half a stride behind, he wondered if Garth meant him.

They were walking towards the edge of a thick stand of trees which stood tall and leafy, catching the morning sun in their tops. Large birds fluttered noisily among the upper branches, their twittering arguments echoing in the morning air. The boy caught a glimpse of a red tiled roof of some huge building flashing between the branches. As they came around the first trees, he saw from its shape that it was a barn. Not an ordinary barn, such as every farm in the region boasted. Those barns were modest structures with thatched roofs, just large enough to hold a cow and a donkey. This building was so large that it seemed to the boy to fill up the horizon and rise half way to the sky. Its roof was not thatched, but of the finest red tiles, such as the boy had seen only on buildings rising up above the castle walls. But tiles were only for the king's houses. And this was a barn from the looks of it, in spite of its immense size.

"That's Star's home." The guard had caught up with him. "He lives in there. In there now." He was watching the boy, looking for some reaction. The boy was excited, but he forced himself to walk steadily and breathe calmly. Suddenly the guard said even more quietly, as if not wanting Garth to hear, "Boy, I think you're going to do all right."

The boy glanced up at the guard and a smile flickered across his brown face. Of course he was going to be all right. He had made it in, hadn't he?

They rounded the long side of the building. The whole shorter end of the barn was without a wall. It was one immense open door, from ground to roof, side to side and corner to corner. Coming around the side and looking into the depths of that monumental building, the boy stopped in his tracks. He was not prepared for what he saw. Before him, lying on his belly, his neck outstretched, chin on the ground, so close that within twenty more steps the boy could reach out and touch him, was Star. He was indeed the largest living thing the boy had ever seen. And every bit as big as a mountain.

"That's him, boy." Garth had come over to stand next to him. "That's who you came to see."

The dragon had been napping. At the noise of their footsteps crossing the dirt, one pointed ear swiveled in their direction and he half raised a scaly eyelid. His dark emerald eye peered lazily towards the visitors. Suddenly both eyes were open and they darted to the side and followed something. Then the boy heard the footsteps and realized another man had joined them.

"Who's the boy, Garth?" he asked.

"Morning, Mali. Some street urchin. Wanted a closer look. Soon as he gets it, he'll move on."

The boy felt the dragon's eyes scan the three familiar men and then settle upon him. He had heard old men tell tales that the dragon's gaze had a force all of its own. It was as if two mighty arms had reached around the boy's back and had begun gently yet irresistibly tugging him forward to come closer to that immense head. The boy took a halting step forward. Then another. He did not know how to resist. He was not at all sure that he wanted to.

"That's the dragon's charm," muttered Garth behind him. "It has him firmly."

A few steps more, and the boy stood before the dragon, directly in front of the right nostril, which was so large that if he stooped a bit, his head and shoulders could easily slip into its cavernous opening. He felt the dragon's hot breath in rhythmical waves scouring his body. He felt himself pulled irresistibly forward by the dragon's gentle and powerful in-breath, nearly pulling him off balance.

He's sniffing me, the boy thought. *He's learning my scent.*

Then the dragon opened his mouth, wide, wide, wider, large enough to drive a carriage and six into, exposing row upon row of razor-sharp teeth, as if the boy had stumbled upon a mad reaper's storehouse of scythes. The dragon's tongue was thick and fire red, the throat was as wide as a tunnel and as dark as a well. For a brief moment, a shock of fear seized the boy that the dragon was about to eat him. Just as quickly, though, he noticed the tongue curl and he relaxed with the realization, *He's yawning.*

"Amazing," Garth muttered behind him. "How he holds his ground."

The dragon's breath mystified the boy. In spite of his past experience, he was ready for it to smell disgusting, of rotted flesh or something equally unnerving. Instead, he found it to be delightful, exactly as he remembered it. Star's breath smelled sweetly of flowering trees in high spring.

Star closed his mouth with a loud crack as he snapped his jaws together and his teeth met. It was the sound of a large branch breaking in the ferocity of a winter storm, and the boy stumbled back a step from the force of the movement. The dragon continued to regard the boy calmly, his chin resting on the ground.

The boy looked over this mountain of a dragon. He was completely awed by the scaly skin that stretched out from him towards the endlessly distant tail. The scales had a greenish hue overall, but when the light hit them in a particular way, they shone with the colors of the rainbow. In fact, the dragon looked like a moving, walking, living rainbow. The boy returned his gaze to the head. He realized with joy and relief that he had not loved the dragon in vain. Star was quite worthy of his love and more than fulfilled his every expectation and daydream.

"He's beautiful," he sighed.

The gentle sound of chimes blowing in the wind filled the air. It was coming from the dragon's throat.

"I'll be," said an astonished voice behind the boy. "He's purring."

"Well," said the guard softly. "Looks like Star has a new stall boy."

Chapter Three

The Stall Boys

They were standing beside a closet built into the wall of the barn, just large enough to hold some buckets and mops. Workers were scurrying about their business, passing them by, giving the boy sidelong looks. Garth had a bucket in each hand and was looking at the boy. He was trying to figure something out. He knit his thick brows and frowned.

"I have to hand it to you, you're more than you seem. I've watched seasoned warriors, I mean prime fighting men who have soaked themselves in the blood of their foes on the field of battle, I've seen those same men faint dead away at one of Star's yawns. I did not see you even flinch. Mali thinks you were even enjoying it."

"He's really very beautiful," the boy said softly. The encounter with Star had left him dazed. This was the most coherent thing he could manage to say.

"Yes, I know," muttered Garth. "You said that before." He arched his eyebrows and laughed in exasperation. Then with an awkward gesture, he simply handed the buckets to the boy.

"Anyway, if you want to be one of the stall boys, you'll start with these. And of course the brooms, plenty of brooms. And you'll need to know where the mops are. And scrubbers. You'll find closets like this one up and down the inside walls of the barn with plenty of each."

The boy could not shake off the light-headedness he was feeling. He could hardly believe that everything he had hoped and yearned for had so suddenly come true. He wondered if Garth was waiting for him to say something. He looked down the long wall of the barn which faded away in the feeble light that filtered through the few high windows. He opened his mouth to speak, and then closed it again. He just did not know what to say.

Garth filled in the silence. "The dragon is led away every day for a wash and scrub in the river. While he's gone, it will be your job to sweep the floor and lay down a new bed of straw. Portions of the barn are floored in stone. Those you'll mop down after you've swept them, before putting down new straw. Think you can handle it?"

The boy looked around at the size of the space he was going to be cleaning. The barn was truly immense. It echoed with the different work being carried on beyond the dragon where he could not see. Garth sensed his hesitation.

"Don't worry," he said with a wry smile. "You'll not be working alone. It goes quicker than you think, and there are plenty of other chores as well. I'll have Mali introduce you to the other boys. Star loves a clean barn when he comes back from his bath, and the stall boys work to keep him happy. Mali!"

Garth suddenly left the boy holding the buckets. He turned on his heel and walked away down the building towards the great gaping entrance. The boy turned and faced the flank of the dragon twenty feet away. Even in the dim light the dragon's scales showed rich tones of green and turquoise. His immense sides slowly rose and sank with his great even breaths. The boy could only continue to murmur to himself, "Beautiful. A really beautiful dragon."

As he stood there admiring the dozing dragon, the boy suddenly sensed that someone was watching him. He forced his gaze away from the dragon. The young man he had seen earlier was now standing a few feet away.

"The Dragon Master told me to show you around. He said you are a new stall boy." Mali stood there sizing up the boy. He liked what he saw and smiled slightly. Mali was a good ten years older than the boy, almost a man by the telltale fuzz on his chin. He had a pleasant, friendly face with broad cheeks. He also wore a tunic with the dragon emblem emblazoned across it. The boy sensed this was someone he could trust and go to with questions.

"You look like you could use a good meal," Mali said. "And a wash, for that matter. We'll get you some new clothes as well. Food first, though. Come with me."

Mali said this as a fact that needed taking care of and not with any intention to shame him. He was glad of that. He was so tired of being taunted and judged by how he looked. The time when his hair was not a nest of tangles and his clothes were clean and mended was still very alive in his memory.

Mali turned and began walking down the length of the long barn, moving towards the tail of the dragon. He took several steps and then turned around to see if the boy was following him. The boy had not moved. He continued to stand there with the buckets still in his hands staring after Mali.

"It's all right," he chuckled. "You can leave the buckets and the brooms there for now. They'll be waiting for you when you come back. You don't have to start work yet. Let's get you settled in first. For now, come with me."

The boy shook himself out of his reverie. He was still trying to get used to the fact that he had not only been admitted to the dragon compound, but that he was now a stall boy. He put the buckets down and hurried to catch up with Mali. *Food,* he thought to himself. *That sounds very good.* He realized how hungry he was.

They walked together following the wall of the building. Mali asked in a matter of fact tone, "When is the last time you had a good meal?"

"Early this morning," the boy lied. He had eaten exactly two small scraps of dried meat, really more gristle than meat, and one fistful of old bread that had tasted moldy.

"Well, then," Mali said, watching the boy carefully, "join us for our morning breakfast meal. It's nothing special, other than it comes every day."

"I'd be glad to," replied the boy, trying not to let the excitement over getting something to eat show in his voice.

As they continued to walk, the mountain of dragon beside them grew gradually shorter, as the dragon's body tapered off towards its immense tail. It was constantly in movement, twitching and thumping on the ground.

"Keep an eye on the tail," Mali commented coolly as they passed by. "It can have a mind of its own sometimes."

The boy saw what he meant. As they passed it, the boy thought the tail resembled a huge snake, as if there could ever be a snake as thick as a tree trunk with great spikes growing out of its back.

At the back of the great barn were a number of doors and open storerooms. Other staff were going to and fro about their business. They all wore tunics with the emblem of the dragon emblazoned on the breast. Many of them looked at the boy curiously as they went about their jobs. He saw a number of boys who looked to be about his own age. They eyed him more closely than the others. Mali walked up to a double door on the right and went through, the boy close on his heels.

They came into another room, this one also quite large, although modest compared to the barn they had just left. It was filled with rows of tables, some with small groups of staff sitting and enjoying a meal together.

"Let's start with some soup," Mali said walking up to one of the windows nearest to them.

Start with soup? thought the boy with wonder. If he ever saw as much as half a bowl of thin soup for his midday meal he considered it a holiday.

At the window Mali greeted a worker who waved to him from the kitchen beyond. He winked at the woman ladling soup into bowls. "What's good today, Nellie?" he asked.

"It's all good, Mali. Since when did you become particular? You're on the early side, aren't you?"

"I have a hungry new friend here," he explained.

"Who's the boy?" She glanced at him sharply and then went back to stirring her pot.

"New stall boy," Mali said in a matter of fact tone.

The boy watched Nellie's eyebrows arc in surprise. "New stall boy? Garth know about this?"

"Garth's the one who let him in."

"Well, I wonder what else is going to change around here." She glanced again at the boy and chuckled. "It looks like he brought the stall with him."

"Give him a few days and he'll learn to leave the hay and dirt where they belong," Mali replied. He gave the boy a big wink and a friendly grin. "Give us a couple of bowls with some bread, too. We're hungry."

Nellie handed over two bowls of steaming soup and two great hunks of bread.

"Over here," said Mali with a nick of his head. They went a few paces and sat at a long, roughly hewn table away from everyone else.

The boy sat staring at his bowl. It was brimming with vegetables in a buttery broth, and, by its earthy smell, he could tell there was some barley in there as well. He still held the bread in his hand. It was fragrant with a thick crust. Above all else, it was not a week old. The boy could not recall the last time he had been able to get fresh bread. What he was used to eating was either rock hard or slightly green.

"Hey, aren't you hungry?" Mali sat there with his spoon poised looking at the boy intently. "Go ahead. You can eat. It's good food, and there's more after that if you're still hungry." The boy had a surprised look on his face, and then he smiled broadly. He tore a big bite out of the bread and had to force himself to chew. He wanted to swallow it whole. It tasted so delicious and he was voracious.

It did not take long before the boy sat there in front of an empty bowl which he had wiped clean with the last bite of his bread.

"You eat like a hungry dragon," Mali commented.

The boy was embarrassed by this, but Mali smiled at him so warmly that he could not resist smiling as well. Then a question occurred to him. "What do you feed him?"

"Who? Star? Nothing, of course. 'Hungry as a dragon' is just a phrase, you know. Refers to wild dragons." Seeing the boy's confused expression, Mali explained. "Star's a Luck Dragon, you know."

This did not explain anything to the boy. Mali wondered if everyone else in the kingdom was as ignorant of their good fortune as this boy appeared to be. It had been a long time since he had spent any significant time away from the compound.

"Look," he began, choosing his words carefully. "Star's a Luck Dragon. He lives here in our land completely by choice. Why, tomorrow, he could be gone again, although it would be highly irregular for a Luck Dragon to leave a place he's settled in. Especially if he's treated nicely. And we do everything we can to make him comfortable."

The boy nodded his head but did not really understand this very well. It had never occurred to him to question why the dragon was there. "The dragon's always been here, hasn't he?"

"You're young, boy, and I realize that for you, for your short life, the dragon has always been here. But that is not the case, you know."

The boy's earliest and most vivid memories were of the dragon. Maybe that was why he loved him so much. He recalled more occasions than he could count when he was held up to see the dragon passing by in procession. Every time, the dragon paused a moment, bowed its immense head and sniffed him tenderly, surrounding him with the scent of flowering trees. The dragon's breath always tickled him and made him laugh. As he would begin to giggle, the great head would raise itself and move on, before the boy's eager hands could have a chance to reach out and grab anything.

These were old memories, though. It had been awhile since anyone had lifted him up to see over the heads of others and get sniffed by the great dragon. Those strong, gentle hands were gone. He had wept many tears at her passing, yet he had learned that tears would not bring her back. Instinctively, he felt for the piece of embroidered, dark blue cloth that he kept tucked away beneath his thin shirt. He brushed away the memory to listen. Mali had continued to speak as the boy was lost in his memories. It was a word that Mali had spoken that brought him back to pay close attention.

"Galifalia, you know. They all say that if it hadn't been for her the dragon never would have—"

"Who?" the boy interrupted. "Who did you say?"

"Galifalia. The Lady. Now don't tell me that your granddame never told you stories about Galifalia."

"How do you know her?" the boy asked, astonished.

"How do I know...? Now I know you're pulling my leg. Why, if it hadn't been for Galifalia, there would be no dragon here. Nay, greatest, most noble Lady our land ever saw. Of common birth, too, they say. She could have been rich and had a room in the palace for what she did. But no, she never took as much as a wooden soup bowl for her part in it. Some say that's why the dragon settled here. It was for the purity of her heart that he stayed. She was a good one. Nay, most likely the best, and King Pell and his father before him honored her for the blessings she brought us."

The boy was completely puzzled. How could this man who spent his life in the compound know anything about his beloved Galifalia? He was still holding onto that piece of cloth tucked underneath his thin shirt. There must be a mistake, or simply another woman by the same unusual name. That must be the answer.

He was about to ask a question when he saw a group of boys, all around his age, moving unmistakably toward them. He stiffened. On the streets, he had learned the hard way that when a group of boys came his way, it always meant trouble. His instinct was to run.

Mali followed the boy's gaze and saw them coming. "Some of the other stall boys," he said. He sensed the newcomer's tenseness and placed his hand reassuringly on the boy's shoulder. "Relax. Word travels fast here, and they're curious about you. It would have been better if I had you cleaned up first, but that can't be helped now."

The boys walked up and made a small crowd around them. They all wore tunics similar to Mali's, with the same design. Some had friendly smiles and nodded their heads in silent greeting. Others looked the new boy up and down with no tell-tale expression on their faces.

"Which of the dogs dragged in this ragged piece of trash?" said a tall, strong-limbed lad who simply glared at the boy. He made some exaggerated sniffing noises and scrunched up his face as if he smelled something disgusting. "By the stench of it, looks like it's been lying in the muck-pens for awhile. Even dragon dung smells sweeter." There was a ripple of guffaws from the boys at this remark.

"Hey, Flek," said Mali addressing the tall lad. "A kind word and a helping hand would be a better greeting for a new boy joining your company."

"He's to join us? Is that even allowed?"

"What Garth decides is allowed," Mali said with finality.

"Garth had to rake through the compost bin to find this," Flek said. Then he turned to the stranger and asked, "What's your name?"

The boy paused a moment. Fact was, he didn't know his name. His grandmother had only ever called him 'Boy.' It had never occurred to him to ask her for more. It was not until he was living on the streets that he realized that 'boy' is generic and he lacked something specific. On the streets, he'd been given nicknames, none of them complimentary.

"Boy," he responded, having nothing better to offer.

"*Boy?*" Flek spluttered, with obvious disbelief. "Your name is *Boy*?"

"Yes," he answered softly, embarrassed, but ready to defend it.

"In that case," Mali stepped in to help him, "Boy it is until we find better."

"How about Dung?" Flek countered with a broad grin. "Or Privy?" There were hoots of laughter. "You let him in here, Mali, he'll bring us all into disgrace," Flek spat out, looking around at the others. "He's what we spend all our time sweeping off the floor. After he passes by, we'll have to sweep a second time." Again his taunting provoked chuckles.

"Don't you worry about that," said Mali. "After I've cleaned him up, he'll look as good as any of you. After that, if you have any complaints, you come straight to me. Is that all right with you, Flek?" He addressed the tall lad, and he paused, waiting for an answer.

Flek just nodded his head a couple of times. Then he said, "I'll let you know." He turned on his heel and stalked out of the commissary. Most of the boys followed him directly, but one of the smaller lads lingered behind, waiting until the others were out of earshot. He had dark, curly hair, freckles and a very sweet smile, though there were some gaps where teeth were still growing in. Glancing over his shoulder to make sure that no one else was able to hear, he spoke quickly to the boy.

"Don't worry about Flek. He's all right once you get to know him. Good to meet you. I'm really glad you've joined us." He held out a sooty hand in greeting. After a moment's hesitation, the boy took it and smiled shyly. Then the freckle-faced boy was off, running to catch up with the others.

"That's Colin," said Mali. "He's a good friend to have."

"And Flek is a bad enemy to make," added the boy in a soft voice. Mali looked at him with raised eyebrows. "I know his kind from the streets," the boy continued. "He wants to be in charge of everything and everyone. And if you don't let him bully you around, he'll do everything he can to squash you."

Mali was silent a moment considering this new stall boy. There certainly was more to him than met the eye.

"Well, even though it's true that the dragon has brought peace to the land, it takes longer to change human nature. I cannot deny the truth of what you say. Give the boys a chance, though, before you're too final with your judgments."

"Looks like I'm the one who's already been judged," the boy said in a low voice.

"All the more reason to get you cleaned up then," Mali said with a wry smile. "Had enough to eat?"

The rest of the day passed in a confused yet joyful whirl. The boy was taken to a wash area where he was told to strip off his old clothes and bid them farewell. He was given a strong-smelling soap with which he scrubbed his body and his hair. He doused himself with several buckets of cold water, dancing around to shake off the chill. He then dried himself off, using the thick, rough towels Mali had left for him. He rubbed himself hard and was soon warm all over again. Then he found the new, clean clothes Mali had laid out for him, including a tunic with the dragon emblazed across the front. He would have stood admiring it the rest of the afternoon if Mali had not walked in to check on him and pressed him to hurry and dress. The boy hastily stuffed inside his tunic the only thing that connected him with his old life: the piece of cloth dyed dark blue with stars embroidered on it.

He was given a brief tour of his new surroundings. He already knew the great barn and the commissary. He was shown the various workshops as well as the smaller barns where the working animals were kept. There were the barracks where the garrison was stationed and the different gates along the wall, some of which were guarded, others just left barred shut. He recognized the gate through which he had gained entrance that very morning. He could still hardly believe his good fortune. The guard who had let him in waved at the boy enthusiastically and called out something which he could not understand. Whatever it was, it made Mali laugh.

Just as in the town, cats roamed freely and there was the occasional dog sunning itself in front of a doorway. Last of all he was brought to a building which Mali referred to as the dormitory. "I assume that you're going to stay here with us."

"You mean I can sleep here?" the boy asked quickly, looking up at Mali.

"Unless you have some place back in town that you prefer. Most of the boys choose to stay here, visiting their families when they feel homesick. You don't have to stay, you know."

"Oh," the boy said quickly. "I'd love to stay here. Just show me where I can sleep."

The building was large and had several floors. They walked up the stairs to the first landing. "Boys your age sleep on this floor," Mali was saying as they entered a large room with rows of mats laid orderly along the walls.

Colin suddenly appeared out of nowhere and hurried up to them. "I was thinking I would meet you here," he said with a big grin. He stepped back and admired the new boy. "You look really great, all cleaned up. Look, I set you up a mat over here." They walked half way down the row of mats and Colin pointed out one that had been newly arranged.

"I put it next to mine. I hope you don't mind. Did Mali show you everything?"

"Everything," answered Mali, "except his new friend. Thank you, Colin, for making Boy feel welcome. Would you be willing to finish up the tour and then bring him back to the commissary for the evening meal?"

"Be glad to," said Colin with a big smile. And then to Boy, "Come on, I'll show you where it's off limits and where we can go anyway."

As they hurried away, Mali called after them, "Don't get him in too much trouble quite yet, Colin. Give it a day or two." He laughed to himself watching the two rush down the stairs side by side, thinking that this new stall boy would do all right.

Chapter Four

Straw Boy

The next morning, it did not take long before trouble found Boy. He had slept well in his new home. He liked being with the other boys in the dormitory and sleeping under a clean blanket on a soft straw mat. After living an uncertain life on the streets, he was hungry, not only for the healthy meals life in the compound offered, but also for work. He was ready for his days to begin early and end late, filled with a succession of chores. He was joyful at the prospect of living a useful life again, punctuated by warm meals and good company.

The first day he had managed to avoid any more contact with Flek. Colin had steered him to other boys who had welcomed him and seemed friendly enough. They all assured him that they worked hard and had a lot of jobs to complete all day long. They were tired by the end of the day. This did not bother him in the least. He could hardly wait to learn his new responsibilities.

He awoke in the early morning light before the sun had kissed the treetops. As soon as he sensed the first boys stirring, he was up and eager to begin his day. Colin was still asleep, so without disturbing him, Boy smoothed out his blanket and quietly walked down the aisle of sleeping and stretching boys to go outside. He did not realize that several pairs of eyes followed him as he left.

Outside, it looked like it would be a glorious day. The air was still cool and the sky was a deep shade of blue. Boy could smell the strong scent of the trees as they breathed out their aroma in the pre-dawn air. He went directly to the well outside the front door. Flek's comments from the day before still stung. He wanted to make sure that no one had grounds to tell him that he smelled.

He went to the well, drew up a bucket of water and set it on the stone rim. He dipped his hands in the cold water, and it numbed them. He quickly cupped them together to catch the water in his palms. He bent his head over the bucket and, taking a deep breath, plunged his face into the cold water. It was invigorating and chased away any remnants of sleep.

He was about to douse his face a second time when his whole world turned suddenly upside down. He was completely confused and a bit frightened as he was lifted off the ground. He was falling into the well! He cried out in shock and fear as he tumbled head first. Throwing out his hands to stop himself, his arms banged against the stone walls of the well, slick and slimy with moss and algae. Then suddenly his forward motion stopped with a jerk, and he hung suspended in the air. He could not imagine what had caused him to fall in the first place, and even less could he understand what now held him hanging in midair.

Then he heard the voices and became aware of the pressure around his lower legs. There was laughter, and the tightness on his legs was several pairs of hands holding onto him.

"Time for your morning wash, Straw Boy," a voice called out loudly above the others. It was unmistakably Flek's. The boy realized that Flek and his friends had snuck up on him while he was washing. They had picked him up and were dangling him inside the well. He was furious at the indignity and at being caught off guard.

"Let me out of here!" he bellowed. His voice echoed dully off the stone walls surrounding him on all sides.

"Oh, Straw Boy has a temper," Flek mocked him from above. "We need to cool off his hot head in the water. What say, fellows, should we let him go?"

"Pull me out!" Boy yelled. "Get me out of here!"

"It's not enough to wash only your face. Straw Boy is in need of a dunking."

The boy was struggling and about to yell again when he heard another voice. He stopped squirming for a moment and tried to follow what it was saying.

"...out or you're in big trouble, Flek. All of you. Pull him out."

Then there were other voices, closer, around his feet.

"...ugh, he's heavy. Slipping. What do you want us to do?"

"Drop him," Flek's voice said decisively. "Let him sink."

"You're all in big trouble, then," said the voice again.

"What are you going to do, Colin? Tell?" Flek asked threateningly.

"Doesn't need to," spoke a clear, commanding voice. Boy was certain that was Mali. There was a lot of murmuring now, and he felt the hands on his legs tugging him up and heard the boys grunting in their effort. His legs and stomach scraped against rough edges on the stones, leaving both his body and emotions raw. He came out in time to hear Flek's excuse.

"Just a welcoming joke, Mali, nothing to get excited about. We do it to all the guys when they first arrive."

"Strange I never heard about it before," Mali said calmly.

"Because it's nothing to get excited about. No one ever complains. Straw Boy's all right. See for yourself."

They had left him sitting on the rim of the well. He began to rub gently where the skin was scraped raw, but stopped when he realized he was smearing blood up and down his leg. He could see deep, red marks where the boys had dug their nails into him. Those spots were slowly turning into swollen welts. He glared at the boys and, in particular, Flek. Flek was looking at Mali, shrugging his shoulders as if nothing had happened. The other boys, four in number, looked rather sheepish.

"Hey," Flek said, shrugging his shoulders. "What's the big deal? We wouldn't have dropped him. He'd ruin the water. We'd have to block the well." The other boys laughed and Flek smirked. Mali was just about to scold Flek for his prank, but he never had a chance. The boy sprang from the edge of the well where he had been sitting and landed his fist into the side of Flek's face. Both boys went tumbling to the ground.

Mali acted quickly before they had a chance to begin grappling with one another. He forced himself between the two of them; he grabbed hold of Boy's tunic. He quickly realized that he had taken hold of the wrong one and let go to face Flek. "Don't do it, Flek," Mali cautioned him.

Flek had stood up from the ground with a fist-sized rock in his hand. He was spluttering and furious. "I'll break his head open!" he bellowed, trying to get around Mali who kept pushing him back.

"Any time," the boy said calmly. "Just come ahead." He stood there solidly, holding his ground.

"Let me at him!" Flek continued to struggle against Mali and was again forcefully pushed back.

"That's enough!" Mali commanded. Flek stared at both the boy and Mali with hatred. The side of his face where the boy had planted his fist was already beginning to turn a dark shade of purple.

"That's enough from both of you," Mali said, glancing behind him to see if he needed to push Boy back as well. He saw him standing there, waiting calmly for what might come next. For his small stature, he stood there strong and confident.

"I want justice," Flek cried. "He hit me without provocation."

Mali laughed bitterly. "I'm not sure anyone will agree with you, Flek. Perhaps the revenge was greater than the original deed, but you did provoke."

"I want justice," Flek cried out again hoarsely, holding one hand to the side of his head.

"You received it, Flek. Now let it rest. This is the boy's first day, and I want you two to come to some agreement with one another. You need to work together. Can the two of you call it even?"

"I'll take whatever Flek is willing to offer," Boy said firmly.

"I'll give him what he deserves," sneered Flek.

Mali sighed. "Is that the best I can get from the two of you?" Neither answered. "Well, I'm not satisfied. I want you both to promise that you will not lay hands on one another. If we can't settle it here, we'll go to the Dragon Master."

"Fine," Flek sputtered. "I'll keep my hands off of Straw Boy. I wouldn't want to soil them." Saying this, he spat at the ground towards the boy's feet. The other boys around him grew very quiet. Mali decided to ignore Flek's spitting and see if the boy would accept the offer.

"What about you, Boy?" Mali had turned to him.

"Like I said, I'll take whatever he offers." Then, after a pause, he added, "And I'll give the same in return." And he spat at the ground towards Flek's feet. Mali had to suppress a smile at the boy's spunk. He also had to stiff-arm Flek to keep him from lunging at the boy.

"All right, you've heard it, Flek. You get back what you give. Now don't let me catch you starting any nonsense like this again. Time to move on."

"Don't worry," Flek answered warningly. "You won't catch me doing anything." He turned on his heels and walked off, followed by his four companions.

"Ah, me," Mali sighed. "Yes, I can imagine you won't let me catch you next time. Well, Boy, I'm sorry that you had to begin this way."

"I'm satisfied," the boy shrugged. "If he keeps his promise. I'm glad to get it out of the way so soon. I saw it coming yesterday." Colin had pulled out a pail of water and was leading Boy back to the well to wash off the blood and the slime.

"You're a tough character," Mali commented.

"I'm not afraid of a fight, if that's what you mean."

"Just as long as you're not the one starting it."

"Not me," the boy responded smiling as he splashed in the water. "But, Mali, don't expect me to run from them, either." He looked up suddenly. "Did we miss breakfast?"

"I'm glad this hasn't affected your appetite."

"I so like the food here," Boy said with a broad smile.

"Come on," Colin said. "I'll go eat with you. Then I'll show you your duties."

"That's what I came for," Boy said, shaking the water off his wet hands. The two boys walked off towards the meal room. Mali watched them go, trying to figure out this newcomer.

Colin steered the boy back to the commons which was buzzing with workers getting a quick bite before starting their daily chores. Some sat, others just milled around, chatting in groups. Breakfast was simple and intended to be taken quickly. From a counter, Colin and Boy took steaming clay bowls filled with a broth similar to the one of the morning before. A large hunk of bread, left over from the day before, went with it. Since the bread had hardened somewhat overnight, they dipped it in their broth to soften it. The boy liked the crust the best: chewy and full of flavor. He already loved the broth; it had cut vegetables floating in it and was very savory. What was merely a light breakfast before beginning chores would have been a feast back on the streets. He knew he was going to like living in the compound.

Colin led the boy over to a group of other stall boys. Boy had shared supper with two of them the evening before. There were now three, and Colin introduced them again so he could remember their names: Frog, Mixer and Stomp.

"They're nicknames, of course," Frog commented.

"They got these names from the kind of work we do," Colin explained. "They just sort of stuck. You'll probably get one, too, before long."

"Flek already tried to give him a couple," Stomp said with a smile.

"Let's not go there," Colin said.

"Hey," Mixer said, "it was funny. It's not like we're going to use them."

"So, do you know the rules?" Stomp asked.

The boy looked blank and asked if he meant lights out.

"There are some other rules besides lights out," Frog began.

"Like fighting," Stomp continued.

The boy was curious about this one. "You mean we're allowed to or we're not allowed to?"

"Both, or neither, depending how you look at it," Mixer said.

"Well, you sure made that clear," Stomp said, giving Mixer a dig with his elbow. "What he's trying to say is that they know we're going to have disagreements that can turn into a fight, so they don't bother to make a fuss about rules. There's only one thing we have to avoid."

"No fighting around the dragon," Frog said. "That's it."

"If we're private about it, they let it go, although they'll stop us if they catch us, and Mali is pretty good about smelling out trouble," Mixer added. Boy had already experienced that.

"Also," continued Colin, "we're not allowed to mess with the dragon."

"What does that mean?" The boy wanted more details.

"You don't poke him, you don't prod him, you don't try and get his attention, you don't get in his way," Frog was counting off.

"You don't even talk to him," Stomp added.

"But we all do it anyway," Mixer said quickly. "Just talk to him nicely, and don't get caught."

"By Mali?" Boy asked.

"Nah, he doesn't care, as long as we talk sweetly," Frog explained.

"Garth doesn't like it," Colin told him. There was a pause as they munched their bread and sipped their broth from the edges of the bowls.

"Anything else?" Boy asked.

"Yes," said Stomp, "but the rest you'll figure out as you go along. Like, no leaving the compound under any circumstances without special permission. Don't know why, but Garth is very particular about that one."

"No worry on that account," said the boy. "I waited long enough to get in."

"Time to go," Frog said. Many workers had gone already and others were moving to the doors. Bowls were stacked up on a side table.

"Who does the cleanup in here?" the boy asked, curious how it all worked.

"The kitchen staff cleans up after breakfast," Colin explained. "But we take shifts for the other meals. It's just part of our work." As the others headed for the door, Colin took the boy by the sleeve and led him in another direction. "Before we go out, there's someone else I want you to meet," he said.

They went through a corner doorway that was closed only by a hanging curtain and entered into the greater kitchen area. Both men and women were working in here, all of them wearing large aprons. Here and there Boy also saw children their own age bustling around with bowls. Many of the kitchen staff stood at tables, kneading dough or chopping. There was a lot of conversation and occasional laughter among workers collected around the same table. A woman passing by glanced at the two boys as they entered. She turned away from them and called out, "Alis! Colin's here."

"Stand quietly," Colin said in a low voice. "We're not really allowed in here, you know."

A moment later, a girl around their age appeared. She was wearing an apron like the other workers, a wisp of dark hair showing from under the scarf tied behind her head. Something about her looked oddly familiar, but the boy could not figure out what it was. Had he met her the day before?

"Hi, Alis," Colin said with a big smile.

"Hi, Col." She was obviously glad to see him. She looked at the boy and said, "This is him, isn't it?" She had a very pleasant face, some freckles, and a very welcoming smile. Why did she look so familiar?

"We've already heard all about you," she continued, not waiting for Colin to answer. "You've created quite a stir. I'm glad to meet you. My name is Alis."

The boy looked from Colin to Alis and back again. Then it dawned on him. Same freckles, same color hair, same pleasant, friendly face. "You're related, aren't you?"

"She's my sister," Colin admitted with a shy grin.

"Twin sister," Alis added. "And I'm older."

"Barely," said Colin.

"And I can still beat you at running," she added.

"Barely," said Colin again, and they both laughed.

"You'd better get going. Don't make him late for his first day in the barn," Alis warned. "Here, I brought you something." She handed them each a piece of sweetened cornbread.

"That's why we came," Colin said, already stuffing some in his mouth.

"What?" Alis said, acting shocked. "I thought you came to introduce him to me."

"In truth," Colin said, mumbling through the cornbread. "That, too. Come on, we have to go."

"'Bye," Alis said, turning to go. "Visit me after lunch."

"We have no choice," Colin said, turning back to the doorway. "We're on cleanup duty."

As they walked, Boy ate some of the bread. It was deliciously sweet.

"You have to eat that quickly," Colin said. His was already gone. "You don't want the others to see."

"Right," said the boy, happily stuffing the rest in his mouth. He knew this rule from the streets. If you don't eat something quickly, it will end up in someone else's mouth.

Chapter Five

Proper Care of a Luck Dragon

When Colin and the boy entered the great barn, the other stall boys were already beginning to line up. The boy would have stayed standing in front of the door, mesmerized by the beauty and overwhelming size of the dragon that lay in the middle of the floor. Colin dragged him by the tunic over to a portion of the barn wall where fairly large pieces of parchment were tacked.

"Good!" exclaimed Colin after briefly examining the first parchment. "He did it."

"Who did what?" Boy asked curiously.

"Mali. Look, he's already added your name." On each parchment was a set of colored symbols the boy could easily recognize, a rake, a pitchfork, a wheelbarrow, and a bucket. Next to each symbol was a list of names. Colin was pointing to one of them on the first parchment.

"There you are," he said, sounding satisfied. "He squeezed you in right underneath my name. We're in the same work group."

The boy looked but recognized nothing other than the symbols. He knew the marks below the symbols were writing, but he could not decipher them.

"There it is," Colin said pointing. "There's my name, and he wrote 'Boy' right below it." He paused a moment to look at his new friend and then it dawned on him. "You can't read, can you?" he said.

Boy said nothing, but continued to stare at the parchment, biting his lip.

"That's all right," Colin reassured him. "You don't need to read to do our jobs. Just your name, anyway. If you want, I'll teach you."

The boy brightened up at this promise. "Really?"

"In truth, it's not hard. Just not right now. We've got to line up with the others. This is the way it works: You look every day for your job. Every day something new, but the order never changes. You'll remember it after a couple of weeks. We're on brooms today, see?" He pointed to the drawing of a broom at the head of their list of names. "Now we grab ourselves each a broom and line up."

Colin pulled him by the tunic again, this time over to the pegs on the wall that held brooms. By this time, there were only a few left.

"Why do we line up?" Boy asked, as they each took down a broom.

"We say goodbye to Star," Colin answered.

"Goodbye?" Boy asked shocked. "Is the dragon leaving?"

Colin was hustling the boy over to find a place in the line together with the others in their work group. They all held brooms.

"Of course. The dragon goes away every day. Didn't you know?"

"I remember Garth mentioned something about it when he was showing me around. But I forgot where they take him."

"Down to the river for his wash. If he didn't leave, we couldn't clean up."

He stared down the long line of boys, all arranged in groups. Each boy held an implement for cleaning up the barn. He felt proud to be standing among them in his new, clean tunic. He saw Mali walking along the line encouraging some boys to stand up straight, others to settle down.

Garth, the Dragon Master, appeared at the wide entrance to the barn. With him came four young men with long poles that were pointed and barbed.

"Who are they?" Boy asked quietly.

"That's Garth, of course. And the others are the dragon guides. They make sure Star doesn't get out of line."

"You mean, Star doesn't always go where they want him to?"

"I've heard he has a real mind of his own," Colin whispered back. "But I've never seen it myself. Here in the barn, he's more cooperative than a milk cow, if you ask me."

The boys stood in place as the four dragon guides stationed themselves two on either side, each near one of Star's massive legs. Garth stood near the dragon's head and began speaking to him, but the boy could not hear.

"What's he saying?" he asked Colin.

"Oh, just telling him that it's time for his bath, and that he's a beautiful dragon, and would he be so kind as to go with them, and other sweet words. When it's our turn with the pitchforks, we'll stand at the front of the line and then you'll be able to hear."

Suddenly the dragon came to life. With a great whooshing sound he rose from the floor. The air around the boy was stirred up, ruffling his hair. The four dragon guides had their poles ready, but they merely tapped the dragon with the side of the pole, not the barbed point. Star walked lightly out into the sunlight, leaving behind a straw-strewn, immense, empty barn. A moment later, Star disappeared from sight altogether.

"Now we get to work," Colin said with a big smile. "Just do what I do."

Over the following days, Boy learned that there was always work to be done. While the dragon was off at the river getting his daily wash, the boys were busy cleaning up the floor and preparing it to receive Star when he returned in the late afternoon. And every day, the boy learned a new aspect of cleaning. The floor needed to be raked and swept and washed. The old straw had to be loaded onto wheelbarrows and carted off. The dragon's fewmets were gathered in other wheelbarrows and carried off to the dung heaps. The stall boys worked with brooms, pitchforks, rakes, buckets, mops, scrubbers and wheelbarrows. Cleaning the floor completely kept them busy right up until the midday meal.

While they worked, Colin explained the reason they cleared the barn of straw every day. “Even though it doesn’t look much used,” Colin said, letting a handful sift through his fingers. “There’s another part of the compound where the straw is mixed with the dragon’s fewmets.”

“The farmers take it away by the cartload to cover their fields,” Mixer added. “I often work there after lunch.”

“They claim it’s worth its weight in gold,” Colin said. “Their harvests are double what they are elsewhere.”

“Neighboring kingdoms trade whatever they can for the straw that Star has slept on for one night,” Frog said.

“That’s a Luck Dragon, for you,” Colin winked.

By noon the floor was cleaned and the portions that had been scrubbed were now left to dry. All the workers made their way back to the kitchen area. As they approached, the boy was delighted to be greeted by the mouth-watering smells of freshly baked bread and something savory.

The bowls they had sipped from that morning were once again in use. This time, though, they were filled with a steaming stew, thick with barley, vegetables and pieces of meat. The bread was still warm from the ovens and delicious. As a treat after the meal, there were trays of cut, sweetened cornbread, the very same Alis had snuck to them that morning after breakfast. Boy was so engaged with his meal that he ignored the happy chatting of the others around him.

Once they were finished eating, Colin explained that the boys on brooms always have lunch cleanup duty. They walked outside where several large tubs of hot water were set up along the wall. The first three were soapy, and then there were a number of rinsing tubs. At the end of the line of tubs were drying racks for the clean, dripping bowls. The boy was impressed with how well organized everything in the compound was run. It was all set up to be done efficiently and quickly.

Rolling up the sleeves on their tunics, he and Colin were walking over to the sudsy tubs, when someone called out, "Hey, Straw Boy, catch!"

Boy looked over his shoulder just in time to see an object flying right towards his head. He ducked in time to avoid being hit, but his tunic was drenched with a shower of cold broth.

"Clean up, Straw Boy. You're a mess!" It was Flek and two of his friends. They were openly laughing at having drenched him. All morning long the boy had been happy to forget about Flek's dislike for him. Flek and some of his friends had been working in another part of the barn altogether. The barn was large enough that they never had any contact—until now.

The boy was furious at this unprovoked attack. He would have launched himself at Flek had not someone intervened at that moment.

"Flek!" boomed a loud voice from the kitchen door. A wide, red-faced woman stood there with her hands on her hips. A large apron over her work clothes covered her generous frame and her hair was partially tucked underneath a scarf. "Flek, don't you like my cooking any better than that?"

"Matild, I love your cooking," Flek protested. "We were just bringing our bowls to get washed."

"And now you'll be bringing yourselves into the kitchen to work with me. I've got pots that need scrubbing."

"Matild," Flek protested, "we're not on cleanup today."

"You are now," Matild answered. She did not look like someone to argue with. She narrowed her eyes at Flek as if to say she did not tolerate trouble. "Any questions?"

Flek's mouth moved silently as he tried to figure some way out. Then he just turned to the boy and muttered, "I'll get you for this."

"And I can use your two buddies, too," Matild added. "My pots haven't had a good scouring for weeks. Today's the day. Get going."

Flek and his two friends scowled at Boy and slouched into the kitchen area. Matild walked behind them to cut off any thoughts of escape.

"Is she the boss?" Boy asked Colin as he was taking off his tunic.

"That's right. She looks after the kitchen. She makes sure that everything runs smoothly. We all worship the ground she walks on."

"Do you think I can wash my tunic in the tub?" Boy wondered.

"Good idea. Then just hang it in the sun. It's warm enough, it'll be dry before long."

Once his tunic was hanging on a tree branch to dry, Boy set to the washing with great pleasure. He enjoyed splashing in the warm water and cleaning the bowls, surrounded by the rest of the boys from the broom detail. There was a lot of work since they were washing up for everybody in the compound. As they were coming to the last of the bowls, Colin told the rest of the crew he and Boy would finish up what was left. The others were happy to go and begin their rest.

"It's worth waiting around for Alis," he winked to Boy. They were just finishing when Alis came out the door of the kitchen.

"I thought I'd find you here." She glanced at the shirtless boy. "You really get into cleaning up."

"We had an accident," Colin said, indicating the tunic hanging in the tree.

"Wouldn't have anything to do with our new pot scrubbers inside, would it?" she mused.

"Might," answered Colin without further explanation. "What do you have today?"

"Just bread and honey," she answered, offering them two large chunks. "Hope you don't mind."

"Mind?" exclaimed Colin taking from her a fist-sized piece of bread slathered with honey. "My favorite!" The three of them sat on a low bench along the wall while the boys ate their bread.

"What happens now?" Boy asked.

"Well, after lunch we all have a rest," Alis began. "Then I go back to the kitchens to get supper ready. All of you barn boys gather in front of the dormitories. You've got it easy. You can lounge around or play games."

"Some of us can," Colin corrected. "We have to be there because sometimes they need help in other parts of the compound, and they come looking for us there. They come and ask for volunteers."

"What if no one wants to go?" Boy wondered.

"Then they don't ask, but just pick someone," Alis laughed. "The work has to get done."

"It's not so bad, though," Colin added. "Not everyone ends up going, and those who go don't work that long. Our work in the barn isn't done yet. We still have to lay it with fresh straw. We only finish up right before Star comes home again."

"And then we're done for the day?"

"Not quite," Alis said. "All of us, even the kitchen staff, stand in attendance while Star eats."

"He eats?" the boy said puzzled. "But yesterday Mali told me that the dragon doesn't eat."

"Oh, wait and see," said Colin. "You'll like it. Anyway, after that are supper and cleanup, then we're free until it gets dark, and then, lights out. But you got all that part of the day yesterday."

"Every day," Alis continued, "it's pretty much the same. We work hard, the food is good and we have the honor of taking care of the dragon. It doesn't mean much while we're in here, but you'll see, when we go out into the town, people do nice things for us all the time."

"How long have you two been here?"

"Two years," Alis and Colin said at the same time, and then they laughed.

"Actually, more like two and a half," Alis said.

"Do you ever miss your family?"

"I do," Alis said quickly. "I really miss Mother. But it's so strange. We go home regularly to visit. And hardly have I spent a day there, I'm already longing to come back again."

"Well, maybe your parents could come live here and work."

"Are you kidding?" Colin said. "They are much too busy for that. Mother is a lady-in-waiting to Queen Meg and our father is one of the king's ambassadors."

The boy's eyes grew very big. "You mean that your parents are of the nobility?"

Colin looked at him surprised. "Of course they are. Didn't you know? Everyone who works here comes from families that are of royal blood."

Boy thought about this a long moment. "Except me, right?" he finally asked.

"Well, that's why everyone's talking about how Garth let you in," Alis confided. "But as long as you work hard, because we all do, you'll do fine."

"Now I understand why Flek hates me so much. I take it that Flek is also of a noble family."

"Of course, and Flek has a special rank," Colin responded. "His father and King Pell are cousins. That puts Flek into the line of succession, if a lot of other people suddenly died. Like Frog, for instance."

"Why Frog?"

"You don't know?" Alis asked. She looked at Colin and frowned. "Didn't you tell him anything?"

"I thought he knew," Colin said shrugging his shoulders. "Frog is next in line. His father is King Pell. But he's not stuck up about it. He works just like the rest of us."

"Well, in that case," Boy concluded, "I'd better make sure that I do my work, too. Let's get over to the dormitories. Thank you, Alis, for the treat. It was really tasty."

"My pleasure," she smiled. "Just stick with Colin and you'll get more. No one'll mind if I give something to you, too. Fact is, I think everyone is sort of looking out for you. Like Matild today. She came down hard on Flek because he was baiting you. Anyone else and she would have just told them to settle it outside the kitchen and get back to work."

"Well, anyway, my tunic's dry now," Boy said slipping it back on. "Come on, Colin. I'm ready for my next shift."

The boy was determined not to give anyone a chance to question his right to stay there. Even now on his first full day, when the craft people came looking for extra workers, he was one of the first to step forward and volunteer. Boy continued this habit for as long as he was working in the barn. On this day, he went off to work with Ole Max, the potter. This old man had a kind smile, wispy gray hair and big hands that looked fit for both hard work and fine detail. He spoke slowly and sucked on a briar pipe which half the time was never lit.

"So yer the new boy," Ole Max said, as they walked to his workshop. Boy nicked his head. He figured word of his coming had become common gossip. "Well, let's see what ye can do," Ole Max concluded.

In the course of the afternoon, the boy helped Ole Max clean out the kiln and prepare it for a firing of clay bowls, the very kind meals were served in. He swept the shop, stacked a new load of firewood next to the kiln and washed down the counters.

"Ye'll do, boy," Ole Max said with a smile. "That was a good piece of work."

Over the following weeks Boy also worked for the shoemaker, the weaver, the tailor, the cooper, and repeatedly for the washers. They often needed help to wring out the freshly washed clothing and set it out to dry in the sun. He returned regularly to Ole Max, who sought him out in the afternoon when he needed an extra hand. "Worth three stall boys," he would mumble contentedly, as the boy hurried off after helping him.

Each day, after a couple of hour's work, Boy was sent back to the barn, where all hands lay to with rakes to spread fresh hay evenly around the barn floor. To make sure that everyone did his fair share of the work, each boy had a portion of the floor assigned to him. It was a point of honor to make sure that each assigned area was well padded with straw and evenly joined to the neighboring ones. Boy dedicated himself to his particular portion with enthusiasm. He had received an area that was directly beneath where Star usually lay. This was considered a much more critical area than around the edges, where the thickness could be less consistent and even taper off.

The stall boys were just hanging their rakes back onto the pegs along the long barn walls when word went around that Star was returning from the river. All of the workers filed out of the barn and the kitchen, and the boy joined them to stand outside across from the large open doors.

Star arrived, accompanied by his keepers. Not only did they have their long prodding poles, but now they also had long-handled scrubbers propped on their shoulders. Star was back from his outing, cleanly scrubbed. Then something astonishing happened.

As soon as Star arrived in the large open space before the barn, two of the dragon guides put aside their prodding poles and took down long-handled padded hammers that were hanging on pegs just inside the barn. They stepped over to a large bronze disk hanging outside the opening to the barn. They struck the disk repeatedly, and its deep vibrating tone filled the air. The sound struck a memory in the boy, but he did not have a moment to think about it.

Without warning, Star stretched out his great expanse of wings and then simply took off, rising almost straight up. The boy's mouth fell open in astonishment as he watched. He had a moment of panic, thinking that Star was escaping. Yet no one around him appeared to be in the least bit surprised.

Up, up Star sailed with very slight movement in his wings until he was high above their heads. Then he began to soar over the compound and the fields beyond. No matter how far away he flew, he always returned to make a large circle, keeping the compound in the outer circumference of his circuit.

The moment the dragon was soaring above their heads, the keepers ceased striking the bronze disk. The sound, though, did not fade as the boy expected. The deep tones of the vibrating metal continued, now coming from above him. It was Star's song.

For the first time the boy understood something that had mystified him when he had lived on the streets. Occasionally he had heard this same sound at the end of the day, but he could never figure out from where it came. The narrow streets and tall buildings prevented him from ever seeing the dragon soaring out over the fields. When he had asked others, older folk insisted it was the dragon's song, but since he could make no sense of it, he had shrugged off their explanation.

It was the most remarkable sound the boy had ever heard. It was at once soothing and rousing. His soul felt satisfied, as if he had just filled his body with foods from a great feast. He stood there mesmerized, watching Star fly and listening to his song.

After watching spellbound for several minutes, the boy could not contain his curiosity any longer. He saw Colin nearby and went to stand next to him. "What's he doing?" he whispered. He dared not speak loudly, afraid to break the spell.

"He's feeding," Colin said simply, also gazing up at the circling dragon. Most of the boys were watching, although a few huddled in small groups chatting. When their quiet chatting turned into laughter, Mali shot them a warning look.

Boy let all this sink in for a minute. But Colin's explanation raised another question. "What's he eating?"

"Air. The light of sunset. Mosquitoes. No one knows, really. No one has been able to get Star to answer that question," he said, chuckling at the thought that Star could talk to them.

"Does he do this every day?"

"He goes several times a week. We never know when, so we always line up in case he does go. It's a sight most of us don't want to miss. No one knows why he chooses to go or to stay. Just his way."

"Isn't Garth afraid he'll fly away?"

"Fly away? Now, why would Star do that? His time isn't up for at least another nine years. No, he's all ours until then. Unless someone riles him."

"Riles him? What do you mean?"

"You know, if someone messes with him and makes him wild again. But that's not going to happen. That's why we're all here. We make sure that Star is happy and well-cared for and no one has a chance to turn him to his wild ways again."

"What do you mean by wild ways," the boy persisted.

"Oh, gosh, don't be so thick. I mean fighting with him. Trying to do the knight-and-dragon-battle thing. That's why there's a stockade around the compound. It's not to keep Star in, it's to keep others out."

"But Nogardia needs no guarding," the boy muttered, repeating the phrase he'd heard so often repeated in the city.

"Nogardia doesn't need any guards," Colin said. "But Star does. And that's why we're here."

This had never occurred to the boy: The stockade was there to protect the dragon. The thought that there might be someone who would want to fight Star mystified him. Who would ever want to challenge to battle a creature as beautiful, magnificent and powerful as a dragon? He hoped never to meet such a person.

As the boy stood there taking in the sights and sounds of a feeding Luck Dragon, he felt a deep sense of happiness. It was a feeling he hoped would last him the rest of his life.

Chapter Six

Straw

The boy's life took on a regular rhythm and routine. He could not have been happier. He enjoyed the purposeful work, the food was plentiful, he had friends, and best of all, he could be near his beloved dragon. Star, after all, was what had drawn him to the compound. It was the hunger to be around the dragon that had given him the courage to stand before the gates every morning for those two months.

As Boy became more familiar with the daily and weekly routine, he began to leave the meal room early and visit Star before the work day began. Not that he ever had Star to himself. Usually there were several other workers organizing the tools and making sure that everything would run smoothly once the barn boys entered. Since the barn boys were his responsibility, Mali was often there early, checking lists and seeing that everything was in its place.

"Morning, Straw," Mali would always greet him. Colin had warned him that he would get a nickname unless he provided something more usable than 'Boy.' Flek's attempt to insult him had backfired. Flek had been calling him 'Straw Boy,' and the others kept the 'Straw' and dropped the 'Boy.' This nickname fit all the better when the others noticed that the boy was very thorough in spreading Star's bedding at the close of day. This new name also reminded everyone that Flek's prediction had not come true. The boy contributed as much as anyone to keeping the barn clean and supporting the daily needs of the compound.

"Straw, I'd say that living here agrees with you," Mali would comment.

"Yes, sir," the boy would respond. "It agrees with me very much."

And then Mali, always busy, would move on. Occasionally, Garth, the Dragon Master, would bustle through, brusque and impersonal behind his bushy, graying beard. He would glance at the boy, nod his head, the flicker of a smile lighting up his eyes, and then he'd be gone on whatever mission he was on.

Most of all, the boy enjoyed meeting up with the Barn Master, whom everyone called Keg. As his name suggested, he was a round, squat man and always had a smile on his face and amusement in his eyes. The boy was comfortable around him. Keg liked to keep the barn tidy and well organized; he worked with a serene calmness and hummed to himself when not giving directions.

"Mornin', Straw," he would call out when he saw him. "Wonderful day to be tending to a dragon, wouldn't you say? He's in a good humor today. Watch that tail, though. You never know when it will get into mischief."

Keg liked that the boy would come early and ask to do something that needed attending. He rarely failed to occupy the boy until the rest of the crew gathered for their daily work, and Straw looked forward to the jobs Keg would give him. Sometimes Keg sent him on errands to other parts of the compound, and he enjoyed getting to know new people that he would not meet otherwise. Occasionally, he was asked to do something directly for the dragon, and those days were rare and very special.

One day, Keg handed the boy a stiff brush and told him to go clean Star's long toenails. "He passed through some deep mud on the way home yesterday, so it seems. They're still caked over. I want you to brush 'em clean. Think you can handle that?"

"Oh, yes, sir, yes," Straw gushed with wide eyes. This would be the closest he had ever gotten to the dragon.

"Well, with two yeses I expect a double good job," Keg laughed and went about other business. "Just remember to talk sweetly to him when you set to work."

The boy approached the dragon's front left foot. He stood there looking up at the immense figure before him. The curved nails on the foot, if they would be straightened out, would probably be nearly as long as he was. He shuddered with excitement, anticipating brushing those powerful talons.

Straw spoke to the dragon the whole time he worked. He scrubbed and he brushed and he never stopped talking. He was working on the fourth foot when he realized that Keg was standing a few steps away watching him. "Am I doing all right, sir?" He was worried that he was doing something wrong.

"Just fine," Keg responded with a smile. "And Star will never lack for conversation around you."

"I like talking to him, sir. Is that all right?"

"Star doesn't mind, as long as you speak respectfully. Just don't expect him to keep up his side of the conversation." Keg wandered away, chuckling to himself.

The boy did not need any response. The fact that Star listened was enough for him.

It did not escape notice that Straw was going into the barn early every morning. "Why do you want to work more?" Colin asked. "The other boys are beginning to wonder what's wrong with you."

"Colin, I came here because of the dragon. I like being around him. And when we all come in, Star leaves, so this way I have time with him. I don't always work, you know. Sometimes I just stand and visit with him. I don't mind doing something extra, anyway. I like being around Keg and I like working."

"Wait a minute. You visit with Keg or the dragon?"

"Why, with Star, of course."

"Like you talk with him?"

"Of course I do. I mean, isn't that why you're here? To be with Star?"

Colin looked at him with disbelief. "The reason I'm here, and all the other barn boys as well, is because our fathers and mothers worked here when they were young. It's what the families of the nobility do. We serve in the compound. It's great being around Star, and it's an honor and all, but, well, truth is, I never thought about it more than that. It's just what we do."

The boy considered this a moment before speaking. "You know, Colin, before coming here I was living on the streets. I didn't know from one day to the next if I was going to have food to eat or where it might be safe enough to sleep that night. Still, I could think of only one thing: get to the dragon. Now that I'm here, I'm going to spend as much time around him as possible."

"That's fine by me," Colin said. "But you should know that there are others who don't like that you go off like this. Flek is using it to make the other boys distrust you."

Straw laughed. "Did we expect anything different from him? I reckon I can deal with whatever Flek thinks up. Besides, he hasn't bothered me for a long time."

"You've been lucky so far because the masters favor you. I suspect that Flek is only waiting to make his move until they stop watching over you so closely."

"Thanks for the warning. Not much I can do about it anyway."

Since being caught by Matild, Flek had kept his distance from the boy. Several weeks had passed without any more incidences. Straw took this for a silent peace declaration and a sign that Flek and his companions had finally accepted him. It turned out that Colin was closer to understanding Flek's plans.

It began with subtle tricks that Straw mistook at first for oversights on his part. One evening, he was standing to the side chatting with some of the boys after he had finished covering his portion of the barn floor. Keg came hustling over to him.

"Straw, stop your jawin'. You've left your portion bare. Go take care of it." The Barn Master knew which part of the floor was covered by each of them. Straw was certain Keg was mistaken, but when he went to take a look, sure enough, his assigned space was bare. He thought it odd, but shrugged it off and completed the work.

The second time this happened, he scolded himself for inattention and swore he would not make that mistake again. The third time it happened, he suspected someone was setting him up. He never caught the culprits, but he found out that on the days when he kept his eye on his work after walking to the side, there was never any problem. It happened only when his back was turned. By enlisting the help of Colin and Frog, he discovered who of Flek's companions were going over to Straw's area to sneakily rake the straw away. The boy was ready to fight this one out.

"No fighting," Colin warned. "They'll deny doing it and you'll get in trouble for causing a disturbance in the barn."

"I don't want to have to cover my area twice," Straw protested. "And get in trouble with Keg over it."

"Look, we'll take turns keeping watch. If they know we're watching, they won't do it."

This worked but did not stop the harassment. Flek and his friends had many more tricks up their sleeves. Straw had to endure a long series of pranks. When he went to bed, he would find handfuls of straw under the covers on his mat. His shoes would be missing in the morning and he would find them next to one of the water pumps filled with mud. Repeatedly, as he balanced a full bowl of stew while passing one of the tables, a leg would shoot out and trip him. Once he was locked in the outhouse and had to shout for help until someone came and released him. Another time, he went to his mat in the evening only to find it altogether missing. He found it eventually on the pitched roof outside the dormitory window.

Straw had to deal with these pranks about once a week. They were annoying and inconvenient, but never involved personal injury. The boy stayed on his guard and accepted this treatment stoically and patiently. He expected that with time they would get bored and give it up. Little did he suspect that one of Flek's schemes would change his life forever.

Chapter Seven

Just a Coincidence

The leaves on the trees were beginning to turn, but not yet fall in any great numbers. The weather had been deliciously warm for weeks, but this day was overcast and misty. The boy knew that out in the fields, the farmers were busy preparing for the fall harvest. The Harvest Festival would come soon, which culminated with a procession including Star. It was an annual event, and this would be the first time the boy would experience it as a member of the compound. He was very excited and looking forward to it. There was a stir among all the staff, as special decorations were prepared and holiday clothing sewn.

The day had begun routinely enough. After grabbing a quick bite, he had gone into the barn to visit Star. Keg was glad to see him, since there were many things to prepare for the Harvest Festival. He asked Straw to help with an inventory of tools until the other boys arrived.

After lunch all the boys were kept busy around the compound. Straw spent the whole afternoon helping Gil, one of the compound's resident carpenters, to balance the wheels of a cart. It was fascinating work for the boy, learning how to align and tighten the spokes just right so the wheels would roll smoothly. Once they were finished, he decided to check in with Keg to see if there was some small job he could do in the barn before it was time to spread the straw. He had just set out when one of the other stall boys came up to him. Straw did not know him very well. His nickname was Green.

"Keg's been looking for you," Green said. "He wants you to bring him some boards that a joiner left outside the northwest gate." He pointed out the direction and went on his way. There were gates and doors all around the compound, and supplies might be delivered to any one of them. The northwest gate was nothing more than a door in the wall. It looked like it was not used very often. It lay off to the side, behind one of the smaller storage buildings. Grass had grown up all along its base. Straw expected to find some of the other boys there as well, since a load of lumber would require many hands and probably even a cart. Green had not mentioned that he should bring a cart himself, so he figured that someone else had.

The area was deserted and quiet. Maybe he had just missed them carrying the first load away. The door was ajar, and he had to force it against the high grass to get it to open wider.

Strange, he thought. *How did they get the wood through this small opening?* He slipped through the doorway. It was the first time that he had stepped outside the walls of the compound since he had been admitted months before. He had not once in all this time had the slightest desire to leave. It was strange now to walk so casually outside. He was on the back side of the compound, opposite the town. He took in the wide open fields stretching out before him. The grain had been harvested, and small flocks of birds were rising and settling in the stubble. The scent of wood fires was in the air. In the far distance he could make out a line of mountains. Not far away stood the edge of the forest.

He breathed in the moist air and felt a deep sense of satisfaction with how his life had changed. It was only then that he realized something was wrong. He looked around, but there was no sign of any lumber. There was not even a cart track showing that someone had made a delivery. Had he come to the wrong door? It was not normal for a gate to be left open for no purpose. What was going on?

That was when he heard the soft thump of the door being shut behind him. He whirled around and watched the narrow gap of the doorway close. He heard the bolt being pushed into place, barring his way back in.

"Hey," he called out running up to the door. "Hey, I'm out here. Open up!" He pounded on it with his fist. It made a dull sound. It was solid oak, but he was certain he was making enough noise to be heard on the other side.

"Hey! Open up! It's me, Straw. I'm out here! Open up!"

There was no response from the other side. He put his ear to the wood, but it was too thick to let any sound through. He pounded on it several more times. "Hey!" he yelled, now angry. "Let me back in!"

No one came. Had someone closed the door without looking to see if anyone was outside? He was annoyed with their carelessness. At the same time he suspected that he had been set up and tricked. He was furious that he had walked into a trap.

He pounded a few more times, and then he kicked the door in frustration. He needed to find a way back in. He looked up and down the walls. Maybe there was another gate open. He knew that he would be in trouble if they found him out here. If he could find an open gate, he could explain what had happened and maybe the whole thing would be overlooked.

He considered the wall. If he could grab onto something, he was certain he could scale it. The wall was made of stone that had been cut and dressed. It offered no handholds. He jumped twice, trying to grab onto the top ledge. He succeeded in doing nothing more than scraping the palm of his left hand.

He looked around for a tree to help him climb over. Or for large rocks he could pile up against the wall. Nothing. In the end, he chose a direction and began walking. Maybe something would show up.

He considered walking around until he came to the front gate and pounding on it until someone opened up. He was wearing a compound tunic, so they would have to let him in. But that way, Garth would hear about it. To make things worse, he was so far away from the front gate that he would miss his barn duty. That meant double trouble. This was not an option. He had to find a way over.

After walking for awhile and finding every gate and doorway shut and barred, he turned and jogged back in the other direction. Still no luck and it was getting late. He just had to get back in.

He walked a few yards away from the wall and sized it up. It was not a particularly high wall, but he was not a particularly tall boy. It was just too high for him to jump up and reach the top. If Colin were there, he could give him enough of a lift to get over. He took a running start and when he came to the wall tried putting his foot against it to give himself a boost. He scraped his hand again, but he did feel that he had gotten higher.

This gave him some hope. He walked out into the field and finally found some stones that looked like they would work. He needed several of them, and they had to be flat enough that he could pile them on top of one another next to the wall. They were heavy, but he managed to turn them on their sides and awkwardly roll them to the wall. By the time he was finished, he was in a sweat, and one finger was numb from getting pinched between two stones. The back of his left hand was bloodied, but he could not remember how it happened. At any rate, it was now worth a try.

He walked away from the wall into the fields and took a running start. When he came to the stones, he used them as a step and then leapt. The momentum of his movement did the rest. He crashed against the wall, felt a blow to his face and was stunned. At the same time, however, his hands managed to reach and hold onto the top of the wall. He hung there a moment, shook his head and caught his breath. His head was jarred and he gingerly touched his teeth with his tongue to find out if they were all still there. He was staring at the stones pressed up against his cheek. It was all blurry. His handhold, though, was secure.

Pulling with all his might and using his feet to push against the wall, he slowly raised himself up. He grunted and in the end yelled out loud to give himself the strength to lug his body onto the top. He got one elbow up, then the other, and once his head cleared the edge, he knew there was no way he was going to let himself fall back down.

He heaved his body onto the flat top of the wall and rolled onto his back. He lay there staring at the sky, breathing heavily and feeling thankful that the wall was flat on top and not spiked. An enemy army could scale it easily. But why bother? Who would attack a dragon?

He was proud of himself for making it on top. He had no time to lose, though. He suddenly realized the sun had long since set and dusk was turning into darkness. That meant only one thing: He was late. He had missed strewing his portion of straw on the barn floor, and there was no way Keg would not have noticed. Everyone would be at supper by now.

On the one hand, this would be welcome. If he hurried, he could still get there before the barn was closed down for the night. He might still have a chance to do his work. Keg would probably give him a scolding, but it would not go any further.

He rolled off the wall on the compound side and let himself down as far as he could before he dropped. It was still a long fall for him, and he hit the ground hard. He got up and wanted to run to the barn, but immediately fell over again. Something was wrong with his ankle. He held it and felt around, but fortunately, although it was tender and weakened from twisting, it did not seem broken. He got up slowly and gently put weight on it. It was sore, but it held. Limping, he made his way as quickly as he could towards the big barn.

It was as he suspected. Star had long since returned and the stall boys had finished their raking and moved on to eat their supper. The barn was now lit by many lanterns which cast a warm, golden glow all around. The dragon, due to his immense size, lay mostly in deep shadows.

Although the part of the barn where he stood was empty of other workers, Straw was worried that Keg would still be bustling around. He heard some faint conversation at the far end of the barn. The great expanse of the dragon lay between him and those voices, bodiless echoes bouncing off the high ceiling. He still had a chance. He took a rake down from its rack on the wall and walked over to where he usually worked. As was his custom, Star had lain down right on top of the area Straw needed to cover with fresh straw. He could tell that it was still bare. If he could tell, then Keg had also noticed. He had to do something. There was not enough straw on the ground that he could move what was there around and make it look finished. He put down his rake and, taking a pitchfork, carried three big loads of straw over to Star from a pile that lay to the side.

Straw looked up at Star in despair. He was lying across the bare spot. How was he going to get him to move over so he could finish?

"Star," he began, looking beseechingly up at the dragon. Hearing his name called, Star looked over his shoulder to see who was speaking. He seemed to be listening to what the boy was saying. He had never done this before, although Straw frequently addressed him. Star's attention surprised him and, at the same time, gave him courage to continue. He was not quite sure how to go about this.

"Star," he repeated, "I know you probably don't understand what I'm saying. But I didn't have time to lay out my section of straw, see. Some of the other boys played a trick on me, and I was locked out of the compound, and I had to, well, anyway, I couldn't finish up here. Star, if you could just move over, I can put down fresh straw for you to lie on more comfortably. See, I have it right here, all ready. Just about ten or fifteen feet over would do it."

Then the pure foolishness of what he was doing struck him and he just laughed bitterly to himself and muttered, "I guess not."

Star, who had listened intently to the boy's request, against all expectations, shimmied away from the boy and looked down at the area freed up as if to ask, "Is that enough?"

The boy could not believe his eyes. There was no mistaking it, though. The dragon had actually moved over. *Surely,* the boy thought, *it must be a coincidence.* It did not matter. He could now finish his work.

"Oh, Star, that was wonderful," the boy stammered. "Thank you!" Sincere relief and gratefulness flooded him. He quickly grabbed his rake. As he began to fill the area in with straw, he wondered, Had it been mere coincidence? Or had Star actually understood him and done what he asked? He stood there a moment biting his lip. He just had to find out. It was too great a temptation to resist.

"Star, most beautiful dragon, another five feet would make it perfect," he said, expecting nothing. Without hesitation, Star shimmied over a second time, giving him a full ten feet extra.

The boy could only stand there and stare. He was not sure why the dragon was willing to do what he asked when even the Dragon Master had to use a star-pole to direct the great beast to go where he wanted him.

"That was magnificent," he whispered. "Thank you, Star!" He immediately set to work to complete his job and get out before anyone noticed.

Unknown to the boy, though, he *had* been observed. The voices he had heard upon entering the barn were those of Keg and Garth. They had been discussing preparations for the upcoming procession when they noticed the dragon move. Garth was surprised to see the dragon shimmy over, not once but twice, and they both wondered what could have caused that. Silently, they walked around to the front of the dragon in time to see the boy complete his work and put his rake away before hurrying off.

"That's Straw," Keg said.

"I know the boy," Garth commented dryly. "Didn't know he had a name now."

"Nickname, you know, like many of them carry. Anyway, I was wondering what had happened to him. Didn't show up to lay the floor this evening. Not like him to leave his work unfinished. He's a right good worker. Often helps me out in the morning before the others come in. He likes being around the dragon as much as I like having him around me."

"Seems that boy's got a way with Star," Garth pondered.

"Sure looks that way," Keg said. "Probably just a coincidence."

"Probably," Garth repeated. When Keg turned to go back to what he had been working on, Garth stood there a long time looking where the boy had worked.

Straw had made it into the commons just as the cleanup crew was finishing. Normally, missing a meal time meant missing a meal. Matild, though, had seen him wander in.

"You, boy," she commanded, pointing directly at him. "Into the kitchen. Right now." It was her way to volunteer anyone she wanted at any time. No one argued with her. Straw had already been through a lot this day, and he figured he was going to have to face some more. Dutifully, he followed her into the kitchen.

"I've got some pots here that need scrubbing," Matild informed him. "But they need emptying first. You know where the bowls and spoons are."

Matild was gone to another part of the kitchen before he realized what she had said. When he looked inside the pots, he saw there was enough stew left over for about two bowls. Even if he had to scrub pots for it, he was grateful for dinner. When she saw him sitting on the table eating, Nellie brought him a piece of bread. As he ate, he sighed happily.

After he had cleaned the pots, Matild found Straw a few other chores to do, and this kept him in the kitchen until nearly bed time. While he worked, Straw had plenty of time to think about what had happened in the barn. He was itching to tell someone. He had to find Colin.

Before the lanterns were turned out, Straw dragged Colin out of the dormitory into the night. Fireflies flickered in the branches above their heads. Straw told him about being locked out of the compound.

"Those rats," Colin growled. "They ganged up on you this time. But I'd say that's pretty good getting back in all by yourself. They're going to be all agog when you don't get into trouble. Now I understand why they were so cheerful at supper. Let's fill Flek's shoes with fewmets. He hates fewmets. I'll be more than glad to help."

"No, I don't care about that. We can save the fewmets for another time. Look, if I hadn't been late, I would've never found out that Star listens to me."

"What are you talking about?"

The boy explained what happened in the barn.

"He moved over for you?" Colin asked incredulously.

"I still don't believe it," Straw said.

"He did it twice?"

"That's why I had to tell you. It was remarkable."

"Star doesn't even glance at me when I talk to him," Colin said with big eyes.

"Look, Colin, I had to tell somebody, but promise to keep it to yourself. I don't think anyone else should know about it."

"Not a soul. You could get in trouble for that, you know. We're not allowed to mess with Star."

"I know we're not allowed to mess with Star. But I didn't really mess with him. I just had him move a bit so I could finish my work."

"Are you going to do it again?" Colin was all excited at the prospect. "Can I watch?"

"No," Straw said earnestly. "I can't afford to be seen doing something like that."

"All right," said Colin a bit disappointed. "I understand. But if you do it again, let me watch, all right?"

"Oh, gee," Straw said rolling his eyes. "It's not going to happen again. It was probably just a coincidence anyway. Come on, let's get back before lights out." He started back towards the dormitory.

Colin followed behind saying, "Well, the next time there's a coincidence, remember to tell me about it ahead of time. I have to see Star taking directions from a stall boy. That is just too much."

Chapter Eight

The Procession

The day for the harvest procession finally arrived. The trees within the compound had turned a blaze of fall colors. The sky was full of white, streaky clouds against a deep blue background. There was a slight nip in the air, a reminder that summer had come to an end.

"No mind," said Alis cheerfully. "It'll keep my flowers from fading too quickly."

Straw noticed that Alis was wearing a garland of flowers in her hair. She was no longer dressed in her kitchen smock, but wore instead a white linen dress stitched along the edges with blue forget-me-nots. She wore an apron that was finely embroidered with flowers and butterflies. She had transformed herself from a scullery maid into the daughter of a noble house.

"You look grand," Straw admired.

"Thank you," she said, her cheeks flushing red. "You look grand, too."

"These are the only clothes I have, I'm afraid," he said, shrugging his shoulders and looking down at what he wore every day.

"Well, they fit you well," Alis said honestly. "One day you'll have more. You know, Colin, you could have given him one of your festival shirts. You have enough to share. And you could have put one on yourself."

"Um, you're right, I guess. It didn't occur to me," Colin said abashed. He also was wearing his work-a-day clothing. "Next time for sure. Come on, let's get into town. Who cares how we look?"

"You will, if we run into any of our family," his sister said.

The three children were headed for the great front gates of the compound. Suddenly Straw held back.

"What's up?" Colin asked.

"It's strange," Straw said. "I haven't been out of the compound since the day I came. Except when they locked me out, but that doesn't count, because I climbed back in as soon as I could. It feels strange to leave. A part of me doesn't really want to. I've found a new life here, and I don't want to risk it."

"Don't worry," Alis said, hooking his arm. "We'll make sure you get back."

"We'll just stay together all day," Colin said. "That way we'll be sure to be in place on time. If we're not in position when the procession begins, Garth will have our hides tanned and hung on the wall of the barn as a warning to the others."

Laughing, the three children walked arm in arm out of the compound and into the town. Colin and Alis kept Straw between them and all three stayed together wherever they went. The whole town was decked out in its finest. Flags flew in the light breeze and banners hung from the houses. The air was thick with the scent of cooked foods, and the streets were lined with vendors selling all things imaginable from shoes to wigs. Everyone was in a festive mood and laughter hovered in the air.

Straw was amazed how they were treated when they approached any of the food booths. Small portions of whatever was for sale were pushed into their hands for free. "It's because we work in the compound," Colin muttered, as he shoved a buttered bun into his mouth and then wiped the grease off on the backside of his pants.

"They even give us sweetmeats," Alis said.

"This is amazing," Straw admired. After Galifalia's death, shopkeepers had treated him to only kicks and curses.

As the day wore on, the three made their way to the open fields where knights were giving demonstrations of jousting and sword fighting. There was a lot of dust, neighing of horses and clanging of metal against metal. The three children were delighted with the excitement it created.

"They don't do anything to get hurt, you know, but it's still fun to watch," Colin commented.

"Ooh, ooh," Alis said pointing. "Over there."

"That knight," explained Colin, "the one with the purple and gold ribbons on his helm. That's our uncle. He was in charge of the garrison in the compound until two years ago. He's a highly honored knight." The twins waved enthusiastically, but their uncle did not seem to notice them.

"Visor," explained Colin. "He said you can't see much through it anyway."

When the knights took a short rest, the children ran off to see the festival games on the green. Watching some farmers try and catch a greased pig, they laughed until their sides ached. In the tug-of-war contest, they joined in and pulled with all their might, being very careful not to fall into the mud pit in the middle.

They bobbed for apples, and Colin was so determined that he dove nearly to the bottom of the barrel to get his apple. He came up wet to the shoulders, but shrugged it off with a laugh that the sun would be his towel. Both Straw and Alis had to hang on, one on each arm, to keep him from trying to climb the pole greased with oil to get the basket of sticky buns perched on its top. Only when Alis promised him a double portion of bread with honey for the next three days did he agree to just stand by and watch. Straw could not remember when he had laughed so much.

Finally, in the late afternoon, the horns sounded. "That's the signal," said Alis. "We've got to get in place."

"Out in the great fields," said Colin. "Say, when you lived in town, you went to the processions, didn't you?"

"Yes," said Straw quietly. "With my grandmother. I even remember where we stood." Then he had an idea. "Say, I'd like to go stand there again. Do you think it'd be all right?"

"No problem," said Colin. "We don't have any special order other than to be present and stand in a line along the crowds. We form a sort of living fence between the people and the dragon. So no one gets the idea of running out in front of him."

As they walked along the procession field, Alis said to Straw, "Colin told me about what happened in the barn."

"Colin!" Straw said surprised. "You promised me you wouldn't tell anyone else."

"She's my twin, Straw," Colin said hanging his head. "Telling her is like talking to myself. We don't have secrets from each other. I'm sorry."

"Straw," said Alis, "I believe that Star did move over for you. I really do."

"It was a coincidence," Straw said. "You know, I'd like to just forget about it."

They walked in silence until Straw suddenly said, "This is it. This is where I used to stand with my grandmother. I recognize it because of the two apple trees over there that have grown all tangled and twisted together." Not far away had been Galifalia's cottage and garden, but he did not mention that. Soon after her death, the house had been burnt down, the fence around the garden pulled out, the garden torn up. He never understood why, and he had fled, fearing for his life.

"Then here we'll stand and watch the procession," Alis said.

There were other workers from the compound there as well, and they made a widely-spaced line with their backs to the crowd.

The boy remembered many such processions held in the spring to bless the fields and in the fall to celebrate the harvest. It was always the same. First flocks of geese were driven down the field. They waddled and honked in protest as they went. Then came the sheep, bleating their loud complaint. Herds of goats followed next, walking slowly, looking around for something to nibble. Last of all came the cattle, garlands of colorful flowers braided around their horns. The calves of the springtime were now half grown and frisked in front of the more serene mature cows and steers.

Next came donkeys, also decked out with flowers and pulling the field carts. The carts were piled high with every manner of fruit and vegetable. The first ones were overflowing with apples, pears and grapes. The more perishable leafy and soft vegetables followed. Behind them were carts holding the sturdier squashes and root crops that could be stored over the winter months. Finally many carts laden with sacks of grain followed. Behind this procession walked the farmers with their rakes, shovels and pitchforks over their shoulders. People applauded and cheered as they passed.

The different guilds were next in the procession: the bakers in white, carrying beautifully braided loaves of bread, the shoemakers wearing their shiny leather aprons, the weavers carrying bolts of colorful cloth spanned between them, the washers and dyers lugging their tubs, the builders with long rulers balanced on their shoulders, and finally the many different artisans, each displaying some token of his art. The people watching clapped and called out hearty greetings to those they knew. Finally the nobility came, flanked by finely dressed pages blowing long handled horns. In their midst walked King Pell and Queen Meg, waving to the cheering crowds. It was all so very grand. The whole town had shown up in their finest.

"There's Mother," Alis cried out.

"Which one?"

"On the queen's left, right next to her."

"She's beautiful," Straw said sincerely.

"I know. I so miss her. Mom! Mom!" But the cheers of the crowd were louder. Straw glanced at Colin. He looked slightly embarrassed by his sister, but he was waving as well.

Last of all came Star. He wore trailing garlands of ribbons and flowers and was flanked by the dragon guides carrying their long poles. Garth, the Dragon Master, walked before him. He wore a brightly embroidered tunic and waved to people in the crowd who hailed him. Straw sighed, remembering all the times his grandmother had brought him and held him up to see over the line of stall boys. And now here he was one of them. It was a dream come true. He was very happy and content.

Just as Star was passing where the boy stood, something went wrong. The great dragon hesitated and shook his massive head once. He stood in his tracks and would not move. The dragon guides were quick to act, calling out loudly their encouragement to Star to keep walking, prodding him with their long poles. Star ignored them, looking into the crowd as if searching for something. When his glance found the boy, he stared straight at him. By this time, the crowd was aware that something unexpected was happening. The dragon guides were openly agitated, but Star utterly disregarded their efforts to get him walking again and was intent on doing something else. He turned toward the crowd and ambled right over to the boy until he towered above him. The people behind Straw had grown extremely quiet, although he could hear many gasps of surprise and fear.

Then Star lowered his head. Down, down it came, until his great nose was directly above Straw's head. He could feel the dragon's sweet breath pouring over him.

Star's smelling me, he thought. He felt no sense of danger. It brought back the memory of every other procession when the dragon had come over to greet him. It all seemed so normal. As a young child, it had never occurred to him that this was out of the ordinary. No one ever seemed to mind when his grandmother held him up for Star to sniff.

Now, however, there was a great deal of commotion. As suddenly as he had come, Star moved on again, as serenely as if nothing out of the ordinary had happened. There was a lot of shouting around the boy. He was too stunned to understand anything that was being said. He only felt someone tugging hard on his tunic.

"We have to get you out of here," Alis said urgently into his ear. "You have to come." With Colin on one side and Alis on the other, Straw let himself be hurried away from the field and toward the compound gate. He was so grateful to pass behind the walls and away from the noise and commotion in the procession field.

"What was that all about?" Colin demanded as soon as they were safely inside the compound walls.

Before Straw had a chance to answer, Mali came running up to them. "Straw, I hope you have a good explanation. The Dragon Master is in a fit over what went on out there. He said nothing like that has happened since Galifalia was alive. He wants to see you immediately."

Straw looked up blankly at Mali. He was not sure what to say. Why was Mali talking about Galifalia? What did she have to do with this?

"Get going," Mali ordered.

"Where? Go where?"

"To the barn," Mali said. "Garth is just settling Star down and wants to see you there."

Straw took a deep breath and started to walk. He had no explanation to offer Garth. He had done nothing wrong. He had not called Star over to him. Star always came over during processions and smelled him. How could he know it was not allowed?

As Straw came around the trees, he had a view of the whole open side of the barn. His eyes were drawn by some motion. He saw an old man with a long flowing beard, wrapped in a traveling cloak standing in front of the dragon. Star was looking intensely down at him. Then the old man turned and disappeared into the darkness of the barn. On the other side of the dragon, Straw saw Garth standing next to the wall. The boy walked over to him.

"Sir, you wanted to see me?" Straw said.

Garth looked distracted, as if trying to figure out some riddle.

"Sir?"

Now Garth saw him. "Ah, there you are," he said. "Thank you for coming."

"Sir," Straw began. "I'm not sure I can explain what happened out there. I only know that—" He was ready to tell about his experiences as a child, but Garth did not give him a chance. He waved a hand to stop him from speaking.

"I don't need any explanations," he stammered. "I only wanted to see if you were all right."

Straw looked up at him and blinked. At best, he had expected to be scolded. At worst, to be sent out of the compound. He did not expect the Dragon Master to ask after his wellbeing. "Yes, sir, I'm all right."

"Good," said Garth. "Then you can go back to the others. Have something to eat. Get some rest."

Straw stared a moment at the Dragon Master, then shrugged his shoulders. He turned to go, then stopped. "Sir, I have a question."

"What is it?"

"Who was that man I saw as I came around the trees? He was standing in front of Star, and it looked like he was talking to him."

"No," said Garth, looking at him sharply. "You're mistaken. There's no one else in the barn but me. I'm alone. I assure you, I'm alone."

"Yes, sir," Straw said. "Thank you, sir." He did not wait to be told twice that the old man was none of his business. He made his way back to find Alis and Colin and share with them his strange encounter with Garth.

Chapter Nine

Dragon Boy

At dinner that night, Colin and Straw watched Flek's eyes grow wide with astonishment when they walked into the commons together. Flek was not the only one. There was murmuring, side-long glances and open stares from half the people there.

"You can't blame them for gawking," Frog commented. "We're all amazed. If this had happened to anyone else, we'd have packed our bags and headed back to our parent's home in disgrace. You lead a charmed life, Straw."

"I understand as little as the rest of you what's going on," Straw grumbled. "I just wish they wouldn't stare at me so much. It's not like I did anything wrong."

"Oh, no, nothing much," Mixer said. "Just interrupting the harvest procession so Star could come over and eat out of your hand."

"He did not!" Straw protested.

"Well, that's what everybody's saying," Frog said.

"Lay off, will you?" Colin said. "We're supposed to be on his side."

"We are, Col," Mixer said. "But you have to admit, it's weird. You do see that, don't you?"

"Oh, just forget it," Straw said, getting up.

"Hey, Straw, don't go," Colin said.

"I want to be alone. I need time to think about this." Straw took his bowl and went to the washing lines. He was not as troubled by

Star's attention as he was by Garth's acting so unconcerned about it. And who was that old man he had seen with Star, and why did Garth pretend he had not been there?

Out of the corner of his eye, he could not help noticing the glare from Flek as he passed by. It was icy cold.

The next morning at breakfast, Flek again stared at him.

"He can't figure out why you're still here," Colin said with satisfaction. Straw rolled his eyes. The evening before, whenever he had passed by other stall boys, they had grown silent. The moment he was out of earshot, their gossip became animated.

"Look, I don't want to talk about it any more," Straw said. "Can't we just forget it?"

"Forget it? You may want to forget it, but how are you going to stop everyone else from talking about it?"

"Oh, gee, just leave me alone."

All morning Straw worked in the barn in silence. He would not talk to anyone. By lunchtime he had no appetite at all. He wandered off to be by himself. He found a clump of trees where he could sit in the shade and look into the empty barn.

This was the first day since coming to the compound that he did not volunteer to help after the noon meal. He sat under the trees outside the barn and just wanted to become invisible.

He did not leave the trees until it was time to lay the straw for Star's return. Once his duties were done, he did not join the rest as they wandered off to dinner. His appetite was still gone. He returned to his clump of trees, deciding to wait there until lantern lighting. There was at least another hour of daylight, so he made himself comfortable. Maybe something useful would occur to him. At least he did not have to watch the other boys gossip about him.

He was frustrated. All he wanted to do was spend time around Star. He did not want to cause any trouble; he just wanted to do his work and be left alone. He looked over at the dragon lying in the barn. Star lay stretched out, his great head resting between his feet. He appeared to be dozing, his eyes only half open. The boy sighed. The dragon was so beautiful, whether he was resting, flying or walking. Straw could not get his fill, no matter how long he watched him.

"I can't believe you're still here." Straw was startled by the voice. He looked up to see who had spoken. To his surprise, there were a dozen boys walking up to him. In their lead was Flek.

"Why haven't you been thrown out of here yet?" Flek asked. His tone was not friendly. "I don't get it. You're making a mockery of us."

"Not now, Flek. Can't you just leave me alone?" Straw was in no mood to deal with this.

"Oh, sorry, your majesty. I didn't know you were busy. Should I come another time when it's more convenient for you?" There was some snickering among the other boys. "You know what your problem is, dung boy? You're still just some trash one of the dogs dragged in. Carrying dragon dung is even too good for you. We should throw you back into the compost where you came from."

Straw knew he was being baited, but this did not make it any easier to resist jumping Flek and pushing his nose into the dirt. He also knew that this was just what Flek was waiting for. With so many other boys watching, they would all agree that Straw had hit Flek first. No one would think to mention that Flek had taunted him.

Straw noticed that Colin had walked up to the group as well, together with Frog and Mixer. "What's going on?" Colin asked.

"What makes this piece of trash so special?" Flek asked. "He smells like any normal pile of dung."

"Give it up, Flek," Colin said. "Can't you just leave him alone?"

"What are you afraid he's going to do if I don't? Hurt me? Maybe sic his pet dragon on me? Go on," Flek challenged Straw. "Go on and try and hit me. I won't mind. You're so small, I won't feel it anyway."

When Straw said nothing, Flek added, "Not only are you small, you're a coward."

Straw did not know how much more of this he could take. He clenched his fists and held his ground. Inside he was seething. He considered his choices. He could turn and walk away. But this would not end Flek's taunting. Straw could smack him and start a fight. He was not afraid about whether he could hold his own. On the streets he often had to tangle with some bully bigger than he was. And being small, it had been necessary to make sure everyone knew not to mess with him. Here in the compound, it was different. He had been warned not to start a fight. Did he just have to suffer Flek's abuse as long as he lived in the compound? This was a depressing thought.

"Not only are you small and a coward," Flek continued, obviously enjoying himself, "you're a weakling. You can barely push your broom. You're always the last done, and you can't even cover your area. We've all heard Keg complain about you. And you're slow. You're so insignificant, it's a miracle that the dragon hasn't rolled over yet and squashed you. He doesn't even know you're there."

Straw wanted to shout out that if his area was not covered well, it was because Flek and his friends kept undoing his work. And he was last to finish because he stayed to be alone with Star, because he loved Star. It burned hot in his soul when Flek said that Star did not even know he was there. Star did know. In fact, Star honored him above all of the other boys. It was to him that Star had come during the procession.

"You think everyone is impressed because the dragon came to you out there," Flek continued, as if reading the boy's thoughts. "Star hadn't noticed you yet. He was looking for a place to crap and saw an empty spot where you were standing. The dragon pays about as much attention to you as he does to a fly."

"That's not true!" Straw blurted out. His blood was boiling. The words tumbled out of him before he could stop them. If his fists were not allowed to fly, his tongue would. "That's a lie! Star knows I'm there. He came looking for me. He has always come to greet me in the processions. Star will do whatever I ask him to. I can get him to do whatever I want, I can!" Straw was not quite sure why he was saying this, and he had no idea if it was true. But it was too late to back down now.

"I could take him all alone down to the river if I wanted, and bring him back as well. He'll do whatever I want." He glared at Flek as he said this. He glanced over at Colin, who looked pale and was slowly shaking his head back and forth. Colin must have realized Straw had gone too far. Flek just stood there with a greasy smile on his face. A moment later the boy understood why.

"Is that so?" drawled a deep voice from behind him. The hair on the back of the boy's neck stood up and he whirled around to see who had spoken. Behind him, with his hands on his hips, stood Garth, the Dragon Master. Beside him, with a puzzled look on his face, was Keg. Mali was walking towards them from the barn.

"So you think that Star will do whatever you ask him to do?"

"Yes, sir," interjected Flek quickly. "This arrogant trash, who can't even sweep properly, has been bragging that he can make Star do whatever he wants. It's shameful to talk so, isn't it, sir? He should be punished."

Silently, Garth sized the boy up, pondering, most likely, the most severe punishment he could devise. Perhaps he would even expel him from the compound. Straw opened his mouth to speak, but no words came out. His throat constricted and his mouth went dry.

"Well, before anyone is punished," Garth began slowly, "I have to determine if there is any ground for punishment." He looked questioningly at Flek.

"Well, the others heard him say it, you can ask," Flek answered, uncertain what Garth meant. The other boys looked down at the ground, not wanting to either accuse Straw or defend him.

The Dragon Master looked searchingly at the boy. "Well, is it true?" he asked at last. "Did you claim that you could get Star to do whatever you ask him to?"

Straw did not know how he was going to get out of this. He could not deny that he had said it. He looked down at the ground and nodded his head.

"You see," Flek spat out victoriously. "He admits it."

Straw was near tears. He knew the rule that even though the boys might quarrel among themselves, they had to keep the dragon out of it. He had crossed a forbidden line and there was no going back.

"All right," Garth continued. "So much is clear."

"Punish him!" Flek shouted out.

"Not so fast," the Dragon Master said firmly. The others looked at him questioningly. Even Straw looked up. "I can punish the boy only if what he said is *not* true." They all looked at one another, trying to figure out what he meant. It was Flek who understood first.

"Let's test it out," he said gleefully. He wanted nothing better than to watch Straw humiliate himself in front of everybody.

"That's right," said the Dragon Master and pursed his lips. "Let's test it out. Boy, I'd like you to step out in front of the barn and call for Star to join you there. If what you say is true, he'll do what you ask of him."

At these words, Straw grew very hot and broke into a sweat. All of them were staring at him, waiting to see what he would do. He was so embarrassed, his first impulse was to run away, but he was too proud to turn tail in front of Flek. He was not going to give him that satisfaction. He looked at the faces around him, some taunting, others looking as frightened as he felt.

Mali was standing beside him, and Straw looked up into his kind face. Mali placed his hand on the boy's shoulder and spoke to him softly. "Do what the Dragon Master asks. You won't be punished if he tells you to try."

"Go on, show them," encouraged Colin in a low voice. "You've gone this far, show them all."

Straw had no choice but to try. He knew what had happened before between him and Star must have been some kind of fluke, some sort of coincidence. Still, it had been so real that he truly believed that Star had understood his requests and willingly complied.

Straw glanced up at Star lying with his great chin resting on his leg, closely watching the knot of stall boys across the yard. It seemed to Straw that the dragon had been following their conversation with interest. How much language did Star actually understand? Probably not more than single word commands, much like a dog.

"Go on," said Garth in a quiet voice. "Give it a try and let's get this over with."

The boy had no choice. He walked slowly out into the great yard in front of the barn. He walked far enough away that the dragon would be able to clear the bulk of his body past the doors if he came out. If he came out?? What was he thinking? The dragon wasn't going anywhere.

"That's far enough," he heard the Dragon Master call. Straw stopped walking and turned to face the barn. All the boys were watching him. Flek stood there, his arms folded across his chest, a big grin across his face. He was almost hopping from foot to foot, barely able to contain himself. Mali, Garth and Keg stood apart from the boys, and Garth was whispering something in Keg's ear. Straw looked over at Star, who was staring at him with great interest.

Straw took a deep breath and let it out slowly. He opened his mouth, but closed it again. *What's the use?* he thought. Who was he fooling? Only himself.

Time stood still. He felt a shift in his chest and everything around him became vividly clear. The sky was as blue as a periwinkle, the billowy clouds above his head were the brightest white he had ever seen. The birds in the trees sang their evening song with intense clarity. Every shadow was as vivid as wet ink on paper.

The boy's vision blurred with tears and he reached up to wipe them on his sleeve. He loved this dragon so much, he could not stand the thought of having to leave the compound. He felt a dull and heavy pain in his chest. He drew in a ragged breath and knew he had to get it over with.

"Star," he called out in a hoarse voice, raising one hand above his head, his palm facing the dragon in a gesture of greeting. "Oh, Star, love of my life, come to me. Please, come to me." He lowered his arm with a decisive, beckoning movement.

For a brief moment, Star just stared at him, and the boy thought, *They'll have me out of here before lantern lighting.* Then suddenly, in one fluid movement and a great swooshing sound, Star raised himself nimbly up onto his feet.

"I don't believe this!" Flek gasped. "Stop him. He's mad." There was a shocked murmuring from the stall boys standing around.

"Ya-hoo!" Colin celebrated.

Star walked lightly out of the barn straight towards Straw. He stopped in front of him, towering over his small figure, looking down his long snout, all of his attention on what the boy might ask next.

"Just as I suspected," muttered Garth, but only Keg heard this comment. Then he called out loudly, "Boy, tell him to raise his legs one at a time and put them down again. You know, put him through his paces."

Straw could not believe his eyes. Star had actually done what he had asked. He did not just shimmy over to make it easier for Straw to sweep, Star had actually left the barn at his command. Tears welled up in Straw's eyes and began to stream down his face. Straw raised his right hand with his palm open toward Star's great head. The dragon lowered his neck down so that the boy could reach up and touch him. The boy caressed the side of the dragon's long snout, and everyone could hear the subtle sound of chimes coming from deep in the dragon's throat.

"Star," the boy sobbed. "Star, I love you."

The dragon nudged the boy on the shoulder, and, although for a dragon it was done gently, Straw lost his balance and nearly fell over. The dragon nudged him again, and then again, as if to tell him to get on with it. The boy began to laugh. What the Dragon Master had told him to do finally registered.

"Star," he spoke in a clear, commanding voice. "Raise your right foreleg."

Star raised his leg and held it suspended in the air.

"Put it down now," the boy commanded. Star put his leg down.

"That was beautifully done, my love. Now the other foreleg, please," Straw said. Star did as he was told.

The boy had Star raise each leg in turn and put it down again. Then he told the dragon to turn in a big circle. Star began to rotate his body around, his immense tail clearing the ground by only a few feet. The onlookers were standing so close that, as Star turned, they realized his tail was going to sweep right across their path. There were stifled screams and some of the group scattered and ran, while others dropped quickly to the ground, trusting the tail would pass over them. When the tail actually reached them, Star raised it high over their heads.

Garth was one of those who had pressed himself to the earth. When the tail passed high above them, he noticed that Star was looking over his shoulder to see the effect of his joke. "Rascal," Garth muttered gruffly, but he smiled nonetheless.

"That's enough," Garth called out loudly. He got back to his feet and slapped the dust out of his tunic. "You've proven your point, Boy. So, Flek," he said, turning to look for him, "do you have any more questions?"

Flek had been one of those who had tried to run for it, but in his panic he had tripped and fallen flat on his face. He had skinned both hands and his cheek. A small trickle of blood ran down to his chin and he wiped it away with the back of his hand. He stood up and dusted off his clothes, moving his mouth but not saying anything. He looked over at Straw with pure hatred. Then without answering the Dragon Master, he turned and walked away.

"Well," said Garth, "I'll take that as your answer. All right, the rest of you, haven't you got any work to do? Let's get on with the day. Go on."

The small group of boys reluctantly broke up as they wandered back towards the barn. Garth, Keg and Mali walked over to Straw.

"That was truly great," smiled Mali and patted the boy firmly on the shoulder.

"I've never seen anyone move Star with that much ease," Keg beamed.

"Nor have I," said Garth severely. He turned to the boy. "How long have you known you can do this?"

Straw began to sputter that he had done it once by accident but had never really tried again because he knew it was not allowed. He was sorry if he had broken any rules and promised never ever again to ask Star to do things for him. He would have gone on, but Garth stopped him.

"Boy, I'm not looking to punish you. But you have to realize that you've lost your position as a stall boy. You will not be sweeping the barn ever again."

The boy's heart felt a stab of grief. He was going to be sent away from the compound after all. He had broken the one rule upheld above all others: Do not mess with the dragon. It was too dangerous to keep him around. He understood they could not take the chance that he might be tempted to try again. He began to plead. "Please, oh, please, I promise never to do it again. Please don't send me away. I promise never to talk again when I'm around Star. I'll be as silent as my broom. I'll clean anything you want me to. I'll collect donkey dung all day. I'll work double shifts. I'll work for the washers. Oh, please, don't send me away."

"Boy, your days of cleaning the barn are over," Garth said sternly, interrupting him. Straw felt his world was coming to a ruinous end. He turned to Mali, hoping he would speak in his defense, but Mali stood there smiling broadly. The masters were of one mind: He had caused more trouble than he was worth. He was, after all, what Flek said, just some trash the dogs dragged in.

"But I can't accept that you won't talk any more around Star," Garth continued. "In fact, that is exactly what we'll need you to do. If you refuse this, you'll have to go."

The boy stood there stunned, trying to make sense of the Dragon Master's words. It was Keg who set him straight. "You're not a stall boy any longer because the Dragon Master needs you to be a dragon boy. You'll need a new tunic, I dare say, to mark your new position. If I understand correctly, it will be your job to tell Star what to do and where to go."

"I don't understand how you do it, boy," said Garth. "But the fact is, he obeys you. I said it when you came, there's more to you than meets the eye. You'll work directly under me now. You'll take orders from me or Keg, no one else. You realize yourself that I'm taking a big risk keeping you around, but I have a feeling I can trust you. Come inside and I'll fill you in on your new duties." He began walking towards the barn. He stopped after a few steps and turned back to the boy.

"Before you come, put Star back in the barn, please. No need to make a spectacle of him out here." He smiled and continued to walk away with Mali and Keg, leaving Star completely in the boy's care. Straw watched as Garth made a swooshing motion with his arms like trying to move a flock of stubborn geese. The crowd of gawking kitchen and barn staff reluctantly dispersed.

"Well, I'll be," the boy said. This was the last thing he expected. He looked up at Star who continued to watch him intently, as if waiting for his next command. "Oh, Star, love of my life, you are so beautiful."

The dragon began to purr, and the sound of chimes filled the air. He nudged the boy, and as before, Straw had to take a few steps backwards to keep from falling over.

"Star, the Dragon Master would like you to return to the barn, now. Please."

Holding his tail high, the great dragon deftly turned around and ambled back to his place beneath the great roof and made himself comfortable on his hay. Straw let out a whoop of joy and skipped gleefully behind him all the way back.

Shortly thereafter, Straw presented himself to the Dragon Master.

"I want you every day to take Star down to the river," Garth explained. "Give him a good scrubbing. All over. That's your job. It will keep both of you entertained until late in the afternoon. After what has happened, I think it'll be best for you to stay away from the compound as much as possible for awhile. I have a rough idea what you've been through with Flek, and I don't think he's going to be satisfied leaving things as they are. Let's give his wounded pride a chance to settle down again. Anyway, it will be a good opportunity for you to bond with the dragon. I expect that you'll have a lot to do with him from now on."

Straw still could not manage to speak. The very thought of being with Star from morning until suppertime made him giddy. He was afraid he might float right off the ground. He was startled out of his euphoria by Garth's voice.

"Don't think I'm giving you an easy job. Fact is, you'll work harder than ever you did sweeping floors. Harder than anyone else here at the compound, I daresay. Understand, I'm sending you alone."

"Alone?"

"That's right. No dragon guides, no scrubbers. Just you and the dragon. Think you can handle it?"

The boy looked up at this bear of a man with his wild beard and fierce eyes. "Um, how, uh, I mean..." A question, almost a doubt, was forming in his mind. "I mean, how will I get him there?" The immensity of the task—to move a mountain of a dragon down to the river and back again, and have him hold still long enough to scrub him—was a disturbing thought.

Garth laughed gruffly. "Don't worry about that. From what I saw today, Star is as much in love with you as you are with him. Trust that feeling, and the rest will follow. I'm confident the two of you will work it out."

Part II

The Dragon's Many Secrets

Chapter Ten

A Voice Like Bells

"This is far enough," announced the boy. "Let me down."

The great dragon slowly lowered his head to the earth and the boy climbed down. Straw had become pretty good at this by now. He knew by heart enough hand-holds and flat spots where he could get good footing as he clambered down the maze of the dragon's immense head. There were so many spikes and dips and mounds he had to maneuver, and he had been quite clumsy at first. Always, Star was patient. No matter how long it took the boy, the dragon waited, still and quiet, until Straw reached the ground. But that all seemed a long time ago. By now Straw knew the quickest way down without having to think about it. He threw his buckets and scrubbers ahead of him, and they tumbled and scattered on the grassy bank. The boy raced himself down to the ground, then he looked up at Star and said with a jerk of his thumb, "Get in."

Straw watched the great dragon with pride and admiration. He was more than a little smug that Star would follow his every command. Here was a beast as great as a mountain following the directions of a boy still small for his age. He watched happily as Star walked gracefully down the bank and slid into the water, waded out to midstream, and lowered himself down flat on his belly onto the riverbed. The water rose as it swirled around him. Star left the tip of his tail on the bank to give the boy a dry path from the shore to his back. Straw picked up the scrubbers and filled his buckets before stepping up onto the tail. At first he had to hold his arms out, buckets sloshing and scrubbers waving in the air in order to keep his balance. But very soon the tail was wide enough for him to walk confidently along the row of spikes. He slung the pole of the scrubber over his shoulder and the buckets hung from the pole. Today he had a long walk, all things considered, and he savored every step of the way. When he reached the base of Star's neck, he set to work.

Straw's job, for all intents and purposes, was to scrub the dragon. Since it was a bigger job than he could do in any single day, he had worked out a rotation whereby he scrubbed on the dragon by sections. He would begin at the tip of the tail and work his way towards the head. Every day, he mentally marked the place where he stopped so he would know where to begin the next day. Once Straw finished the back, Star would turn over and he would repeat the process on the belly side. Scrubbing the dragon front and back, from tip of the tail to the point of his snout took him roughly ten days. When he completed his task, Straw simply began all over again.

He was finished scrubbing the back and had come to the part he enjoyed the most: Star's head. He scrubbed more carefully on the head, and yard for yard, it took more time to complete than any other area on the dragon, for the head presented much more than a flat surface. There were ledges and protrusions and special swirls of flashy scales. Star had horns on his head, three sets of them in increasing size. He also had fins of a sort, not so much for the sake of flying, but more like the mane of a lion that increased his magnificence.

Although this work was far more detailed and time-consuming than elsewhere, this was the place the boy looked forward to the most. Straw felt a stronger connection to the dragon when working on his head. He could watch Star's eyes following his every move, or the ears swivel to catch his conversation. He liked that the dragon watched him and took an interest in his activity. It made him feel important. It also provided him with much needed companionship. Since taking over the care of the dragon, Straw had lost much of the contact he had with his friends in the compound. Most of the boys avoided him now and even Colin gawked at him in awe. Only Mali and Keg had remained unchanged towards him. But Garth had been true to his word about keeping him away from the others and out of trouble. He rarely saw anyone except at dinner, and more frequently than not he ate alone.

As a result, Straw liked to talk to himself while he worked. It helped him to while away the tedium of scrubbing and also took away the loneliness. Although he did have a whole dragon to keep him company, Star, as Keg had once joked, was not much of a conversationalist. The fact was, the only noise Straw ever heard Star make was the sound of chimes in the wind when he was half asleep and seemed happy and content.

This particular day, the boy was puzzling over something. The more he scrubbed, the more puzzled he became. He had next to him two full buckets of clear river water, and he was sloshing them generously over the bridge of Star's snout. He was always careful to scrub in the direction the scales grew, in order to avoid jamming any dirt up underneath them.

"These scales are just about the most beautiful thing I can imagine on any beast." He was addressing the dragon directly. Normally, he did not. After all, most parts of the dragon where he spent his time scrubbing were so far away from the head that Straw rarely had the sense that there was anyone there for him to talk with at all. Today, with the dragon eyeing his every sweep with the scrubber, he had a captive audience.

"There's one thing I just don't understand," he shared. "It has baffled me from the first time I ever saw you, and you are my oldest memory, you know. You and Galifalia." The dragon had been holding his great head as still as a boulder in the river. But then something unexpected happened. At the mention of Galifalia's name, he suddenly twitched and the boy nearly lost his balance.

"Whoa!" he called out, throwing out his arms to regain his footing. "What was that all about?" He looked up and saw the dragon not just eyeing him carefully, but with fully raised eyebrows. The three rows of horns on the top of his head stood more erect and towered over the boy's smallness perched there on the dragon's long muzzle. "Did I say something wrong?"

The dragon slowly calmed down. The horns settled a bit onto his head.

"Well, I'm glad at least that I have your attention," he continued. "Although, I can't imagine what I've said to make you so interested. Anyway, you see, it's like this. This is important to me to find out," and he paused with his work to lean on his scrubber and look directly into the dragon's eyes.

"Look at these scales. They are just beautiful. Splendid! Spectacular, even. Each one looks as if it were reflecting a rainbow out of the sky. And when I scrub them with water, why, the rainbow shines even brighter. Reds and golds, and every blue tone imaginable, and then lots of turquoise and greens. It's just phenomenal, even if you are a dragon and already beyond remarkable. So now that I have your attention, can you tell me, why are you called Star and not Rainbow? I don't see a star anywhere. All I can see are rainbows! How in the world did anyone ever get the idea of naming you Star?" As if to prove his point, he lifted his arms wide and indicated the whole landscape of the dragon that swept out before him.

At this, the dragon considered him for a moment silently, with a look as if he might be about to say something. The boy noticed this, and laughed out loud at the thought that the dragon could talk.

"Not that I'm expecting you to know why." He said this in the same way he would talk to a dog, knowing it responds to the energy in his voice, not to the actual content of the words.

"Anyway, I've been thinking a lot about this, seeing that I know every inch of your scales by now, several times over, and I can assure you, there is not a star in sight." The boy had gone back to his scrubbing as he said this, now speaking partly to the dragon, but mostly to himself.

"I even asked Keg about this once, but he insists that you came with that name. Whatever that's supposed to mean."

"It means that there is more to me than meets the eye, which is saying a lot, considering my size."

The voice was so soft, so smooth, so deeply musical that the boy was taken completely by surprise. The voice was coming straight out of the dragon himself. Straw's heart leapt into his throat and felt as if it would burst out of his ears. He screamed out of shock, completely lost his balance and toppled head first off the dragon's snout, right into the river.

The boy was so astonished that he gasped for air, but since he was underwater, all he got for his troubles was to begin choking. This brought him quickly to the surface again, where he began frantically to tread water, sputtering and coughing violently and finally spitting up water. He bellowed in a desperate attempt to clear his lungs, coughed deeply and spit up some more water. He noisily heaved at the air, trying to suck in as much as he could and clear his lungs. He coughed again. He looked up at the dragon who stared down at him in the water with seeming unconcern.

"You can talk!" the boy yelled so loudly he was shrieking. "I heard you talk to me!"

"Of course I can talk," the dragon commented dryly. "What sort of ninny did you take me for?"

Hearing the dragon speak again was so shocking, the boy screamed, stopped treading water and went under for a moment. He came up once again sputtering and spitting water. Straw was growing exhausted from the exertion. The water suddenly swallowed him up for a third time and closed over his head. With a great effort, he propelled himself to the surface once again, but not without swallowing what seemed like half the river. As he came to the surface he was coughing hard.

"Star," he finally squeaked, gasping for air. "Help me out. Please."

He had hardly gotten the words out when he felt the dragon's mighty leg rising slowly and gently beneath him. He landed on it turtle-like with arms and legs spread wide and he was lifted safely a few feet above the surface of the water. Straw lay there a moment intermittently panting, coughing and wheezing, trying to arrange his jumbled thoughts. He shook the water out of his eyes and ears and coughed some more. When his breathing was nearly normal again, he looked up at the dragon and, for the first time since coming to know him, felt something close to fear. Straw had grown cocky. He thought that he knew every inch of this mountainous creature from top to bottom, that the dragon held no secrets from him any longer, and that he had complete control over him. The dragon had become tame, docile, predictable and an object of curious reflection. All of this certainty had now been shaken.

The dragon had many secrets still, which knowing every inch of him from the outside obviously did not reveal. Was the gentleness the boy had grown to accept and depend upon also something he should not be taking for granted? Was his life in danger? Was it possible for Star to suddenly snatch him up with a flick of that long, tongue and swallow him down without a second's hesitation? His disappearance would never be questioned. After all, there would be no one to give answers. It would be assumed that he had slipped, fallen and been swept away by the current of the river. Had this ever happened to any other scrubbing boy? He realized that he had never asked.

Star was patient, as patient as the mountains themselves. He waited for the boy to stop coughing, catch his breath, and ponder all of these questions in his heart. He knew no hurry. A being with a life that stretches over centuries does not question the passing of minutes.

Just as quickly as they had arisen, all of Straw's fearful feelings suddenly passed. Star would never harm him. Of this the boy was certain. So he returned to the origin of his shock. "Star, you spoke to me."

The great dragon turned his head to look at him down his long snout, but said nothing.

"Is that it? Once, and never again?"

"Well, that all depends," the dragon said finally. "I don't care much for idle chatter. I won't talk about the weather, how much milk the cows are giving or the price that barley is bringing." This was followed by a sort of chuckle, as if the dragon had amused himself by what he had said.

Hearing Star's chime-like voice took Straw's breath away again, although this time he kept his balance and did not fall into the river. But his jaw did drop and he placed his hand to his lips. "Your voice is beautiful," he whispered. "Like the rest of you." First and last, the boy was awestruck by the beauty of this dragon.

Then there was silence again. Straw became aware of the squawking of birds in the trees along the bank. He heard the rushing of the water below him as it bubbled against the dragon's great bulk. He could hear his heart beating wildly.

"Why have you never spoken to me before?"

"Before today," the dragon answered slowly, "you never addressed me with a question I was compelled to answer."

"Is it really that simple?" The boy was still completely astonished. "I mean, do you have conversations with the Dragon Master all the time, when you are both alone? Keg never let on for a second that you could talk. I'm sure he would have mentioned it."

There was silence for awhile, as if the dragon were deciding how to respond to this question. For a moment, Straw panicked that he would never hear his voice again. Would he conclude later that he had been hallucinating, fell in the water by accident, hit his head on a stone, imagined he had heard the dragon speak? But that would not be necessary. The dragon did speak again.

"It is rather peculiar, I must say, that you can understand me. It has been a long time since I have had a conversation with anybody, let alone a whiff of a scrubbing boy. It is, in fact, most peculiar. I must think upon this."

The boy looked up into those great emerald eyes that peered at him with such intensity. "Will you be willing to tell me when you are done thinking and ready to talk again?"

Star gave one great nod with his head, which the boy interpreted as agreement.

"I'm going to lie down and rest. And also think this over," the boy said. He climbed up Star's leg and onto his great scaly back. He lay down and snuggled up against a row of spikes in order to lie in the scant shade they provided. Although it was autumn, the noonday sun was still hot. He heaved a sigh and looked up at the irregular clouds that puffed up here and there on the great blue of the heavens. He watched them floating along the currents of the sky and tried to recount to himself everything that had happened since coming to the dragon compound. Had there been any rumor that the dragon could speak? Had he ever overheard someone saying, suspecting, even inferring that Star could speak? These thoughts swirled through his brain as the breeze swirled through the branches of the trees, scattering clouds of dried leaves. He fell into an exhausted sleep.

"Now, how is it that you come to mention the Lady?"

The boy heard this question from very far away as he floated up among the clouds. It was not spoken in a normal voice, but sounded as if chimes could speak. It was the voice of the dragon. Suddenly Straw was wide awake and sitting up straight. He looked around to regain his bearings. He was still on the dragon's back, the sun was still hot, but shadows on the bank told him that the afternoon was no longer young. His clothes were dry and the shade from the spikes in which he lay was more generous. "What? What did you say?"

"How did you happen to mention the Lady?" the dragon repeated. "You seem much too young to have known her."

Straw was baffled by this question. "What lady? I don't remember talking about any lady?"

"Ah, but you did," Star responded. "Up until then I had been ignoring your prattle, as I do every day. But when you mentioned her name, I paid special attention. Did you know her?"

"Who? Who are you talking about?" The boy did not have a clue what the dragon meant.

"The Lady," was all Star said. The boy scrambled from the dragon's back and, using Star's leg as a bridge, sat down on the bank so that they could converse snout to nose, so to speak.

Straw paused a moment before he next spoke. "Look, Star, I don't know any lady. I grew up in a small cottage together with my grandmother. She kept a beautiful, magical garden and spent most of her time tending it, and I spent most of my time playing in it and, as I grew older, helping her. She kept to herself, but helped the villagers when they were sick, having babies, or in trouble. She certainly never helped any ladies, if you mean the nobility. She didn't seem to have many friends, and of the few she had, none of them was a lady. But she died three years ago. The day after she died, our cottage was torched by the villagers and they chased me away. I lived on the streets until I came to the compound. I've never known any ladies."

"That explains everything," Star said and then was silent, as if all questions had been answered.

"What's explained?" asked the boy, thoroughly puzzled.

"The Lady was your grandmother," Star stated as a fact. "And it was you she held up during processions for me to bless. I was certain you smelled familiar the first time you came to the compound. Dragons do not forget smells. I liked your smell from the very first. It was for the sake of that smell that I accepted you and have been willing to obey you. Your smell reminds me of the Lady, and while she lived, I was willing to follow her anywhere. So I followed you. In spite of the familiar smell, I never put the two of you together, she so old, you so young. I just accepted it as one of those oddities of life. By my age, I should know better than to ever accept coincidences. Yet I was lulled into foolishness just the same. At any rate, now I understand why you smelled so familiar."

Straw thought for a moment about what the dragon had been saying. It was just not possible, but there was no other explanation. "Do you mean to say that you knew Galifalia?" he finally asked.

"Galifalia was the Lady," Star reverently responded in his chime-like voice.

"But Galifalia was my grandmother," the boy said quietly, still trying to unravel the mystery.

"It makes sense to me that you were connected to her, seeing that you understand the ancient tongue," the dragon commented. "Although there is still a riddle to be solved, because she was not of the ancient race."

The boy did not pay attention to what Star had just said. He was still trying to bring his grandmother and the dragon together as having known one another. Surely she would have mentioned something so important. "Maybe it was someone else of the same name," Straw suggested.

"Do you remember her holding you up at the seasonal processions?"

"I remember it vividly," the boy answered fervently. "I looked forward to every procession because it was such a treat when she held me up for you."

"And did I not every time walk over to you and bless you?"

"You did. But didn't you bless lots of children?"

"Not along the procession route. Only at the beginning and end. The ceremony requires that I walk the full length of the commons without wavering to one side or another."

"Of course," Straw said, smacking himself in the forehead. "That's why Garth was so angry at the procession when you walked over to greet me."

"And so it always was," the dragon said. "Whenever I saw the Lady, I could not resist going to greet her. The respect and love I owed her was greater than the rules of ceremony. After all, it was only right. If not for the Lady, I would never have come to live three generations in this land."

Now Straw was beginning to remember the stories that Mali had told him during his first meal at the compound. He had thought Mali must be talking about another woman of the same name. It was so queer to hear about someone he thought he had known well and find out there was a whole history that he knew nothing about.

"You came here because of Galifalia?"

"Yes, the Lady Galifalia won my heart, even though she could not speak with me as you do. I suspect that she was not truly your grandmother."

"What are you talking about?"

"If she had truly been your grandmother, then she also would have been of the ancient race and could have spoken with me. But I tried many times without any success. Hers was a pure heart; she always understood what I meant without comprehending my words."

"Wait, wait. What ancient race?"

"There is a race of men as old, or at least nearly as old, as we dragons. There are not many left today. It has been many generations of mortal men since I last spoke with one. They are an old, tired race and I have often wondered if they might have died out, much as we dragons are doing as well. Perhaps you are the sole survivor. It's hard to say."

"Who are these ancient people?"

"Why, they are the dragon tamers, of course. It was they who first discovered our inner nature and turned it to good rather than evil. It is they who learned how to tame us, to bring good to others. It is from them that people today have the term 'Luck Dragon.'"

The boy's head was swimming. There were so many questions to ask, so many riddles to solve. He did not know where to begin. A cool breeze ruffled his hair, and for the first time he noticed that the sun was now low on the horizon and shadows were growing very long.

"I have to get you home," he said quickly. "Otherwise, I'm going to be in big trouble. I'm still being watched carefully, that I can do this right, and the Dragon Master will think I can't control you and then…" Straw did not want to finish that thought. It would mean that he could not come out alone with Star any more, and it was more important than ever to have time to talk with him.

"Do you think you could hurry home?" he asked hopefully. "I know you like to sort of stroll back, but do you think…?" But he never had a chance to finish his request.

"Climb back on," Star commanded. Once he had taken his position, Star muttered, "Hold on, Boy," and almost before Straw had a chance to grab hold, the dragon took off at a gallop.

The boy gasped. The dragon heaved himself out of the river with a great rushing and crashing of water. Trees and hills flew past as the dragon headed home with amazing speed. The ride was extremely smooth, and Straw wondered if they might be airborne, skimming just a few feet above the surface of the earth. The two miles back to the compound were covered in a speed that made him nearly dizzy, and although they were on the late side, it was not late enough to cause raised eyebrows. Everyone knew that the dragon could be awfully slow, so if they were a bit later than usual, no one was alarmed.

When they arrived, as every day, the stall boys and kitchen staff were lined up to greet Star at his return. Star lowered his head to give Straw a chance to dismount. Then, as the bronze shield was struck with its padded hammers, the dragon rose up into the air and began to soar. Star flew in great circles around the compound, much longer than usual, and his evening song was far more joyous than Straw had ever heard before.

When Star finally landed, he walked over to the boy to be led into the barn. Just as they were entering that great space, Star glanced around to see if there was anyone else within earshot. Then he chuckled to himself at his own unnecessary caution. He could talk with the boy in full sight of anyone, including the Dragon Master. The others would hear only his chime-like voice, but give no meaning to it. He leaned toward Straw and whispered, "You were curious about my name. Come tonight, after the lanterns have been put out. That should answer your question."

The boy turned around to look at Star with amazement. Another riddle to be solved, he thought. "But no one is allowed to come near you after lantern snuffing," he puzzled.

"Then come carefully," the dragon replied.

Straw found the barn keepers and officially turned the dragon over to them.

"A bit on the late side tonight, boy," Keg commented dryly.

"Sorry," he said, and shrugged his shoulders.

"Well, look, let me give you a tip. When I was younger, I used to take Star out for a wash, although I was never alone like you. He's big, he's beautiful and he's slow. It's hard to get him moving, but then, there's a lot of him for his legs to carry around." Star began chuckling at these words, and the boy realized that only he knew that the sound the dragon was making was laughter. He also realized that the Barn Master had no idea how fast Star could move when he wanted to.

"So here's my advice," he continued, interrupting Straw's thoughts. "Just leave earlier. It's that simple. Just give this lovely mountain of a blessing all the time he needs to saunter back from the river. No way to rush him, so just give him more time. We've got to have time on our end to finish our work too, you know, before lantern snuffing. Will you give it a try?" He was looking straight at Straw with a broad smile on his friendly face. When the boy did not respond, Keg looked at him searchingly and pursed his lips. "You feelin' all right, boy? You look like you may have got too much sun out there today."

"No, sir," Straw said quickly. "I mean, yes, sir, I will bring Star home earlier. I am grateful for your advice. I just lost track of time a little today."

"Bless me, I know it can happen," Keg replied, still regarding Straw with a questioning look.

"Think about wearin' a hat out there, to keep the sun off your head," he finally said. "I'm worried about you, boy. You don't look at your best."

"I'll do that," Straw said quickly. "I'll make sure to wear a hat. Gotta go now. I'm powerful hungry."

With this he hurried away, hoping to avoid any further questions. As he walked to the commons, he overheard the Barn Master comment to another worker, "Good lad, he'll do all right. More than once we'd bring the dragon home a bit late. 'Tis precious to spend time with Star."

Chapter Eleven

Stars in the Night

Straw headed for the kitchens, his head swimming. He was famished, but he needed to be alone to figure this out. No matter what, he had to avoid Colin. His friend would notice that something had happened and would not leave him alone until he heard the whole story. Straw trusted Colin, but he knew he would tell Alis, and something this big she might not be able to keep to herself. Ancient races, talking dragons and his own grandmother the Lady of the land was more than he was ready to share with anyone, even Colin.

He walked around the back of the kitchens and went in the server's entrance. He stood around until he could get the attention of a woman who was carrying out an empty pot. He made up a story about not feeling well and wanting to go to bed early. Actually, this was more true than not. She willingly filled him up a bowl and brought it to him.

Straw retreated to the stand of trees from where he could look into the barn and knew that no one would bother him there. If he sat just right, he could see the entrance to the dormitories through the bushes. He had to figure out how he was going to get downstairs and out before it was time to go in to bed.

Absently, he watched the barn keepers put the last of the large doors into place, closing up the barn for the night. How was he going to get back in there?

But first, he had to eat, just eat and satisfy the gnawing pain in his stomach. He began stuffing his mouth, enjoying the wholesome flavor and warmth of a good meal. After the first few bites, he was able to slow down enough to enjoy it. He was still grateful every day for the food at the compound. When he lived on the streets, he had too often gone without eating. Now he could eat his fill, and this often meant several helpings.

Tonight, though, there was going to be only one helping. He did not want to risk seeing anyone who would start asking questions, any questions. He had too many of his own to answer. For instance, how was he going to sneak out of the dormitory tonight after lantern snuffing to go visit Star in the barn? And afterwards, how was he going to sneak back in?

Going through a window was not a solution. He slept on the second floor, and there was no reasonable way to let himself down. He could just spend the night out and think of some good story about where he had been. The only problem with that plan was that it was unlikely anyone would believe his story.

Then he wondered about the front door. Was it actually locked at night? He had never thought about it before. Why in the world would they lock it? After all, there was nothing to fear in the compound. He slapped himself on the forehead. Of course, he could just walk out the front door. This was, after all, the dragon compound, the safest place in the whole land.

He laughed at himself for thinking it would be complicated. He just needed to go to bed early and get a couple of hours sleep. In the dead of night he could sneak out, visit Star, and then sneak back in before dawn.

Delighted with his plan, Straw contentedly made his way to his dormitory room. It was growing dark, and several beds were already occupied by sleepers who had early shifts and got up in the predawn light. He had to keep that in mind and return before they rose.

As Straw lay in his bed, he wondered if he would be able to fall asleep with all of the impressions of the day still rushing through his mind. He doubted it, but closed his eyes anyway.

Suddenly, his eyes shot open and he stared into the darkness. With a shock, he realized he had slept, and that he had no idea how late it was. He listened carefully to the sounds around him. He heard the steady breathing and soft snoring of others in the beds around him. He wondered for a moment how much of the night he still had. His bed lay near to a window; he rose slowly and quietly in order to look out of it.

During his years on the streets, Straw had learned how to gauge time by watching the progression of the stars in the sky. Although they changed with the seasons, he knew what was visible when it grew dark, as well as what the stars were on the horizon right before daylight. He studied the sky and was satisfied that he had not slept long at all.

He oriented himself in the dark room. The starlight through the window did not give much help inside the dormitory. He could make out the dark shapes of the boys asleep on their mats and, more importantly, the walkways between them. Cautiously, he moved towards the door, intent on not bumping into any beds. He found the door easily, not only because it was darker than the wall, but also a strong draft blew through its opening, making him realize how much he was sweating.

Using the railing as a guide, he carefully walked down the stairs, feeling his way with his feet. The cold stone stairs helped chase away any remaining drowsiness.

It was even darker in the entryway. He had to half guess, half remember the direction to the great doors. Then he laughed at himself, because he was making it more difficult than it needed to be. At the bottom of the stairs, he left the safety of the railing and followed the ledge of the last step until he came to the wall. With his hand on the wall, he followed it until he felt the door. He stubbed his fingers on the door frame and stifled a curse. He found the handle, large and cold in his small, warm hands. He pushed down on it and pulled on the door. To his great relief, it was unlocked and a gust of fresh, cool air rushed through the crack.

He opened the door very slowly, in case there was any squeaking or creaking that could give him away. The door hinges, though, were well oiled and made no noise. He was out on the front steps and just closing the great door behind him when he smelled something that should not be in the air. It was the heady aroma of pipe tobacco.

"Goin' for a stroll, boy?"

Straw was taken so by surprise that he jumped and let out a squawk. His hands shot to his heart, as if to keep it from leaping out of his chest.

"Who's there?" he cried out in a breathless voice. He peered in the direction the voice had come from and in the deep shadows saw only a thumb-sized warm glow of light. It danced about like a firefly as the voice spoke again.

"Only Ole Max. Sorry I gave ye such a fright."

Ole Max! He was the potter he had worked for on his first afternoon and on many occasions afterwards. Maybe they did set guards, after all. He had to think quickly in order to come up with a reasonable excuse for being out. He was so rattled, though, by being found out, that his mind was a terror-stricken blank.

"Ole Max, good evening to you." He had to come up with something. "I couldn't sleep and it was, uh, hot inside." Well, almost true, it was an unusually warm night for autumn.

"By the sound of ye, I'd say yer the boy they call Straw," Ole Max's voice was comfortable and soft.

"It is me, Ole Max."

"Haven't seen ye for awhile," Ole Max said. "I miss yer strong arms and willin' nature."

"Well," Straw stammered. "I'm kept pretty busy with the dragon nowadays."

"So I've heard, so I've heard," Ole Max said. "So ye couldn't sleep, y' say?"

"No. It was hot."

"Y' know, at my age I have trouble sleepin', too, whether it's hot or cold. Might as well come on out and have a little smoke."

Straw was relieved that at least he was not guarding the door.

"Of course," Ole Max continued, "as that might be normal for an ol' man, it's not usual for a youngster, by my reckonin'. Partic'ly a youngster that spends his days scrubbin' down a dragon. I'd expect that youngster to sleep soundly all night long."

The boy gulped, not sure what to say.

"Unless the youngster has got a plan," Ole Max continued smoothly. "There's a big dragon out there in the barn, most valuable resident of our land. Sleepin' all alone, no one watchin' him. Now a scrub boy might think it his duty to make sure no one has stolen him away." The boy heard a deep chuckling.

"G'wan with ye," he said quietly. "Hasn't been a scrub boy yet that could resist visitin' Star in the night. G'wan an' satisfy yerself. It's a wonderment it took ye so long to get th' itch."

The boy could only stand there astonished, with his mouth hanging open.

"G'wan," repeated Ole Max. "Time for an ol' man to put his bones to bed. No fear, the door'll be open when ye come back. Don' stay too late, though. The early crew is partic'ler about anyone messin' with the dragon before their shift."

"Thank you, Ole Max, I won't stay long." He was already headed down the steps. At the bottom he paused and turned, remembering his manners. "And I wish you a good night's rest."

Ole Max only grunted at this, and the boy heard a tapping sound and saw sparks flying in the night as the old man knocked his pipe against the dormitory wall. Then his dark shadow moved smoothly and silently to the door, became one with it and disappeared.

Straw stopped a moment to let his racing heart settle. So, there were no locked doors, no guards, and the strict rules that could lead to dismissal from the compound were not always so strict. He had been feeling like a thief in the night, and now he was not only legitimate, he was long overdue.

He nearly whooped for joy, but restrained himself, not wanting to attract any more attention. He had been lucky with Ole Max. He did not want to take the chance of meeting someone else who might not take his midnight stroll so casually.

Now, under the stars, he had an easier time orienting himself. He stood there until he knew without a doubt in which direction the barn lay. It was so large that he could find it easily by the way it blotted out the sky.

He walked towards the barn without seeing anything other than the dark shadow of a cat scurrying across a clearing. Everyone in the compound was soundly asleep. And Star, would he be asleep as well? Or would Star be waiting for him, expecting him? For the first time he began to wonder what he would find when he got there. Star had said he should come if he wanted an answer to the question about his name. How could coming in the dark of night answer that? Well, he would know soon. The barn stood before him, a swallowing darkness against the starry night.

He had watched the keepers closing up the great barn doors, but he knew where to find the small door to the side that would let him in. What if that door was locked? No, that would make no sense at all. What did they need defend the dragon from? Other than nosey boys like himself.

He walked along the great doors until he had nearly reached the corner. Feeling with his hands, he located the door with only a couple of splinters in his fingers for his efforts. He lifted the latch and, as he expected, it was not locked. He let himself into the inky blackness of the barn.

He took one step inside, and his breath caught in his throat. There must be some mistake, because instead of stepping inside, he had stepped outside. Before him and above him stretched the starry pattern of the skies. He was terribly confused and totally disoriented. He shook his head to clear his vision and turned around to find the door again. The door was still wide open and through it he could see the outline of trees against the star-studded sky. He turned again. Before him glistened the starry dome of heaven. It was a breathless, beautiful sight. The stars twinkled and glimmered, some faintly, others with a ferocious burning light that awoke a nameless fear in his soul.

"What in the world?" he mumbled, letting out a long breath.

Then he heard that familiar tinkling of chimes which he had come to recognize as Star's laughter.

"I hope that this answers your question," spoke the now familiar voice.

"Star, is that you? I mean, those stars? I mean, I'm not really outside staring at the sky, but those stars are you?"

"That's right, boy. Now you can see why my name is Star."

"Why, it's magnificent. It's about the most beautiful thing I've ever seen! It's like walking through the night sky. Star, how is it possible?"

"Can't really say for certain. Some things we can just enjoy for what they are."

Straw shook his head slowly. He had never been so close to stars before. It looked like a curtain of starlight spread before him. They danced right before his eyes, and he suspected that if he extended his hand he would be able to touch them.

He stood there a long time in silence, just gazing. At one point, he walked back over to the door to look at the sky. Then he came back and looked at the dragon. He did this several times until he was satisfied.

"You're more beautiful," he concluded. "Maybe because you're closer and I can touch you and you're real. And we can talk." He sighed contentedly.

"I am also happy," commented the dragon. "And I am grateful for your visit. Over the many years of my life as a Luck Dragon in many lands, an untold number of scrub boys have snuck away in the night to get a glimpse of the sleeping dragon. They didn't know what they were coming for, except drawn by some unspeakable desire to visit me after hours, in the dark, alone. For some it was a dare, for others an honest inner desire to be with me. They all reacted as you did, with utmost surprise at the beauty of my coat. Each of them saw the truth of why I am named Star instead of Rainbow. I asked each one, 'Are you now satisfied? Are your questions answered?' You are the first one, in so many generations of scrub boys, ever to answer my question. I am happy that you came."

Straw took halting steps toward the dragon's voice. He felt the warmth of his breath, and he smelled the fragrance of flowering trees as the dragon lowered his head to meet him. Star nuzzled the boy gently, him so large, the boy so small. Straw realized here in the dark that his muzzle was as soft and gentle as a dog's. He wanted to throw his arms around him and give him a hug, which was impossible. Without knowing quite why, he burst into tears, and they were tears of both sadness and joy.

"I love you, Star," he said between sobs. And in his heart, all the pain that he had felt since Galifalia's death, but had never allowed himself to express, poured out as he hugged the dragon's warm, soft snout.

Chapter Twelve

The Dragon Keepers

After that night, Star and the boy began a new routine. They continued to make their daily pilgrimage down to the river for a good scrubbing. But Star no longer sauntered on his way there. As soon as they were well out of sight of the compound, he would tell the boy to "hold tight" and take off at an incredible speed. Once at the river, Straw would set to work with his scrubbing, remaining faithful to his routine and progression around the dragon's body. But now he worked with a certain dispatch. It was no longer the sole purpose and focus of his day. Both boy and dragon waited for that moment when Straw exhaled deeply and said, "Done."

That was when Straw lay his scrubbers and buckets to the side and the two of them would retire to the shade of a great elm tree. Or more exactly, the boy would retire to the shade of the tree, while Star preferred to lay in the warm autumn sunshine, since he could not fit underneath the tree anyway. This was the time they both looked forward to the most. It was their time for the boy to ask and the dragon to explain.

"All right," Straw began one day as huge clouds were piling up on the horizon, suggesting an afternoon storm. "How is it that you come to live here? I mean, why do we have a Luck Dragon and not any of the neighboring kingdoms?"

"Well, first of all, there aren't that many of us left to go around," Star chuckled. Then he grew serious. "Dragons are vanishing from the earth. For many reasons, our numbers, never strong, have dwindled to a very few." Star paused and became very quiet. The boy did not dare interrupt the dragon's reverie. Then, just as quickly, Star came out of it.

"And secondly, a Luck Dragon has to be attracted to live somewhere. That was the Lady's great deed. That is why I live here to bless the land and not in a neighboring kingdom. Every time I need to be attracted to go and stay someplace."

"What do you mean every time?"

"I stay three generation of mortal lives in any one land. That makes about three score years."

The boy looked up, astonished. "Does that mean you might leave here?" He sounded alarmed.

"Not might," Star corrected him. "Must. There is no choice in the matter. We need to spread ourselves around over the course of time. It wouldn't be right for one land to have our blessings longer than the lifetime of the generation that attracted us."

"How soon before you leave?" the boy asked sitting up very straight.

"Truth is, I am towards the end of my stay here. Bit less than ten years left, now."

The boy let out a sigh of relief. Ten years for him was a lifetime. "Where will you go when you leave here?"

"I can't say, myself. After I leave a place, I move on to find a new home. I live wild until I'm attracted to live somewhere new. The time of wandering can last a long time, but it doesn't need to."

"Sort of like bees," mused the boy.

"You mean when the queen sets off with a swarm of her followers? Yes, there is a similarity. When I'm in my wild state, I'm looking for a place to settle, and in the same way it takes a beekeeper to catch a swarm of bees and keep them, it takes a dragon keeper to catch me.

That's why it can take awhile for me to settle, when I wander through places that have lost the knowledge of dragon-keeping."

"Has that really happened to you, that you stay wild for long?"

"It has. It will again."

"Had you been wild for a long time when Galifalia found you?"

"Very long," Star said, sounding almost sad. "The world is changing, as it should, but with change there are fewer and fewer folk who understand Luck Dragons. That is one of the reasons hastening our disappearance."

"You mean, fewer folk who understand you like the ancient people did?" Straw still did not include himself when speaking of the ancient ones.

"Now, that was one of the first big changes, and it came about a long time ago," Star explained. "For some reason, there were fewer and fewer of the ancient race being born. It's like they had grown old and tired; every generation their numbers dwindled. The dragon keepers must have seen that their time on the earth was coming to an end. For untold ages they had held tightly to their secrets of dragon lore. They always kept to themselves and were the ones to mediate between common folk and us."

"So the ancient ones were the dragon keepers?" This thought intrigued Straw.

"Yes, up until a point. Then, there came a shift. There was a lot of squabbling among the ancient people about this, and there was some unnecessary bloodshed as well, I'm sorry to say. It wasn't like them to fall to violent ways, but some of the leaders felt threatened when others wanted to share their secrets before dragonlore was lost forever. Well, as it often does, time won out." Star paused and gazed out over the plains at the distant mountains where more clouds were piling up. He pondered something before he continued.

"There came a day when it was not even a discussion any longer whether their knowledge should be shared. Many realized that if their secrets died with them, then the care of dragons would die as well. They saw that this would bring disaster to the races of the earth. There was one foresightful ruler among them at that time, Soran the Great. I knew him, and he was truly a great man. Not only was he a Dragon Master, but a warrior in his own right, which was rare among them, since they were mostly a peace-loving folk. Anyway, he was the first to choose common folk and teach them how to care for dragons. So, thanks to Soran, the tradition of Luck Dragons continued, and that's why the Dragon Master at the compound knows all about me. Garth was trained by a master named Draco. And Draco was in his turn trained by a master named Nebo."

"Did you know them all?"

"I knew Draco, but I never met his teacher, Nebo. If you ask Garth, he could probably tell you his lineage of teachers all the way back to Soran the Great."

"Did Soran also teach the people how to talk with dragons?"

"Now, that was the only thing the ancient ones could not teach common folk. This was not a secret Soran could pass on. It was a gift. It came through the blood, I guess. I had to get used to being cared for by people who couldn't understand me. It was hard not having anyone to share a conversation with."

"Why is it that we can talk, Star?"

"That's what I keep trying to explain to you, but you don't want to hear it. You are of the ancient people."

The boy fidgeted uncomfortably. "But you said Galifalia wasn't of the ancient ones. How did I get to her?"

"That's a mystery I can't unravel. I had heard a rumor, just a rumor, mind you, that there was an enclave of the ancient ones still living in the far north, beyond the mountains in a remote valley. They were descendants of Soran's people. The story on the wind was that they were a kingdom without defense, relying on the surrounding mountains for protection. Once their valley was discovered, they became open prey for any ambitious prince who wished to expand his territory. Maybe you came from them. Maybe the wizards had their hand in it. I know that the Lady had dealings with at least one wizard.

"Wizards? Do they really exist?"

"As much as Luck Dragons do, and about as rare. They are even more ancient than your folk, and there have never been many of them. They look after the balance of things in the world. It was the wizards who were most interested that the secrets of dragon lore were passed down. They could hear the whispering in the wind and knew what was coming. It was at their prompting that Soran decided to begin teaching commoners about dragons.

"I wouldn't be surprised if a wizard had something to do with your being brought to the Lady. It's obvious, though, that he didn't stick around. He had a lot of faith that the Lady would make sure we met. Of course," he chuckled, "things did work out. But you'd think he'd show up at least to satisfy his curiosity." Star paused and stared hard at the boy.

Suddenly Straw remembered the old man with the flowing white hair he had seen in the barn the day of the procession. "Star, maybe he did come by."

"I doubt it," Star said with a shake of his great head. "Seeing how busy a wizard can get, I expect he's been sidetracked. But you keep your eyes open. You never can tell when one might show up."

"But, Star," the boy protested. "What about that time…"

"Time," Star cut him off. "You're right. It's time to get going." He was looking towards the mountains and the clouds that were building up all around them. "Storm coming, and we don't want to get caught in it."

Straw continued through the fall caring for the dragon and spending the bulk of the afternoons asking, listening and learning. Winter brought some variation to their routine. Snow and ice were rare in their moderate climate. Just the same, windstorms and prolonged rain could keep both the dragon and his keeper under cover at the compound. Storms came and went, leaving days of calm in between. Star and the boy always took advantage of the break in the weather for an outing to the river. The dragon was never bothered by heat or cold. Scrubbing warmed Straw up when there was a chill in the air.

Straw was so content with their routine that he lost all track of time. He was surprised one day to notice new buds on the trees. The Spring Procession was not long off, and once again, the compound was buzzing with activity.

One afternoon after their return from the river, Straw wandered off from the barn, his mind filled with ancient ones and wizards and the nagging question of how he fit into all of this. He noticed a gathering of stall boys at the wall of the compound and walked over towards them. They had piled boxes up against the fortification and were leaning over the top, engaged in animated conversation about something that was going on outside in the fields.

"What's up?" Straw called out to them. Mixer and Frog were up there and, looking over their shoulders, saw him.

"Sparring!" Frog said excitedly. "The knights are sparring."

Straw found an unused crate and dragged it over to the wall. He clambered up and looked over the top. In the fields beyond, mounted knights with drawn swords were charging one another, taking blows on their shields. Their armor shone in the setting sun and Straw had to squint to look at them.

"Marvelous," he whispered to himself. Their swordplay was magnificent. In spite of the heavy armor they wore, the knights wielded their swords effortlessly. They moved with deftness and skill. It looked like an exotic dance as the warriors struck and parried and struck again. The clashing of the swords against one another and upon the shields rang in the air. It was music to Straw's ears.

"Ah, to be a knight," he sighed. He did not understand why he was so attracted to it. Maybe because they looked so grand.

Straw had not paid any attention to where he was standing, and found himself next to a clump of stall boys. In their center was Flek. They, too, were admiring the knights at their sparring, but Flek had also noticed that Straw had joined them. Slowly, he traded places with several boys until he was standing next to the dragon boy.

All of them were shouting encouragement to the knights, waving their arms excitedly, and Flek added his own. "Smack him again! With the pommel! Hit him! Hit him!" he yelled, swinging his right arm in the air. "Like this!" and he swung his arm around, landing his fist in Straw's face.

Straw was stunned by the blow and flew from his perch on the crate down to the ground. He lay in the dirt, blinking his eyes, his hand to his cheek. Flek looked down at him.

"Oh, sorry. I didn't see you there. I was just waving my arms around a bit. I didn't hurt you, did I?" The boys around him burst out in rowdy laughter. Flek snorted and turned back to watch the knights. Straw felt the blood rush to his head and he no longer cared what was allowed or not. The dragon was in the barn, so now it was time to test if it were true that the masters let the boys work out their differences among themselves. He leapt to his feet and grabbed Flek's ankles. Then he pulled with all his might. Flek fell hard on the box but quickly scrambled to his knees.

"How dare you touch me, dirt bag! I'll have you—" but Straw did not give him a chance to say what he would do. His fist landed on Flek's cheek with a crack, and Flek went flying to the ground.

"Oh, sorry," Straw said. "I didn't see you there. I got excited watching the knights. I didn't hurt you, did I?"

Straw did not wait for an answer. He turned and walked away. *Supper must be ready by now,* he thought. He gingerly touched his cheek. *And I could use a good meal,* he concluded.

The next day at the river, after hearing about the encounter with Flek, Star grew pensive. He was lying on the bank with his tail hanging in the river. The water rushed around it, and occasionally the horned tip lifted itself and splashed back down again. "Boy, I've been meaning to ask you."

"What?" Straw asked. "Ask me what?"

"Have you ever thought much about where it goes from here?"

"I don't understand."

"Well, you've become a first class dragon boy. Even the Master acknowledges how well you handle me. You've got a lot of freedom around the compound, we have lots of time together, and lots of folk respect you, in spite of your small size and young age."

"With some exceptions," said the boy ruefully, thinking of Flek.

"Don't let Flek bother you," Star said firmly. "It has less to do with who you are and more to do with what he's struggling with."

"I only wish his struggles didn't include me."

"But since they do, learn to make the most of it. Flek is in love with power, and he has very little of it. He sees that it comes to you naturally. You actually attract power. He doesn't like that. There's a lot you can learn from this."

"You mean like how to keep my face from getting broken." The boy touched his cheekbone. It was still sore.

"That could be very useful to know." The dragon studied the boy. Straw noticed this and felt uncomfortable.

"What are you getting at?"

"There are not many more years left to my staying here. When the day comes, I get up, fly away and look for a new home. What about you?"

Now Straw was even more uncomfortable. "Can't I just go with you? You know, sort of be your personal dragon keeper. Help you get settled in a new home and all that?" He did not sound very convincing, even to himself.

"You're scrappy," Star said finally.

"I'm what?"

"Scrappy. You not only don't mind a fight, I suspect you sometimes go out of your way looking for one."

"Well, I wouldn't mind sticking my fist into Flek's nose again," he said, feeling his knuckles, which were also sore. "I don't turn my back on a fight."

"That's my point. You don't mind fighting. In fact, I think you sometimes enjoy it. Am I right?"

The boy considered this. When he had lived on the streets, fighting was part of getting by. Since coming to the compound, aside from his ongoing feud with Flek and his gang, he had not had trouble with anyone else. Finally he concluded, "Look, I don't go looking for a fight, and I don't run away from one either."

The dragon had a bright glow in his eye and looked at the boy intensely. Straw felt challenged by this look, and he stared back at him with his own little fire burning in his eyes. Finally, Star broke into a hearty laugh, coming from deep out of his belly.

"Boy, that's what I liked about you from the first time you walked into the barn. You stand your ground. You're small, but you're scrappy. And uncommonly strong. You get more done with a brush in less time than any dragon boy I've had in a tree's age."

The boy was still looking at Star feeling suspicious. Where was he going with this? "So? Out with it. What are you thinking?"

The dragon's tail rose and splashed twice before he spoke again. "Look, we've got all this time to ourselves every day. No one to bother us, no one watching, no one expecting us back. Who knows how long we'll be left to ourselves. Why use all our time with talking? Why not a little exercise?"

"What kind of exercise?" The boy was infected by the dragon's growing excitement.

"Fencing. I propose we do a little fencing together."

"With swords?" asked Straw aghast.

"Well, of course with swords. Swords, long-staffs, spears. I mean, I wouldn't have a sword, you would," Star said with all his chimes chuckling. "But I don't need one anyway. You know, boy, when you leave here, skill at arms could come in very useful. You might consider taking up the calling of a wandering knight."

"A knight?" Until now, Straw had only dreamt of this possibility. He had not dared mention it to anyone. Was Star reading his mind? "But knights have horses and armor," he protested. "Where in the world would I get all of that?"

"One step at a time, I say," Star said unconcerned. "When you're ready for a shield and lance, then we'll worry about where to find them. Let's start with training first. What do you think? Interested?"

Straw felt something in his chest expanding and wanting to burst out. His hands began to tingle and he clenched his fists and then relaxed his fingers several times to let the tension flow out. He stood up suddenly and paced about under the tree. His legs felt like two powerful springs, and he wanted to run and jump. He grabbed his own shoulders and ran his hands down his arms in an effort to contain them. Something in him was awakening and he could not keep it down. Even his teeth began to ache, and he had the sudden urge to bite into something, and bite hard. He clenched them together to get the itch out.

In the midst of this, a thought occurred to Straw and it made him pause. It made him push back this rising tide of unbridled strength.

"Star," he said, looking up at the dragon, full of concern, "I wouldn't want to hurt you."

Star's reaction was unexpected. He fell abruptly down on his side, rolled onto his back with his feet pointed up towards the cloud-scattered sky above them. Dust billowed up around him. His whole body was shaken by spasms, his tail thrashed the ground, tearing up clods of sod, and the sound coming from him was so loud that the boy had to cover his ears and open his mouth to bear the intensity of it. It took Straw a couple of moments to realize that the dragon was consumed by raucous laughter.

Time for the new activity was added to their afternoon routine at the river. Straw suggested that every other day he would do a quick scrubbing of the dragon's scales. Once finished, they could retire to the shade of a tree for conversation and give the boy a chance to eat his midday meal and rest. Then they would begin sparring.

"How do we go about this?" Straw asked the first time they sat to work out the details.

"To begin with," mused the dragon, "you need at least a sword."

"Why a sword?" the boy asked. "Won't a stick do?"

"Well, it doesn't have to be a real sword, I mean, iron and all. Something wooden will do just fine at first. But it should at least have the feel of a real sword. Using a stick would be more like a club. Unless you could fashion it somehow."

This gave the boy an idea. There was a small garrison of soldiers in the compound. Even though the kingdom feared no invasion as long as the dragon dwelt among them, the king knew it would be foolish to let his army grow lazy simply because there was no one to fight. King Pell maintained two barracks of foot soldiers, and he rotated them between the town and the frontiers. Dragon or no dragon, trade routes needed protecting. The king kept half a company of soldiers at the compound, more for show than for guarding anything. The foot soldiers were in addition to the nobility who filled out the ranks of knights the boys had been watching the day before.

Straw had often seen the soldiers parading and practicing their martial exercises. What had caught his attention most was their daily fencing drills. They did not use metal swords for this, as a precaution against someone getting unnecessarily hurt. Rather, they used stout wooden practice swords that would bruise and teach a painful lesson, but not cut. The soldiers were not particularly protective about them either. When not in use, they lay in a disorderly pile against the wall of the barrack next to the practice field. Straw was certain they did not keep a clear count of how many there were and that he could help himself.

But how to get one, and then get it out to their place by the river without anyone seeing it? It was not something he could easily hide under his tunic. He turned to Star for advice.

"Getting one is not the problem. You slipped out at night once before. Do it again. Once you have a sword, bring it to me. In fact, bring two or three, so we have some spares. I daresay we'll break a few along the way."

So once again Straw stole out of the dormitory in the middle of the night. He was more confident this time and found his way much more quickly than before. He did not encounter Ole Max or anyone else. He had no problem locating the pile of swords, having memorized the way in the light. From inside the barracks droned a chorus of loud snores. He had little fear of being caught. The only mishap came when he was picking out his three swords.

It was too dark in the shadow of the wall to see much, and he was groping around with his hands. He thought that he was taking three from off the top, but there must have been others lying over the ends of them. When he picked them up, there was suddenly a loud clatter of wooden swords knocking together as the pile partially collapsed, and several of them smacked him painfully in the shins.

The boy sat down hard holding his leg, pressing his lips together to keep from yelling out his pain. He froze, listening carefully to hear if he had wakened anyone. There was a snorting and grumbling coming from the open window above his head.

"Wha'zat?" someone mumbled gruffly.

"Cats, again," a muffled voice answered. "Go back t' sleep.

Straw breathed a sigh of relief and sat there, waiting for the snoring to resume before he dared move. It did not take more than a few minutes before they sounded like a chorus of swamp frogs again.

When Straw got to the barn, he was looking forward to seeing Star's coat in the dark again. Since he knew what was waiting for him, he did not expect it to affect him as it had the first time, but he was wrong. When he walked through the barn door and saw the expanse of stars glimmering and glittering with ferocious intensity, it took his breath away. He could only stand there and stare.

Star broke him out of his trance. "Don't just stand there gawking. Give them to me."

"Oh, of course. I got three, like you said. What should I do with them?"

"Place them here before me. I'll take care of the rest."

Straw walked forward and placed them on the ground at the edge of the field of stars.

"Now, get along to bed. We have a big day ahead of us tomorrow."

Chapter Thirteen

Sparring

Star wanted to begin sparring the very next day. Unfortunately, Straw had been so excited that after he returned to his bed, he tossed and turned most of the night. The next morning he barely made it through scrubbing before he collapsed underneath the tree and fell into the sleep he had missed the night before. He woke up just in time to make the trip back to the compound. He noticed that the swords were lying next to the tree trunk.

"Say, Star, how did you get them here?"

"In my mouth," he said dryly. "They tasted of dirt and sweaty soldiers, in case you're interested. Not my favorite flavor. Maybe it would be best to hide them under some brush. And get some sleep tonight; tomorrow we begin."

The boy was much better rested the following day. They agreed on a short scrub, and afterwards Straw was so excited about beginning, he did not even want to take time to eat the food he had brought.

"How do we start?" he asked eagerly.

"Take a sword," Star suggested. "I want you to get used to the feel of carrying one."

The boy took one of the wooden swords that he had stashed underneath some brush. It felt good in his hand, but at the same time it felt awkward. It was, after all, made for an adult, and he was far from full grown and still small for his age. He swung it several times and noticed that when he was slicing through the air with it, he was more comfortable.

"Well, that's a good place to begin," Star said, and began giving the boy instruction on simple swordsmanship: slices, cuts, feints, thrusts, parry, attack, and retreat. Teaching him to parry was difficult without a partner, but it was still important to go through the motions.

"That's good, move your feet, slice right, slice left, thrust, move your feet, forward, back, slice. Move your feet, I said. Faster, faster!" Star kept this up, leading Straw through a whole series of movements until the boy had broken into a sweat and was panting. He stopped only when Straw began to stumble.

"Now rest," he said, and Straw collapsed in the grass. When the boy's breathing became normal again, the dragon asked directly, "Do you want to eat now or continue?"

"More," Straw said with a gleam in his eye.

"All right," Star began. "You need to develop your footwork. Keep the sword in your hand, although you won't be using it. Right now, your main interest is to not get squashed."

"Not get squashed?" the boy asked perplexed.

"That's right," Star responded. "Don't let me squash you." So saying, he raised his immense head and brought it down right where the boy was standing. With a yelp, Straw jumped out of the way just in time. Star raised his head again and aimed once more for where the boy was standing. Straw was ready for it this time and jumped without the yelp.

"Have you got the idea now?" the dragon asked, pausing.

"I think so," Straw said, his eyes wide. He felt a tinge of panic that the dragon might really squash him if he were not nimble enough.

"Now, it's no fair running away," Star admonished him. "When you can't jump any longer, just yell out and I'll stop." He saw the look in the boy's eyes and added, "I promise."

He began the exercise in earnest now. The dragon showed every intention of squashing Straw if he did not move from where he was standing. At first the pace was slow, giving the boy a chance to get into a rhythm. Then, as the dragon saw him becoming more comfortable with it, he quickened the pace. To the left, to the right, to the left, to the right, Straw dashed continuously, breathing hard.

"Vary it now," the dragon called out without breaking the rhythm. "Move forward and back as well."

Following the dragon's directions, Straw began to change where he landed, and it became a game of cat and mouse. Everything went well until Straw slipped on some loose gravel in the packed earth and fell hard onto his side. Relentlessly, Star's head came straight at him. Straw rolled at the last moment, yelling loudly, "Stop!" as Star's head thumped the ground exactly where he had just been lying.

The boy lay there gasping for breath, staring up at the sky. Terror seized his heart. Had he been he mistaken all this time, foolishly lulled into feeling that it was safe to play such games with a dragon? Star loomed over him, staring down at him.

"Scared you, huh?" he asked. Then his chimes chuckled.

"If I hadn't rolled—" the boy began, not wanting to finish his sentence. It was too frightening to say out loud.

"And if I hadn't acted like I was going to crush you, you wouldn't have rolled," Star explained calmly. "Look, boy, this is training. There are going to be bruises and cuts along the way. If it's not real, then why bother?"

Straw paused before responding. "But Star, I was scared of you for a moment."

"So shake it off. It won't be the last time. I'm a dragon, after all. With enough practice, your fear will turn into respect, caution and skill. That's what we want." The chimes chuckled once more. "Take a break, have something to eat. We'll continue later."

Star turned out to be a very competent trainer. In the following days, he focused mostly on developing Straw's stamina before moving on to more complicated drills. As the days turned into weeks, and the weeks into months, Straw began developing some skills. He was young and well fed, so his body responded to the exercise by growing stronger. The length of the drills grew longer. Straw discovered that, although he might be breathing hard, he did not need to stop in order to catch his breath. He had found a rhythm by which he could do strenuous drills for extended periods of time.

One day they had been playing the cat and mouse game until Straw was drenched in sweat, when Star suddenly stopped.

"Let's keep going, Star. I'm not winded yet," the boy urged.

"I can see that," the dragon said calmly.

"Well, you're not tired, are you?" Straw asked, his chest heaving with deep breaths.

"It's time to try something new," Star answered.

Straw was delighted whenever the dragon introduced some new game or technique. It was always challenging at first, but once he got the hang of it, he found it very satisfying.

"We're going to keep playing the cat and mouse game, but from now on, instead of just hanging onto that sword, I want you to try and smack me with it as you jump out of the way."

"You want me to hit you?" Straw asked, incredulous.

"No. I want you to try and hit me," Star answered patiently.

"Oh, so you don't want me to really hit you," he said relieved.

"I'll try again. I do want you to try and really hit me."

"I'm confused," Straw admitted.

"Look, I just want you to take your sword and see if you can hit me. I don't want you to be frustrated, though, because it's not going to be as easy as you seem to think."

"So you're not going to be mad when I hit you?" Straw asked. "I mean, you're a very big target. It'd be hard to miss.

"I'm glad that you're so confident. Don't worry about me. Just try your hardest. Are you ready?"

"I guess so," he answered.

"Go."

The game resumed with the added variation. As the boy dodged out of the way, he took a swipe with his wooden sword at the dragon's head. Already with the first try, he was astonished at Star's ability to move so quickly. Where the dragon's head had been one moment, the well-placed sweep of the blade found only empty air. After several minutes, it began to dawn on him why the dragon had encouraged him to *try* and hit him.

One day later that week, after returning Star to the barn, Straw headed for the washroom. It had become routine for him to go wash himself after a full day's exercise with the dragon. He was always hot and sweaty, in addition to getting dirty from rolling and diving to avoid getting squashed by Star. He would first wash himself down and then give his tunic a wash. He appreciated having this time to clean up. The water always felt so refreshing, and he could wash the dirt out of his hair and clean up any scrapes and bruises. It was a time he could be alone, because the other boys were still busy in the barn, and none of them washed as regularly as he did.

"Well, there you are," spoke a familiar voice. It was Colin.

"Hi, Col," Straw called out from the tub where he was scrubbing his tunic.

"I've been wondering where you disappear to every day after you bring Star back. Now I understand why you look so freshly scrubbed at supper."

"Well, I like to be clean," Straw answered simply, hoping Colin would not ask any more questions than he wanted to answer.

"Straw, I'd say working with Star has been really good for you."

"What do you mean?"

"You've got muscles!"

Straw had been standing there washing bare-chested. At Colin's comment, he looked down at himself. He could not see any difference. "You think so?"

"I can see it. Look at your arms. Straw, they look twice as thick. And your chest is really filling out."

"Really?" The boy was delighted to hear this.

Colin pulled up the sleeve of his tunic and flexed his arm. "Now why doesn't mine grow like yours? I do a lot of work. I push brooms and wheelbarrows and throw straw around with a pitchfork. You mean that scrubbing a dragon makes that much difference?"

Straw hesitated a moment. He was not prepared to tell Colin what the muscles were really from. "Well, you know, Colin, there's a lot of dragon to scrub."

"I guess so. Anyway, you look great. Gosh, you could probably knock Flek to the floor with one blow."

I already did, he thought but he did not say it out loud. He figured that was the reason since their last encounter that Flek had not bothered him again. And with all the training he was getting, he was probably quicker now than Flek if it ever came to a fight. Then he shook these thoughts out of his mind. Sparring with Star was far more satisfying than any thoughts of fighting with Flek.

"You know what Garth warned," Straw told Colin. "No fighting. I don't want to lose my privileges with Star. It's not worth it."

"I guess you're right. But it is fun to think about. You ready to go eat?"

"If you help me wring out this tunic." The two boys laughed their way through wringing the water out of the tunic and, once it was hung up to dry, went off to another good meal. "I do love the food here," Straw said happily.

The days, the weeks and the seasons passed in quick succession. For Straw, every day was a welcome repetition of the routine from the day before. While everyone believed that he and the dragon were going for a wash at the river, Star was relentless in training Straw in the arts of sword, staff and lance.

Time for the Autumn Festival was again soon at hand. It was now a year since Star had been entrusted to him. Garth, the Dragon Master, was grudgingly satisfied with his work, and never once suggested that their rhythm should change or that anyone should join him at the river.

"You and Star seem to understand one another quite well," he said one evening, keeping the boy behind after their return.

Straw struggled not to show his worry that Garth might know something of what they were doing. "We have a good understanding, sir," he answered cautiously.

"And it seems you can control him as needed?"

"Star will do whatever I ask of him," was Straw's simple reply. It was, after all, the truth. Star had never yet refused something that Straw asked him to do.

"I've noticed that," Garth said looking at the boy carefully. What did he want to know? Straw was feeling uncomfortable.

"I'll tell you what's on my mind," Garth said. Straw braced himself for what was coming. "The autumn ceremony is coming up very soon. As Dragon Master, you know, I lead Star on his ceremonial march. Big crowds, lots of commotion, trumpets blaring, all the soldiers and knights in their finest, foreign dignitaries filling the stands, the king and queen presiding over all of it. There are people who travel for days to see Star. They make the trip every festival. Others travel weeks because they've heard there's a Luck Dragon here and want to get a glimpse at him. So it's a big gathering."

He paused as if trying to figure something out. Then he gave up and continued, "Of course, you already know all that. You know, Straw, you're certainly more than meets the eye. You've surprised me ever since you arrived. What have you been doing to build so much muscle?" Garth was looking at Straw's arms. "I can't say that you've grown that much in height since you've come, but you're really filling out."

Straw felt his face flush. It must be getting obvious if it was visible through his clothing. He had to think quickly.

"You know, the food here is really good and I eat a lot." He added, "And scrubbing down a whole dragon every day, you know, I guess that's what does it. Star's a big dragon, you know." And he smiled, trying to look equally perplexed.

Garth continued to stare at Straw, but he did not reveal his true thoughts. "Well, if you keep filling out like this, we'll have to find you a new nickname," he laughed. "Anyway, I wanted to ask if during the procession you would ride by Star's ears, on his neck, you know, just to give a bit more stability and guidance. The king has it in his head to set off cannons this year, and in case they might startle him, you know what I mean?"

Straw was relieved. He was being offered a great honor. Garth knew nothing of his daily sparring with the dragon. "I'd be more than glad to," he replied, smiling broadly.

"All right, it's settled then. You'll need a special tunic, but we'll have that made for you. Get back to work."

The boy was about to go when something occurred to him. "Sir, I have a question."

"What is it?"

"Will you want me to stay with Star the whole day, or will I be able to go into the village for some of the festivities?"

Garth paused a moment and smiled. "Wouldn't want you missing out on any of the fun, would we? No, you won't be needed until a bit before the procession begins. But you must promise to be on time and not get your tunic soiled."

"That should be easy. Thank you, sir."

Straw turned back into the barn. He wanted to find Colin and see if he was ready to go eat. He could not wait to tell him about Garth's request. Of all the stall boys, Colin remained the most open and happy about Straw's good fortune.

He found him with several of the others just finishing laying down new straw. Some were working, others were leaning on their brooms or pitchforks listening to Flek.

"What a waste of time," he was saying. "We're such suckers working every day for that great lazy hulk of scales. What does he do but get served by us?"

Colin stopped smoothing out the straw to respond. "You'd better watch what you say, Flek. If the Dragon Master hears you, it won't be nice. You know we're not allowed to talk about the dragon around him."

"Aw, I'm not afraid of Garth. I don't plan to spend much longer pushing a broom for a lazy pile of scales, I'll tell you that."

"Just watch what you say," Colin warned.

"Like he can understand us?" Flek challenged, jerking his thumb towards the dragon's back several broom lengths away.

"You willing to take the chance he can't?" Straw could not keep from taking Star's side, in spite of having promised Garth and Mali to stay away from Flek. "He has very good hearing."

"Oh-ho," Flek scoffed with a delighted grin. "And you should know. You clean his ears daily. Don't think you're fooling us, Straw Boy. We know what you're doing every day out there with that dragon."

Suddenly, Straw was uncertain. Could Flek know what they had been doing? "What do you mean?" he asked, not sure if he wanted to hear the answer.

"You don't think anyone believes that you spend all day scrubbing scales. You're dumb, but you're not stupid."

"He washes the dragon," Colin said, coming to his defense.

"Dragons don't need that much cleaning," Flek persisted. "We know what you're really doing out there with no one to watch you."

"What's that?" Straw challenged. He had to find out what Flek knew.

"You're sleeping, that's what you're doing. It's what any of us would do if we had your cushy job. I don't know what you did to kiss up to Garth, but you come from the trash heap and then you get the cushiest job in the compound. How do you rate?"

Straw was relieved to hear that Flek did not have a clue what he was talking about, but just spitting out his usual venom. He actually laughed with relief.

Flek, of course, misunderstood the reason for the laughter. "You think you're so fine, rising so high above the rest of us stuck pushing hay and dung around. But when we leave here, we know what's waiting for us in town. Every one of us will live a life of ease. We have property and servants of our own. When you leave here, you're headed back to the muck bins. Your time is coming, Straw Boy, and you'll come down with a crash." Flek was facing away from the dragon when he said this. He never had a chance to see the tail before it floored him. He hit the ground hard, although his fall was somewhat cushioned by the straw. The blow had been gentle, from a dragon's point of view, so although it threw him to the ground, Flek was only bruised, and jumped to his feet again spluttering.

"Damned pile of useless scales!" He had no time to say more, as he saw the tail coming again and ran to get out of its way. Some laughed, Colin hooted, and they all scattered to avoid getting nailed by that tail that appeared to have a mind of its own.

Over dinner, Straw told Colin about the Dragon Master's request.

"That's just tremendous. What an honor!" Colin's happiness was sincere.

"I'm afraid it won't make me very popular with the others," Straw said.

"Who cares?" Colin challenged. "You came here to work with the dragon, not make friends. That's what you've always told me. Anything change that?"

"A few friends would be nice, though."

"Well, you've got me and Alis and a lot of the others. And Mali likes you a lot. And obviously Garth trusts you."

"Yes, well, fewer enemies in the barn would be welcome."

"When you've got a dragon on your side, who cares?"

Straw had to think about that. Maybe Colin had a point. He looked at Colin and smiled, "Thanks for being my friend."

"Sure," Colin said. "Look, let's go tell Alis we can hang out together at the fair."

Chapter Fourteen

The Great Secret

Following the Harvest Festival, Straw's routine with the dragon took on a new twist. Every day they still went out to the river, and the boy quickly looked over Star's coat and gave attention to places that needed it. But a complete and thorough scrubbing became a thing of the past. The weather had turned cooler, and Straw welcomed the change because it meant he could spar with Star longer before he got too hot and had to rest.

"You know, Star," he said one day, "You're not looking neglected at all. Just the same, before the spring ceremony, I'm going to give you a good old fashioned washing, just like before. You deserve to go into the procession as clean as possible."

"Let's save it for the day before. What you're doing now is good enough. I prefer to use the time we have with training."

"Fine by me."

Truth was that Star was enjoying their daily sparring as much as the boy. It gave him added exercise and, being a dragon, he enjoyed movement.

"I want to teach you something new today," Star said. "So put those things down for a bit."

Straw was standing there with one of the wooden swords and a roughly made shield that he had recently begun using as well. At

Star's request, he lay down the shield and sword and stood there waiting, full of curiosity.

"I'm very happy with how you've been learning, boy." Star was more solemn than usual. Straw wondered what was up.

"You seem to take to this naturally. Your endurance and strength have grown very quickly. It's time that you got yourself a helmet."

"Why's that?"

"Because I can tell that we're going to get rougher with each other. There are going to be more bumps and you can't afford any bad injuries. You have to protect your head. Anyway, if you still want to be a knight...You do still want that, don't you?"

"Absolutely," Straw responded.

"Then you'd better get used to wearing a helmet. Do you think you can pinch one from the barracks? You've had no trouble getting more swords and a few shields."

The boy wondered if they kept track of the number of helmets. The missing swords never seemed to be noticed. "I'll get one," he decided. He'd just go and do it. Sneaking out at night and getting what he needed from the compound was no longer a big deal. He knew his way around and he was comfortable in the dark. After all this time sparring with a dragon, he realized that many of his fears, such as feeling panic in the dark, had vanished. Nothing else much matched facing a dragon.

"Good. Get it soon. Now, boy, there's something you have to know." Star paused, and the boy grew curious.

"It's time that you learned about the secret."

"There's a secret?" What was this all about?

"It's not just a secret, it's the Great Secret. It's the biggest secret about dragons that I can teach you."

"Bigger than the secret that you can talk?"

"Well, I don't consider that a secret. After all, I talk freely. It's just that no one but you can understand me." Straw heard the dragon's chuckling chimes.

"This is the Great Secret that dragons never reveal. But I'm going to tell you because you are becoming a dragon fighter, and since I'm training you myself, I'm allowed to share it. You will need to know this; it will one day save your life."

Star paused to let this sink in. The boy's eyes grew very big and he began to breathe through his mouth, nearly panting.

"There's one thing I want you to understand. You are becoming very strong, very quick and very skilled. By the time we are finished, you are unlikely to ever meet another warrior who will be able to stand against you. You will have every skill a warrior needs and you will know no fear. After all, what is there left to fear after being trained by a dragon?"

The boy listened carefully. Star was giving him a picture of his future.

"Not only will no one ever match your skills, you will not hesitate to stand your ground even when you are outnumbered. If you can battle with a dragon, what child's play it will be to battle against three, five or ten men. You will have the confidence to stand against a whole army, if the need should arrive, although I don't recommend it. Yet with your courage, skill, and cleverness, you could probably pull that off as well."

Straw had never thought about any of this before, but it made sense as he listened to Star describe it. "There will be only one being on the earth that can stand up to you and defeat you. Can you guess what that is?"

Straw was puzzled. What could he mean? If he could take on a whole army, what would be left? Did Star mean some mythical beast that was still rumored to live in the far distant mountains? Or some wild animal whose claws and teeth could slash away at armor?

"No matter how strong you are, how skilled you are, how clever you are, there will always be one being that can defeat you. Against which you will have no hope. Against which you will always suffer defeat. Always."

"What could that possibly be?"

"A dragon."

The boy was thunderstruck. When would he ever want to fight a dragon? Let alone, where would he find one to fight?

"Do you understand me? No matter how well trained you are, you cannot defeat a dragon. The dragon will always win. You might succeed in wounding the dragon, you might bewilder the dragon, you might trick the dragon, but in the end, the dragon will win. Do you understand me?" Star paused.

The boy was confused. Why was Star telling him this? "Well," Straw said slowly, "I better make sure I never pick a fight with a dragon, then. I mean, a real fight."

Star chuckled and the air was filled with music.

"Well, I hope that you're lucky enough to avoid it. But fate has a way of catching up with us. If you're dragon-trained, then one day you're going to go into battle with a dragon. That's why I am going to tell you the Great Secret. It will save your life."

The hair on Straw's head stood on end. He was attentive with all his senses to what was coming.

"Now, when a dragon has vanquished you," Star continued, "it will not kill you outright. That is not the way with dragons. We like to see our enemies suffer in their defeat. We want them to know with every fiber of their being that they have taken up arms against a creature that cannot be defeated. We want them to wallow in their failure."

Straw listened, spellbound with terror.

"We take the warrior we have defeated, and let me repeat that no matter how long the battle might last, we will end up on top. And that is exactly what dragons do. We take our beaten enemy, broken, yet alive, and we place him on our hoard if we have one handy. Otherwise, we simply find a suitably uncomfortable spot near the place of battle."

This was terrifying, yet Straw still held his tongue.

"We drag the broken, barely living warrior to this spot, and then we lie down on top of him. Not enough to totally squeeze the life out of him, but enough so that he can feel the weight of his defeat lying heavily upon him. Let me assure you that the pain becomes excruciating."

Star spoke as if he had first-hand experience. Shivers ran up and down the boy's spine. The hair on his arms was now also standing up. He felt his whole body on high alert.

"And we lie there on top of the ruined knight until we have slowly and with as much pain as possible, squeezed all of the life right out of him. This can take up to three days, depending how strong the knight's will to live might be."

"Star, you're scaring me," Straw finally burst out.

"That's good, because you must take what I'm telling you very seriously."

"I do," Straw whispered.

"Now, unless you've had the good fortune to have learned the Great Secret, only one outcome is guaranteed: You will die. You can struggle if you have any strength left, and you can plead for mercy if you have any breath left, but nothing will do you any good. You will die." It sounded so dreadful, so final.

"Your only chance is to use the Great Secret. And the irony is that the only way to use it is in defeat. Unless you are lying beneath the dragon, you will not be able to make use of the secret I am going to share with you."

Straw was intensely attentive.

"Now, walk right up to me and lie down."

Straw was not quite sure what Star wanted. "You want me to lie down?"

"It's not that complicated. Lie down in front of me with your feet towards my tail."

The boy did as Star asked. Immense, the dragon loomed above him, blotting out the sky.

"Now I'm going to lie down on you. Don't worry, I'm not enraged, and I will hold most of my weight above you. Still, you will feel my mass because I must get in the right position, and there is no other way to do this."

Star lowered himself upon the boy's body, so small beneath the dragon's great bulk. Straw felt the dragon's weight, and it was so crushing that it squeezed the breath right out of him. "Star," he gasped. "…can't breathe."

"Relax," Star commanded. "Take smaller breaths. Find the space where you can still take in air."

The boy did as Star told him, trusting in the dragon's guidance. It was true, that by taking smaller breaths, he was able to still breathe, although he was panting.

"Now, boy, pay attention. I've pinned one hand but left the other one free. Even after a battle it will be like this. With your free hand, I want you to feel above your head along the scales."

Straw could feel his body growing numb under the great pressure from above and his head began to throb. It was true, though, that his right arm was free. What did Star want from him? He did as he was asked and began exploring along the scales above his head as far as he could reach. He was puzzled what this was all about. He was also fighting a mindless panic that he was trapped, never to get free again.

"Stop flailing about with your hand," Star ordered. "Search with your fingers."

What was he talking about? There was nothing here to find but scales. He had been over every inch with a stiff brush many times over. What did Star expect him to find? And then, to his astonishment, it was there. Then he lost it with a jerk of his arm and doubted his senses. Then he found it again. It was really there.

"Star," he gasped. "There's an opening. A slit in the scales." Where had that come from? It had never been there before. He was certain he would have found it before.

"You've located it. Try as hard as you want, you'll never find it when I'm standing up. It opens only when I am lying on top of one of your race's frail bodies. It's the only time."

So that explained why he had never seen it before. But what was he to do with it?

"Now slip your hand within, boy" Star continued. "I want you to press in, as deep as you can."

Straw slipped his fingers into the opening, and then his whole hand followed. He was inside the dragon's body. It was hot inside.

"Further," Star urged. "As far as your arm will reach."

He needed to push only a little more and he could feel a rhythmical, powerful beating. The further he pushed his arm within, the closer he came. He was fascinated. "Star, is that your heart?"

"That, boy, is my heart. Now reach until you can touch it. Don't worry. It is sealed off by a firm membrane, and you cannot hurt me with your bare hand. Part of this secret is that a dragon's heart is very close to the surface. You have slipped between scales, bone and tissue to reach it."

Straw could feel it now with his hand. His fingers throbbed with the vibrations emanating from it. It was clear that he was not touching the heart itself, but was separated from it by a thick wall of tissue. Still, it was so vulnerably close.

"Open your hand and place your palm against it."

Straw could feel his whole hand being pushed backwards and pulled forward with every forceful beat. He was mesmerized by its constant movement.

"Now this is what you must remember, if you are to ever survive a battle with a dragon that has gone wild. Once he has conquered you, once he has broken and ruined your body, he will leave enough life in you to survive at least this long. Once he lies down on you, you must use your free hand to find the passage to the dragon's heart. Then you will have a choice to make."

Star paused as pictures rushed through Straw's mind. The boy swallowed hard, fearing what he might next hear.

"If by some chance, you have been dragged to this spot and your sword is still in reach, you could decide to thrust your blade into the dragon's heart."

Straw flinched at the very thought of doing this.

"This will kill the dragon, and in his death throes, he will crush you. You have, however, another choice."

Star paused again, and Straw demanded in a hoarse whisper, "Tell me."

"Reach in, as far as you are able, and place your palm upon the heart, just as you have done. Then, in a clear voice, confident and free from all fear, speak these words: 'We be of one heart, thou and I. We be of one heart.' Now say it."

The boy took as deep a breath as he could. He felt neither confident nor free from fear. He spoke as loudly as he could, although his voice sounded pinched to him. "We be of one heart, thou and I. We be of one heart."

"And we be of one mind, thou and I. One heart and one mind, we be one together," Star said.

Suddenly the weight was lifted off the boy's body. Straw took a deep breath, and immediately began coughing. He wanted to roll over, but his body was too numb to respond. He imagined that he would find an indentation in the earth beneath him. He painfully wrenched his body over, and began to heave from the deep nausea that suddenly rose in him. Tears flowed down his cheeks. Star backed up to give him room.

After a few minutes, Straw sat up. He could move only very slowly. He wiped his face with his sleeve and his sobbing subsided. A question swirled in his mind. "But what good does it do?"

"This is the way to tame a dragon. Although you cannot defeat one, you can tame a dragon, and this is how you do it. I used to believe it was the only way, until I met the Lady."

"Galifalia?"

"Yes, the Lady. She did not use this method, yet she succeeded without a battle. But the Lady was a very special woman. I am old by your lifetimes, yet she taught me much about love and faithfulness. She had her own ways of taming a dragon's heart." Star stopped speaking and Straw took deep breaths until his head began to clear.

"That is the Great Secret, boy. Remember it. I hope you'll never need it, but I doubt you'll be that lucky. You've been trained for a special purpose, but neither you nor I can foresee what that is. Your path will lead you to places you cannot even dream about. And sooner than you can imagine."

Straw felt sick again at the dragon's words, yet somehow he knew that Star spoke the truth.

Part III

The Making of a Knight

Chapter Fifteen

The Approaching Army

Winter gave way to spring, spring to summer, summer to fall as the seasons turned in succession. The rotating seasons counted off the years, but life in the compound changed little from its routine ways. There was always work to be done and a Luck Dragon to care for.

The Harvest Festival was once again at hand, and the heat of summer had declined. The days were noticeably shorter and, although the nights had not yet turned significantly cooler, the leaves on the trees were tinged with yellow and red.

Over the course of time, many of the boys reached the age when they left the compound. New, younger boys joined and were introduced to the life of caring for Star. These new boys looked on Straw with awe and reverence. One of their own had risen to become the dragon's sole caregiver. Those who knew him from before viewed him either with suppressed jealousy, such as Flek and his companions, or with admiration, such as Colin and his friends.

Star continued to train the boy rigorously. He rarely allowed him a day off. Straw did not mind. His body enjoyed the training, and he loved the sparring. From time to time he wondered how it would be to square off with a human opponent, but knowing how unlikely that was, he never wondered for long. Little did he know how soon an opportunity would present itself.

It was Star who first noticed that something was coming. They were on their way back to the compound after a rousing session. The boy had tripped in the end, scraping both an elbow and a knee. He was riding on Star's head, surveying the cut on his knee, which he knew would heal, and the tear in his pants, which he planned to sew up that night. No one was ever alarmed, even if they noticed that Straw came home with scratches or torn clothing. He was, after all, looking after a dragon. It was a rough job and if Straw was not complaining, then he was obviously able to handle whatever came up. On occasion, Garth looked to be on the verge of saying something, but ended up only muttering in his graying beard.

"There's dust yonder," Star said. It did not sound like he meant much by it. But Straw did stop examining his knee long enough to take notice. He knew that it was not Star's way to make small talk. If he mentioned dust, then—take it seriously.

"What does it mean?"

"I can think of two things. It might be a dust storm, but it's not the time of year for dust storms, so I tend to think it's the other." He stopped talking.

"Well, are you going to tell me?"

"Oh, I thought you'd know. It's an army on the move."

"An army?" Straw felt both alarmed and excited. "What army? Where are they going? Do you think they'll pass by here?"

"So many questions. I can't know whose army, and, yes, I think they will not only pass by, but they are headed here."

"They wouldn't dare attack us, would they?"

"No, not directly. They're after something else, most likely."

"What?"

"Let's just wait and see." Star was reluctant to share more.

Straw was able to get more information at supper. Star was not the only one to have noticed the dust. It was the general talk of the commons. There was an avid discussion going on at one of the tables that included not only Colin, Frog and the others, but Flek and some of his friends as well.

"It's been years since the last one," Frog was saying when Straw joined their table with his food.

"I can't wait," said Mixer. "This'll be more fun than a procession day with all the vendor stands."

"Finally something to break up the tedium," Flek added. "This place could use a little action to wake it up from its stupor."

"What's going on?" Straw asked.

"The guards in the towers have seen dust in the distance," Colin explained.

"And that means we're in for a tournament," Stomp said with obvious pleasure.

"Something more fun than pushing brooms and throwing hay around," Flek said.

"You mean there's a tournament planned?"

"No," answered Colin. "What it means is that some prince or chieftain somewhere has heard about the dragon and wants to make a name for himself."

"Every few years," Frog continued, "some raving idiot of a warrior gets it in his head to come and challenge the dragon in a battle to the death. Garth usually goes out and explains to them that Star's a Luck Dragon that brings prosperity to the land. He explains that the dragon is pampered and cared for and in no shape for mortal combat. Then he offers a tournament so that they don't feel they made the trip for nothing."

"That's why we see the knights practicing from time to time," Stomp added. "The king makes sure that he keeps a good supply of knights on hand for such an event." Straw recalled the many occasions he had been able to admire their skills. Over the past two years, he often longed to go out and join them, but he knew better. Only children of the nobility could become knights, and Flek continued to remind him regularly that he was not one of them.

"What happens if they won't take 'no' for an answer?" Straw wondered. "I mean, if they want to fight the dragon anyway."

"Every once in awhile there's some nut who thinks it's his mission to fight the dragon. Then Garth offers to let the tournament decide. If they lose, they agree to go home peaceably."

"And if they win?"

"King Pell has spent years training knights so that never happens."

"That would be something, wouldn't it?" Flek pondered. "I mean, he's big, all right, but do you think Star could stand up to an armored knight with a pointed lance and a razor-sharp sword? Maybe he'd be the one to turn tail and run. After all, he's had a pretty easy life here, with us doing all the work for him, spending every afternoon out lounging under a tree with Dung Boy, here." He sneered at Straw, who suppressed a smile at these words. He was pleased that he was not even tempted to defend himself.

"What do you think, Straw?" Frog asked. Suddenly they all turned to him. "I mean, could Star take on a knight?"

"Right, what does Straw Boy think?" Flek challenged. "Has Star gotten fat and lazy living here? We know that you're getting plenty of naps and swims in the river while the rest of us work. Does he cozy up next to you and snore away?"

There was some chuckling. Flek had never given up accusing the boy of not working hard enough. Straw had a brief moment when he was tempted to defend Star's ability to do whatever he wanted, even eat a lunatic knight. But how would he explain that he knew this to be true? If the secret he had kept so long were to remain a secret, he had to keep all this to himself.

"I don't like the idea that Star has to fight anyone," he finally answered. "It wouldn't go well for either of them." This was as honest an answer as he could give.

Two days later the heralds from the roving army arrived. They wore leather riding clothes covered by chain mail, and their banner was black with a golden emblem of a sword crossed over a battle axe. Their horses looked hard-ridden and tired. They announced that their chieftain, the Lord Malvise, was approaching with a great host. He was coming, as the boys had expected, to challenge the dragon in single combat to the death.

Garth and Mali went outside the gate to speak with the heralds. Although they could not hear the conversation, the boys could well imagine what Garth was telling them. The rumor spread that the messengers left looking unhappy.

"What happens now?" Straw wondered.

"Nothing much will change until the army gets here," Frog explained. "I remember one other time. Garth took the prince in to see Star, and Star gave him one of his special yawns. You know, all the teeth showing, and that deep, dark throat that looks like a tunnel into hell." Straw recalled getting that very yawn the first time he met Star. It had been beautiful. He also remembered Garth's comment about how seasoned warriors reacted. Frog finished the memory. "The prince nearly soiled himself. They didn't even stay for the tournament."

The approaching army brought Straw's workouts with Star to an end. Garth came himself to deliver the decision. "We're going to keep Star inside the compound until this is over. The last thing you need is to get confronted by an advance party looking for a fight down at the river. That could get very nasty."

"Couldn't we just sort of send Star out to them when they come? I mean, once they get one look at him, they'll think twice about demanding a fight."

"That has worked in the past. But I've heard of this Lord Malvise. He's been ruthlessly expanding his territory. He hopes that by challenging the dragon he'll intimidate the towns he wants into surrendering without a fight. It'd be quite a feather in his cap, to claim giving battle to a dragon. If we send Star out, they're likely to attack him as a body."

"But they can't do him any harm, can they?"

"No, I don't believe they can actually hurt Star. But they could rile him up. Have I never told you about this before? When Star was first brought to us, there was an ancient keeper who cared for him who knew everything about dragons. His name was Draco. Not a bad name for a dragon keeper. I trained with him myself. He taught me that there were two things that could result in Star's leaving us. One was the natural end of his stay after three generations. That's just how long a Luck Dragon is willing to stay in one place. We've gone through most of that time already, and I have a commitment to see it through to the end."

"What's the other way?"

"If Star gets riled. If someone challenges Star to combat and riles him to really fight. Draco said that Star would forget himself in a real battle, and afterwards just disappear, never to return. It's part of our duty to keep him protected so that doesn't happen. That's why we're here. Not just to give him a pleasant place to sleep and scrub him down every day. I know I've told you this before. Don't you remember?"

Garth looked at Straw with such a penetrating gaze that the boy had to look away. It was as if Garth could see into his soul and knew what he had been doing with the dragon. Straw mumbled that he did remember what Garth was telling him and then excused himself. He had to talk with Star about this.

It was not yet time for lights out. The great barn still had several lanterns lit. The finishing up crew was mostly gone, and even Keg was ready to call it a night. No one took special notice of Straw when he walked in. They were used to his coming in and checking on Star. He could even go and have a conversation with Star without anyone getting suspicious. After all, everyone expected Straw to talk with the dragon. When they heard the dragon's chimes, the workers assumed this meant that Star was happy. Everyone marveled at their relationship, but no one saw it as anything more than a youth who had a special way with a dumb beast.

"Come to tuck him in?" Keg called out. "I'm going to put the lanterns out in a few minutes, but until then you can speak sweet nothings in his big ears." And he bustled off to another part of the barn.

Straw walked over to stand before Star's immense head. Star said nothing, but bent his snout down and nuzzled the boy, as a horse might. Straw reached up and caressed the side of the great snout.

"I do love you, Star, so very, very much. Since forever. You and Galifalia. And now I've got only you."

"She was a great woman, the Lady, considering that she was not of the ancient ones," Star said. "I also miss her. But boy, what's troubling you. It's been years since you've come to profess your love to me. Not that I've ever doubted it."

"Star, have I been doing the wrong thing? Might you leave the compound early because of me?"

"Boy, whatever are you talking about?"

Straw repeated what Garth had told him.

"When we fight now," Straw continued, "you seem to really get into it. Not like when we first started, when you wanted me to try and hit you and all I could do was swing at the empty air. I mean, you've shown me your sensitive spots, and I'm fast now. I can really rile you up."

"You've learned your lessons well."

"But aren't I doing the very thing that we're here to protect you from? Isn't it the same as if you would go into battle with this Lord Malvise?"

"It would be, except for one important difference."

"Is it because you and I have a special relationship? That I can understand your speech?"

"No, that has nothing to do with it. When I'm riled, I become blind to who you are. You are my opponent and nothing else. When you rile me, I'm as wild as any wild dragon ever becomes. You have already had to deal with my full fury."

"Then what makes it different? Why don't you just fly off afterwards?"

"You're forgetting the great secret I taught you. I can only say that it's a good thing that you remember it when I'm lying on top of you. That is what tames my fury and brings me back to my senses. If you would forget to do it, then, indeed, Garth's fears would come true."

"Isn't that taking an awfully big risk?"

"Yes. But wouldn't you agree that it's been worth it?"

They were interrupted at this point by Keg.

"Let's go, Straw. Kiss him goodnight and be done."

Straw reached up and embraced the dragon's head. "Goodnight Star," he said. "I'll see you in the morning."

As Straw was walking to the door, Keg caught up with him after putting out the last light. "'Tis a pity, Straw, that the dragon's time is soon done here."

"Why do you say that, Keg?" He knew why he was sad, but he wondered what the Barn Master's reason was.

"Well, watching you with that dragon. You've got a special way with him. You're young. With you around, we could go another sixty years."

"I never thought about that," Straw said. Now he had another question for Star. But it would have to wait for another day.

Chapter Sixteen

Lord Malvise

The stall boys had taken carts and lined them up along the compound walls. They stacked several crates on top of one another on the cart bed, until they could look over the length of wall that separated them from the army's encampment.

Keg fretted over the disorderly way it looked, but Mali overruled him. "Look, Keg, if we forbid this, they'll find some other way. It could be worse." It did not help that the army had been offered the flat fields right outside the compound walls to set up their camp.

Since he could not take Star to the river, Straw spent his time fussing over him, just to keep himself occupied. He was cleaning Star's talons when he overheard Keg, Mali and Garth talking as they walked through the barn. They must have known that he was within earshot but were too involved in their worries to care if he heard them.

"But why so close to the compound?" Mali asked.

"So we can keep an eye on them," Garth muttered. It was obvious that he was not pleased with their arrival. He had become very difficult to get along with.

"You've been a regular fire dragon since they arrived," Keg humphed. "It's not like it's never happened before. No reason to get so ruffled over it."

"I'm worried, to tell you the truth," Garth confided. "The garrison has never looked so weak. We've grown too confident and lax. Most of our knights are untried youths. I don't like the looks of this Malvise, or his army, and I don't know if we have the champion to stand up to him."

That was all Straw heard before they moved on. He looked up to Star. "Did you hear that? I've watched our knights. They look very good at their exercises."

"I'm sure they are, but Garth is right. Our knights are going to be facing seasoned warriors who have many campaigns behind them."

"I hadn't thought of that."

"Nothing to worry about yet," Star said softly.

"I've never seen Garth so upset. You'll let me know when it's time to worry, won't you?"

"Well, from a dragon's point of view, it's never time to worry. Particularly if you're a Luck Dragon."

"Well, how about from my point of view?"

"Then let's make this today's lesson. Even off the fields we can prepare you. It's never time to worry. Practice it. Deal with the moment alone. Right now you're well fed, warm and happily occupied. You're ready for any challenge that comes. I know, because I trained you. So stop imagining the future and give up with it all the worry."

"This will be tougher to learn than the roll and parry." Straw was referring to an exercise he was working on where he dove to one side and rolled, springing to his feet again immediately to parry a blow. He had been having difficulties with it.

"Learning to be in the moment might be your hardest lesson of all. But, who knows? You're a quick learner."

The stall boys knew nothing of these concerns. For them Lord Malvise and his army provided a welcome break from their routine. When Star stayed in the barn, their day's work was considerably shortened. They spent their time alternately watching the encampment and their own knights, who had picked up the pace of their exercises within the compound walls. It had not taken long for them to come to the same conclusions as Garth.

"Look at that Malvise. Did you see how he's dressed?"

"All in black leather. I've never seen anything so sharp. I'd like a set of leathers like his when I become a knight."

"You're never going to be a knight, Frog. Give it up."

"Am, too."

"And look at his knights. They're all seven feet tall!"

"And how they ride around keeping their order with their lances held in the air. They never break form. It's a beautiful sight."

"I think our knights are in for it."

"They look pretty small by comparison."

"Nor as fast."

"Nowhere near as orderly."

"Looks like Star's going to get his battle after all."

"I can hardly wait to see Old Scaly fighting Malvise."

This was spoken by Flek. Straw simply held his tongue. He agreed with everything they were saying. The knights exercising in the compound were a sorry lot next to the army outside the walls.

In an attempt to discourage Malvise's determination to challenge Star to single combat, Garth decided to invite him to visit the barn before the tournament. "It's worked before," he reasoned.

"The others were different," Keg said. "He's not the type to be scared off by a yawn."

"You're probably right. But it's worth a try anyway," Garth responded. "Straw," he called. The boy was hanging around the barn trying to find something to do.

"Yes, Dragon Master," he came over to him.

"I've invited Lord Malvise to view our Luck Dragon. Have a word with Star ahead of time. Let him know who Malvise is and why he has come."

"He knows all about him." When Garth looked at him questioningly, he continued. "I told him already."

"I see," Garth said raising an eyebrow.

"Well, I had to explain to him why we're not going to the river right now. That was all right, wasn't it?"

"You do what you need to do, Straw. I've never known that dragon to purr as much as he does around you."

"Thank you, Dragon Master."

"And Straw, do you think you could arrange for Star to give a bit of a show when Malvise comes? You know, something more than a yawn might come in useful."

"What did you have in mind?"

"I'll leave that to you and Star." And without saying more, he was off arranging something with Keg.

Star had been listening in on this conversation. Straw turned to him and asked, "Do you have any ideas?"

"I think I know what he means. I've got a very good idea." And he began to explain his plan to Straw.

Later that day, Straw found himself in a most awkward situation.

"Star, I just don't see how you think this is going to impress him. To tell you the truth, I feel pretty foolish in here."

"Un-huh-un-nuh."

Straw began laughing. "Sorry! I forgot that you can't talk while I'm sitting here."

"Un-nuh-huh!"

"All right, I see them. I hope this works."

Garth was leading Lord Malvise and three of his knights into the barn. Mali and Keg were with them. Garth was explaining once again that Star is a Luck Dragon, totally unfit for duels to the death. What they saw as they stepped inside was the dragon with his jaws wide open and Straw inside his cavernous mouth, sitting on his tongue. Straw had a long handled brush and a bucket. He was scrubbing away at the dragon's teeth.

The whole group stopped in their tracks. Straw was watching them out of the corner of his eye. Malvise and his knights looked shocked. That was good. Garth looked grave, Mali was growing pale, and Keg, well, he looked amused. Garth spoke into Mali's ear a moment, and he hurried over to where Straw sat.

"Straw, come out of there immediately," he spoke softly. He did not want the others to hear. "Right now, do you hear me? This is the craziest thing I've ever seen. Garth's not at all happy."

"We've got company, Star," Straw said in a loud voice, as if this had been rehearsed. "Now behave yourself." He gathered his brush and bucket and began to carefully step over and between the rows of razor-sharp teeth.

"Really, Straw, I know you have a relationship with him," Mali continued to fret. "But he is a dragon after all. You just don't take chances and do foolish things around a dragon."

Straw stood inside the dragon's mouth listening to Mali scold him. He handed the bucket and brush to him and decided to stand there just a moment longer, for the effect he was hoping to make on Lord Malvise. Then something strange happened. Maybe it was a movement Star made, or a shift in weight, but suddenly the hair on the back of Straw's head stood up. Some inner response alerted him that he was in grave danger. He sprang from Star's jaws and landed right in Mali's arms. The two of them staggered back just as Star's jaws snapped together as if they were spring-loaded. The sound was sharp and decisive. The jaws caught the end of the long-handled brush and snapped it in half. Both Straw and Mali jumped even further out of the way, and Straw felt his heart take a leap.

Mali was unnerved. "You could have still been in there," he gasped.

Straw was also surprised and annoyed. *That's not what we agreed to do,* he thought to himself.

Star had his own plans. A greenish light began to glow in his eyes. He stared straight at the small group that still stood near the barn doors. He lifted himself lightly onto his feet and crouched down, as if he were about to spring. Then he opened his mouth wide, but not for a yawn. He let out a bellow that sounded like a forest of trees being snapped in half. Mali was so alarmed that he grabbed Straw by the tunic and dragged him out of the way to the side of the barn. Star followed up his bellow with a snarl like summer thunder. His expression looked utterly menacing.

Malvise and his knights had a look of terror on their faces. They took several steps back and hastily drew their swords. Keg and Garth immediately ran to the barn walls and took down the long hooked poles that had been used to guide Star before Straw had taken over his care. They held the poles ready and advanced cautiously towards the snarling dragon.

Straw knew the gleam in Star's eyes. It was how he looked when they had sparred to the point that Star was completely enraged at being smacked so often on his relatively soft nose. It was when their sparring turned into an earnest battle and Star stopped teaching and went on the offensive. Straw was alarmed by this. He dragged himself away from Mali's grasp and ran past Keg and Garth to stand right in front of the menacing dragon.

"You stop that right now!" he called out in a loud, commanding voice. "You will not do that! Down! Down, I say!" He spoke forcefully and with full authority, gesturing with his arms. There was no trace of fear in him. With sword or without, he was simply beyond being afraid of Star, whether the dragon was furious or not.

Star growled once more, and then looked down at the small young man facing him. He growled again, but softer.

"Enough! Back down, I say! Down!"

One last growl, just to show that he made his own decisions, and Star rested his long body on the ground again. His head remained upright and alert. The menacing gleam in his eyes, though, was gone.

The dragon boy was satisfied that Star's fit was finished. He turned around to the others. "I'm so sorry," he said. "He's not usually like this. You can probably approach now if you want."

Malvise and his knights stayed where they were, their swords still drawn and held before them. "Tame as a house dog," Malvise snorted. "He'll make good sport, that I'll swear to. I look forward to our match. Dragon Master," he called out. "I take you at your word. Once the tournament is ours, I claim the right to battle with your tame house dragon. Don't disappoint me."

With these words, sword still drawn, Malvise stalked away, followed by his three knights. Garth walked over to where Straw was standing.

"I'm not sure that's what I had in mind when I asked you for more than a yawn." He looked tired. Straw wanted to say that it was all really Star's idea, and that he had improvised much more than they had agreed upon. Then he realized there was no way to say that without a lengthy explanation.

"It was the best we could come up with," he finally said.

"I was frightened for you, Straw. I saw something unleashed in Star that I didn't think was going to be calmed so easily again." He looked over at the dragon lying there as quietly as if nothing unusual had happened.

"He got pretty excited," Straw agreed. "I don't think he likes Malvise very much."

Keg and Mali joined them. "Well, I guess that backfired," Keg said, looking bemused. "But there was no way of knowing how it would go. I'd say you did what you could."

Mali was more concerned for Straw. He had already taken him by the shoulder and was turning him this way and that. "Straw, are you all right? You're lucky he didn't snap your head right off. It was absolutely crazy, what you did."

"I'm not hurt," the boy protested. "Star didn't touch me. I'm really all right."

"Do we have to put a special watch on him now?" Mali asked. "I've never seen him act like that. What was that all about?"

Garth walked over to Star's immense head and held up his hand. Star sniffed at it and let Garth scratch his muzzle. "I don't think we have anything to worry about," he said. "I think we can be confident that Star has returned to his usual sweet self."

"Then what was that show of fury?" Keg wondered.

Garth turned to face them. "Draco, the ancient keeper who trained me, left me with a number of teachings about dragons. One of the most important things to know about them is that they take on the energy of the human beings around them. That's why we keep him so protected and treat him as well as we do. That's why we're so strict about the barn boys not fighting around him." He paused and glanced at Straw, who understood his meaning. "We stay calm and peaceful around him, and he reflects our own inner state back to us. Yet, the opposite is also true."

"Malvise," Straw gasped. He was now realizing the explanation for Star's strange behavior.

"That's right," Garth said. "Malvise is a man filled with anger, hatred and violence. He gathers an army to come here for the sole purpose of fighting a dragon. Why? So he can intimidate other people into accepting his domination. His inner state was so powerful that it spilled over. I imagine Star hooked into it and reflected it back. I almost wish we could let them have their battle. It would be a good deed to rid the world of such a tyrant as Lord Malvise."

"But why don't we, then?" Straw blurted out.

Garth looked very stern when he answered. "I took a very solemn oath to protect Star from violent behavior. His remaining here depends on it. I am not going to break that vow even for Malvise. We will trust in the skill of our champions. Now, Straw, I want you to keep an eye on Star and make sure that no one else bothers him for awhile."

"Do you think we can leave the boy with the dragon?" Mali asked.

"I'm convinced that Straw is the last person we need to worry about. Come on, you two. I want to discuss some options with you."

Garth walked away, accompanied by Keg and Mali. Straw was left alone with the dragon.

"Star," he asked, "do you agree with what Garth was saying?"

"I always liked that man," Star commented. "He knows the ways of dragons quite well. It's a pity that we can't talk. He often reminds me of Galifalia. They knew one another when they were young. And, yes, that's pretty much the way it is. When Malvise came in, I simply focused all my attention on him. I let his inner state do the rest. I just sort of amplified it."

The boy was suspicious. "Star, did you plan to do that? Without telling me first?"

"Well, that was my plan, I admit."

"But Star, how could you know that I would get out of your mouth in time?" This was a very uncomfortable thought.

"I've trained you to be quick. I wasn't worried. You felt it coming. I'm very happy with your progress."

Straw only shook his head, thinking how narrowly he had come to being crushed between Star's immense jaws. "I still think we should let you fight him," he said.

"Garth's right. It's not a good idea. Fighting Malvise would rile me to a fury unlike any even you have seen."

"After you've destroyed Malvise, I could fight with you then. I could quiet your heart again."

"That you could. But there's a very big chance that I would not stick around long enough to engage with you. Most likely, I'd just fly off. I would be so blinded by the battle that I wouldn't recognize you or care about staying any longer. You know, my time is coming to an end soon anyway, and the urge to leave would be awakened early. We did the best thing."

"But we failed. Malvise wants to fight you more than ever before."

"I disagree. I think we were very successful, just in a different way. But you'll have to wait to find out that I'm right. In the meantime, enjoy the tournament."

Straw could get the dragon to say no more.

Chapter Seventeen

The Tournament

Gray banners with the emblem of a red dragon were fixed along the walls at regular intervals. They snapped gaily in the wind and gave everything a festive look. Outside the wall, in the army camp, every tent now sported a banner in front of it. It was the black banner of Malvise with the emblem of a crossed sword and battle axe. These also were whipped up by the wind and made everything look like a celebration.

Now that the barn boys had time to spare, they were set to work burnishing shields and armor, sharpening swords and securing metal lance points onto sanded wooden shafts. They greased leather jerkins to make them more pliable and checked chain mail for gaps. All of the knights' chargers were curried and groomed and their hoofs given a thorough cleaning. The blacksmiths were kept busy day and night repairing, correcting and creating new weapons and armor.

A group of boys under the direction of skilled carpenters took up the task of erecting grandstands for the families of the nobility to sit in during the jousts. A special royal box was prepared for the king, the queen and their family.

Although the boys approached the upcoming tournament as they would any festival, with lots of good humor and chatter, Straw could feel the somberness of the older staff members. None of the adults who worked in any of the crafts looked cheerful or pleased.

Straw had just helped push a cartload of flour from the gate where a miller from town had delivered it. He hoisted one of the heavy bags onto his shoulder and entered the kitchen door. A commotion inside caused him to stop in his tracks. Some of the cooks were openly crying. He could hear Matild yelling in the background.

"...will not tolerate it one bit! Doom and gloom has no place in my kitchen! Scrub the pots! Shine them with your tears, you bunch of silly geese!" When she paused in her tirade, the crying grew to a wail. Straw was not sure what to do.

Fortunately, at that moment Alis came hurrying over to him.

"Alis, what's going on?" he asked in a low voice.

"Put the sacks over here on this pallet," she directed him. "Don't worry about it. Some of the cooks have been over-salting the food with their tears, and Matild has had it."

"What are they afraid of?"

"There are a lot of the older women who believe that if Malvise wins the tournament, the days of the compound are over. For many of them, it's all they've ever known. Many came as children and just stayed on. They're scared. How are the barn boys doing?"

"They think it's a holiday. Some of them would like to see our champions fail, which would force a battle between Malvise and Star."

Alis was silent a moment. The wailing in the background continued, though not as loud. "What about the Dragon Master?"

"He's worried, too. He doesn't think our knights have what it will take."

"Maybe the days of the compound *are* coming to an end. How's Star? Is he disturbed by all of this?"

"Star is not in the least bit worried."

"Yes, I didn't expect a dragon to worry. What about you?"

"I look forward to the tournament. I've never seen one before. As for the rest, I just want to get it over with."

"Well, tomorrow it all begins. Maybe that will quiet things down around here. We could certainly use it."

At first light the next morning, the trumpets began to blare. Each trumpet blast signaled a different gathering. The first was for the judges to gather and mark off the jousting arena. The next signaled the squires to begin getting the knights ready, and the next was to signal the grooms to prepare the horses. It continued like this throughout the morning. Very early, folk from the town gathered to find choice spots to sit and watch the proceedings. They brought food with them to last throughout the day. Vendors had begun the night before setting up stands to sell food, pastries, drinks, jewelry, weaponry, cloth, hats and potions. Straw began to understand why the other boys looked at it as a festival. Overnight it had turned into one.

Garth had wisely given all the boys of the compound the day off after completing bare maintenance in the barn. It would have been too much effort to force them into anything more. Straw was also looking forward to walk the vendor stands and find a place to sit and watch. He had told Colin and Alis to wait for him while he checked on Star before going. He was annoyed that Star did not seem in the least affected by all the commotion, nor did he have much to say. He made only one comment, which Straw found odd.

"During the tournament, boy, keep your eyes on Malvise. Watch him carefully, how he moves, how he attacks, parries, feints, lunges. Watch him until you can begin to predict what his next move will be."

Straw was puzzled. "Whatever for? Is he particularly good at something?"

"Watch him, if for no other reason than to learn how he moves," the dragon said. "Don't trouble yourself with why, but with doing it. You'll find out in due time."

As Straw was coming out of the barn, he saw Malvise leaving the stables that stood along the further wall of the compound and stopped to watch him. Malvise was in his armor, still without his helmet, leading his horse. When he had first arrived, he had declared that he wanted only the best for his horse, and requested, although it had sounded more like a demand, to have it kept in a stall within the compound. It was rumored that Malvise cared more for his horse than for his men. He visited his horse first thing in the morning and last thing at night, and periodically throughout the day. He would let no one else exercise him.

Straw watched him lead his charger out through one of the open gates in the wall. *Study him*, he told himself. He was more inclined to watch the horse than the man. The horse was well muscled and walked effortlessly. But that was not what Star had told him to do. *Well, Malvise is light on his feet, even when he's wearing armor,* was Straw's first impression. *He's going to give our knights quite a beating.* As soon as Malvise walked through the gate, Straw ran to catch up with his two friends.

"There you are! What took you so long?" Colin asked. "We've been ready to go forever."

"Colin is worried about getting a good seat," Alis explained.

"Well, it's not every day that we have a tournament," Colin said, as they hurried toward the gates. "Besides, I want to be able to cheer Corin on."

"Is he also one of your cousin knights going into the tournament?" Straw asked.

"More than that," Alis explained. "He's our brother."

Straw stopped in his tracks. "You have a brother?"

"And two sisters, too," Alis said with a shrug of her shoulders.

"And you never told me?"

"It's not like we get to see them that often," Colin said. They had arrived at the first stands and slowed down to take in their wares. Alis had stopped at one with earrings, necklaces, and bracelets. The boys waited politely while she looked. "They're lots older than we are, anyway," Colin explained. "They had already moved out of the compound by the time we came."

"They were here, too?" Straw said astonished.

"Of course. I told you that all the children from the noble families spend time here. Come on, Alis. You can look later," he urged.

"Oh, all right," she said reluctantly, and they continued to weave their way through the stands. They all paused at the pastry stand and ogled the sticky buns and cinnamon rolls.

"Come on, Colin, let's get some now," Alis said. "They may not have any later."

"You're right," Colin agreed. He took some coins from the pouch at his waist and bought them each a bun of their choosing. At first Straw refused, well aware that he had no money of his own and could never return the favor. Alis understood his reluctance and said, "Come on, Straw, it's like when I give you extra from the kitchen. No one is going with less because of it. We're friends, aren't we?"

"But I can never pay you back," he mumbled.

"Then you'll do something else for me sometime. Fact is, you already have. Flek is much less obnoxious since you began caring for Star. And I don't think it's because he's grown older or more mature. Now take it and stop being so silly," Colin said, pushing a swirled roll at him. Straw took it reluctantly, but once he tasted it, he was glad for the treat

They worked their way through the stands onto the open field. There was already a great crowd gathered. The grandstands were nearly full. Next to the stands was a large gathering of horses, knights and squires, all wearing the emblem of the dragon. Colin headed towards them.

"I want to wish Corin good luck," he said and disappeared into the throng. Straw and Alis had to hurry to keep up. Colin wove in and out among the knights, apparently clear what he was looking for. They finally caught up with him as he was talking with a tall knight who had his helmet under his arm. Straw could see the resemblance. His hair was light brown and he had the same abundance of freckles. But unlike his younger brother and sister, he looked very somber.

"Hi, Alis," he said as they joined them. "Who's your friend?"

"This is Straw," Alis said. Corin now smiled broadly and sized him up.

"I've heard all about you," he said. "You're the talk of the town."

Straw was not quite sure what he meant by this.

"You know," he explained. "Because of what you can do with the dragon. We've all seen you riding on Star's neck at the processions. It's not like it's a secret."

"I just go wash him every day," Straw said, trying to play it down. It made him uncomfortable to think that people in the town talked about him.

"As you wish," Corin said, still smiling. "Anything you say. You show me someone else who can make the dragon sit up and beg like a dog."

"I don't do that," Straw protested.

"Well, just about everything else. At least, that's what people are saying. They're hoping you're going to bring Star in at the last minute to save the day."

The three friends were silenced by this remark. Finally Colin found his voice. "What do you mean, Corin? You're going to send them packing, aren't you?"

Corin was looking grave again. "Look, little brother, we've been watching them for a week now. They're very good. I don't think many of our riders can match them. We've become too relaxed lately, thinking that having a dragon is protection enough. Besides, they're seasoned warriors from the look of them, and most of us have never engaged in a real battle. Before this is over, Star may have to do some fighting of his own."

"But, Corin," Alis protested. "We're here to protect Star."

"And we'll do our best," her brother responded. "But our best may not be enough." This was somber news, and the three friends silently walked across the field to join the picnickers.

The tournament began with a great deal of fanfare which delighted the crowd tremendously. The knights of Lord Malvise paraded before the king's box, followed by the knights of the town. They all looked splendid and the sun glanced off their polished armor. Lances were adorned with small pennants, and shields bore richly decorated coats of arms. Even the horses were festooned and had their tails braided. Drums and trumpets set the tone and the pace of the parade.

The tournament opened with what looked like a general skirmish. The two forces rode down on one another with a clamor and great clash of arms. At some distance from the green, it was difficult for the onlookers to tell who was taking the advantage. This was a kind of warm-up for the knights, but looked every bit like an all-out battle. There was no intention to harm one another, which was another way of saying that no one was out to kill. Bruising, blood and broken bones, however, were unavoidable. The knights bashed and battled one another, attempting to either make their opponents yield or unseat them altogether from their horses. Any knights taken prisoner were thenceforth ineligible to take part in the jousting. This narrowed the field down and eliminated the weaker prospects.

There was a great deal of shouting and dust. The people watched in dismay as one dragon knight after another fell to the ground and was taken prisoner. Cheers went up when one of Nogardia's knights singlehandedly braved the guards holding his companions captive. While his companions kept the main force occupied, he dashed through their line and began attacking the guards. One by one they fell and were in turn taken prisoner by the group of dragon knights that were now freed. Even though they were all on foot, he managed to protect them long enough to get them safely back behind their own lines.

"That's Corin! That's Corin!" Colin yelled, jumping up and down. "I can tell it's him! He's freed them! Go, Corin! Whip them!"

Colin was not the only one jumping up and down with excitement as they watched Corin bring the knights to safety and then turn and reengage. He fought with a fury, and it was clear that the knights of Malvise's army avoided him if possible.

Straw's attention was drawn to another part of the field where Lord Malvise was fighting. He could imagine himself out there. He was convinced that he could do just as well as many of them. He could identify differences in skill level and saw who would not remain long in his saddle. He fancied that he would be able to hold his own. Then he remembered Star's instructions and started paying close attention to Malvise's fighting style.

Malvise was very dynamic and flexible. His blade was never still and seemed to be everywhere at once. Straw began to follow his every move. He realized that Malvise was extremely strong. His sword was always raised, unless he was bringing it down to strike. And he noticed he could unhorse an unprepared knight with a single blow. The more he watched Malvise's swordsmanship, the more a rhythm and pattern began to emerge. Parry left, parry right, parry left, feint, strike. Right, right, left, feint, strike. Right, left, right, feint, strike. Malvise struck hardest after a rhythm of three blows and a feint. His fourth blow was always the one he used to finish off his opponent. He held the advantage because of his strength and speed. But he rarely varied his rhythm. One, two, three, feint, one. One, two, three, feint, one. Pretty simple, he thought. And although Straw had to agree that Malvise was very fast, he could plainly see that Malvise would not have a chance against a dragon.

The melee began to wind down as more knights on both sides were being captured. There were judges riding the field with two purposes. The first was to prevent any knight from becoming involved to the point that he tried to kill an opponent. Their second purpose was to assess when one side had gained an advantage and then bring the fighting to an end. Otherwise, the knights would just continue to battle until one side had completely overwhelmed the other.

It was looking like it might just go in that direction, as Malvise's forces were again taking more prisoners. The judges wanted to make sure that enough knights were left for the jousting. They gave the signal, and trumpets began to blare. The knights were so engaged in their battling that the trumpeters had to ride between them in order to gain their attention. Once a knight noticed the trumpets, he was required on his honor to cease fighting. The knights began to slowly regroup, prisoners were returned, and they made their way towards the grandstands. Malvise's force came at a brisk trot. The knights of Nogardia came much more slowly.

"We got whipped," Alis said sadly.

"That Malvise is too good," Colin said. "But maybe at the jousts, Corin can go against him. Did you see him? He fought like a madman. Hey, Straw, do you think we have a chance?"

Straw had been deep in thought. He had continued watching Malvise and thinking about how to get around him. Colin's question roused him out of his reverie.

"Say, is there any chance that I can talk to Corin? I've got something he needs to know."

Colin was puzzled by this, but answered, "Sure, why not? Come on, let's go find him."

There had been a number of injuries on both sides, and many knights needed tending. Those who had been taken prisoner were not allowed to take part in the jousts. The group of dragon knights continuing to the next stage of the tournament was forebodingly small. Upon their return, they grouped together with their squires, tended to their gear, replaced weapons and shields, and took what short rest they could. There was not a long break before the jousting would begin. This was definitely a battle of endurance to see who could last the longest.

They found Corin sitting on a low stool. His squire was washing a cut on his forehead. "I just don't want it bleeding into my eye during the joust," Corin was saying. "It'll blind me on that side for sure."

Colin ran up to him. "Corin, you were tremendous! We saw what you did. It's like you held them all off single-handed and freed all the prisoners. You were great!"

Corin looked at his younger brother and smiled weakly. "I'm afraid it didn't do much good, little brother. Most got captured again, you know."

"But now you can show them how to joust," Colin said confidently.

"In truth," Corin said. "We'll show them." But his voice lacked his younger brother's confidence.

"Say, Corin," Straw began. "I've been watching Malvise. I know he's strong and quick and all, but I think that you can beat him."

"Once you've got it clean, just hold a cloth to it," Corin said to his squire. He seemed not to have heard Straw. "Maybe that will stop the bleeding."

"Look," Straw tried again. "I think I know how you can beat him."

"By keeping this blood out of my eyes," Corin said standing up. Holding the cloth to his forehead, he muttered, "Have to see to my horse," and walked off.

Straw wanted to tell him about what he had observed, but Corin was too preoccupied to listen. Straw decided to try again and ran after him. "Corin, listen, I know how you can beat Malvise. I've been watching him."

Corin stopped long enough to let Straw catch up. He looked spent. His face was drawn and ashen. "Look, Straw, about the only thing that's going to help right now is if you bring Star in. It may have to come to that anyway. Be ready for it." And without waiting to hear what Straw had to say, he walked on.

"He strikes three times, then a feint, then a final blow," Straw called after him, but his advice fell on deaf ears.

"What do you mean?" Colin had followed Straw. "What do you mean, three times and a final blow?"

"It's three quick strikes, a feint and then a final blow," Straw said. "It's how Malvise fights. It's his rhythm. I wanted Corin to know."

"How do you know how he fights?"

"I've been watching him."

"What do you know about fighting?"

"Oh, gee," Straw began. He did not know how to explain how he came to know this. "I just thought it would help. Come on, let's go back."

By the time they got back to Alis, the riders for the first joust were lining up. Straw noticed some people walking around making bets on how many lances the opponents would break and who would stay mounted. The odds favored Malvise's knights.

Colin went over to a woman who was taking bets and spoke with her for some time. Then he took some money out of his pouch and handed it over to her.

"I put money on Corin," he said. "For good luck, you know."

"Are the odds in his favor?" Alis asked.

"Yes, but he's one of the few they're thinking might win."

Straw fretted silently that he wished Corin had listened to him. *Then he might have a chance*, he thought.

Once again, the trumpets were sounded. It was time for the jousting to begin.

"Star, it doesn't look good," the dragon boy said. He had left the jousting arena after the first run. Not only had the dragon knight been unhorsed, he lay there stunned and had to be carried off the field by attendants.

"I think that everything is coming along splendidly," Star said. A loud cry from many voices went up in the jousting fields.

"Splendidly for them," Straw said bitterly. "I don't know how you can be so confident at a time like this. Do you want to be forced to fight Malvise?"

"I don't believe it will come to that," Star said. Another loud cry rose out of the fields. This time, it carried a sound of despair in it.

"I don't see how Malvise can lose."

"I agree with you there."

"So what is going to prevent him from fighting you?"

"My guardian."

"Your guardian? What guardian? You don't have a guardian. Whatever are you talking about?" Then it dawned on Straw what the dragon meant. "You mean *me*?"

"Look, boy, if anyone is going to stop Lord Malvise, it will have to be you." Once again, a loud cry went up from the fields. Then there was chanting and clashing of arms. It sounded like a victory song.

The door to the barn slammed open. It was Colin. He was pale and breathing hard. "He took Corin down," he said. His eyes were wide and full of fear. "After two lances, they fought with swords. Malvise looked like he hardly tried. He's bragging that tomorrow he comes to fight the dragon. We're lost." He staggered away, leaving them alone again. They were silent for a long while, listening to Malvise's army celebrating.

"I'm not ready to let you go, Star."

"Then do something about it. And do it soon."

Chapter Eighteen

What Happened in the Stables

Straw knew that he was going to have only one try. He feared that he had very little chance of succeeding, and somehow, the hopelessness of the situation gave him the courage to go ahead with his plan.

It was soon lantern lighting. He hurried over to the woodworking shop and looked through a stack of wooden staves stored against the side of the building. Quickly he chose two of roughly equal length. He needed something that would take the force of a blow without breaking. With the two staves in hand, he trotted off to the stable.

The grooms were all gone by this time. When he entered, in the dim light, he saw many heads rise and ears perk. The horses were curious who had come in this late. He hoped he had come in time. He set the staves against the wall and sat down on a low bench. Breathing hard, he tried to calm his nerves. He did not have long to wait.

The door opened briefly and once again heads and ears rose up to see who had come in. Straw was not disappointed. It was Malvise. He came bustling in, a wind of energy around him. He walked briskly through the barn, heading straight for his horse's stall, his movements sharp and directed. Straw stood up.

At the unexpected movement, Malvise came to a sudden halt and took half a step back. He strained in the half light to see. "Who's there?" he asked in a menacing voice.

"'Tis I," Straw said taking a step forward.

"And who might you be?" Malvise asked. Seeing no threat, he relaxed a bit. "Have we met?"

"Aye," Straw answered. "We met, although briefly. When you came to see Star. I was there."

Malvise stood a moment, silent in the dim light, trying to remember the youth's face. Then he made the connection. "Ah, you were that foolish boy cleaning the dragon's teeth. Most idiotic thing I've ever seen. I'm surprised that beast hasn't eaten you yet. Well, after tomorrow..." But he did not finish his sentence. He concluded the boy was nothing more to concern himself with. He continued on his way to his horse's stall at the far end. Straw, his heart beating wildly, stepped into his path.

"Lord Malvise."

Malvise paused and looked at him. "What is it, boy? I'm busy. What are you doing here, anyway? Did they put you in charge of brushing the horses' teeth as well?"

"Lord Malvise," Straw repeated. "Tomorrow morning you will take your army and leave the kingdom."

Malvise could not believe his ears. Then he just laughed. "So you're the village idiot. Now I understand what you were doing in the dragon's mouth. You're mad, boy. It's a good thing for you that I'm in a good humor. Now step aside so I don't be rough with you."

Straw did not step aside, though. He stepped even more in Malvise's way. "Lord Malvise," he said. "You will do as I tell you."

At these words, Malvise's mouth fell open.

"You impertinent pup!" he barked. Suddenly his right arm was swinging through the air, aimed straight at Straw's head. He intended to give him one smart blow to teach him how not to talk to his betters. His arm, though, only swung through empty air. Straw dodged neatly out of the way. Malvise stumbled, and he was surprised and enraged at the same time.

"Boy, you are not worth my anger," he spit. "Stay out of my way." He resumed walking towards his horse. Straw saw only one way to get his full attention. He put out his leg and tripped him. Malvise stumbled and then recovered without fully falling. He now stood and faced Straw. He was furious.

"Boy, how little you value your worthless life to play with me in this manner." His voice was cold and deadly calm.

"Lord Malvise, I am giving you a chance to leave here with your honor," he paused a moment before continuing, "and your life."

"Are you threatening me?"

"You are never going to fight the dragon."

"What are you talking about, fool? Of course I'm going to fight the dragon. I've won the tournament. Tomorrow morning I am going to thrash your hand-fed beast. What could possibly stop me now? There are no knights left to stand against me."

"In truth, there are no knights left," Straw admitted. "But before you can fight the dragon, you must get past the dragon's guardian. That is me. And you cannot possibly defeat me." He said these last words slowly, so there would be no mistaking his meaning.

There was a deep silence in the stable. Even the horses seemed to be listening to every word. Then the space was filled with Malvise's deep laughter. "Boy, you're raving mad. Entertaining, but mad. You're lucky that I haven't my staff with me, or I'd crack your head to teach you a lesson not to mock your elders."

"You're in luck," Straw interjected.

"Luck? What idiocy now? What luck are you talking about?"

Straw bent down and picked up one of the staves he had left leaning against the wall. "I happen to have a staff right here. Will this do? Here! Teach me a lesson." With these words, he tossed the staff right at Malvise. The knight snatched it out of the air before it struck him.

"You poor, misguided fool," he growled. "And you've been set up. I beat you, and King Pell complains I've mistreated one of his cousin's illegitimate brats and nullifies the deal. Did he promise you a fiefdom if you survived the beating? I'm not so easily throwing away my chance of killing your dragon." He threw the staff to the ground and turned away.

Straw had no choice but to smack Malvise from behind on his shoulder. Malvise turned enraged. "What do you think you're doing?" he bellowed. In answer, Straw struck him again.

Malvise's eyes bugged out of his face. "You're about to get a lesson you'll never forget. The only trouble is that I won't leave you with enough senses to remember it." He swooped up the staff and in one motion took three quick steps forward raising it like a club. The blow he delivered was so fierce that, had it connected, it would have knocked Straw unconscious. Instead, Malvise was surprised when his staff did not strike the boy's head, but was deflected by a staff that suddenly appeared in the boy's hands.

"You're quick," he said, the surprise showing in his voice. "Still, that won't stop you from getting the beating—" Malvise never finished his sentence. Straw had dodged to the right, pivoted, turned and delivered a sharp blow to Malvise's unguarded ribs. He ended up standing behind Malvise, who grunted with the blow and bellowed with rage.

Malvise quickly turned with his staff at ready to keep Straw in front of him. He went into a guard position, as he might do in battle. Straw saw this and knew that he would not be able to strike him unprepared again. Malvise was finally taking him seriously. His fighter instincts had taken over. Straw knew his only chance was to do the unexpected.

"Before we engage one another," Straw said. "I want to honor your skills as a knight. They are impressive. I've learned much by watching you." And so saying, he bowed before Malvise.

Malvise's lip curled in scorn. "Fool," he muttered and took a quick step forward with his staff raised, intending to hit the boy across the back while he was still bent over. Instead, he received a sharp jab into his stomach from the end of the boy's staff. As Straw bowed, he anticipated the knight's attack and had followed his bow with forward motion, jamming his staff into Malvise's oncoming body. The knight had the wind knocked out of him and fell to his knees.

Straw knew that he could make an end of it here with one quick blow. But he had a different intention. "Lord Malvise, I want to give you a chance. If you yield to me now, we don't have to continue this. All I ask is that you surrender your right to fight the dragon."

Malvise looked up to where Straw stood. His face was distorted with pain and anger. With a great war-cry emanating from his gut, he leapt right towards his opponent with his staff whistling through the air. Straw was expecting something like this, and the staff thudded against a post of the stall where the boy had stood just a moment before. *Now*, thought Straw, *I'll play with him, just as Star taught me.* This was working out much easier than he had expected. Malvise was indeed fast, for a human being. But Star had the speed of an animal, and not just any animal, but a dragon at that, and the boy was attuned to that pace.

Straw stood his ground in the midst of an open space. Malvise charged him with his staff raised. Straw was ready for what came. One, two, three, the blows rained down on Straw, and he parried each one with his own staff held in both hands. His hands stung from the impact of wood against wood, but he held on firmly. *Now comes the feint,* he thought. He did not wait for it, but made his move. Malvise was so sure of his actions, that he never suspected Straw would not cover himself when he faked a fourth blow. Straw, convinced it was a ruse, let down his guard and instead delivered a resounding crack to his opponent's ribs before springing out of the way.

Malvise was on his knees again, looking up with utter surprise. Straw backed away to give him some space. That was what he had wanted to tell Corin about. Now he was certain that with this knowledge, he could defeat Malvise.

"Are you ready yet to yield?" Straw asked.

In answer, bellowing once more, Malvise attacked. One, two, three, the blows came in quick succession. Malvise was too stunned by the beating he had taken to realize that he should change his fighting rhythm. It had never failed him before either in a tournament or in real battle. Why should it fail him now with this fool of a scrub boy? But fail it did, as Straw sent him one more time to his knees and he struggled to get his breath back. This happened two more times, and each time Straw asked, "Will you yield to me?" But each time, Malvise answered with renewed attack.

Straw was impressed by how much punishment this knight could take. He admired his tenacity and determination to keep fighting. He feared that Malvise would never yield, true to his knightly code to fight to the death. He was careful never to hit Malvise in the face. The last thing he wanted was to leave visible signs that they had fought. He was being merciless with the knight's ribs, though. He was certain that he had already bruised them badly and perhaps cracked a few.

The fifth time Straw knocked the wind out of Malvise, the knight crumpled to his knees. Supporting himself with his hands, he was panting, beaten. He looked up to Straw. "Why don't you just finish me off?" he gasped between breaths. It was obvious that he was in a lot of pain.

"Because you are brave," Straw answered. "And I want you to leave and take your army with you. You've come to fight the dragon. But you cannot get past me, his guardian, and I am still a boy. How do you expect it to go with the dragon? He will not bother to leave you alive, nor be as gentle as I have been."

And now Straw decided to play his bluff. It would be simple now to defeat Malvise completely. But that did not remove his army, which might take revenge on the town for the damage done to their prince.

Star had warned him that in order to defeat an army, he had to be not only quick and strong, but also clever.

"Listen to me, Malvise. If you refuse to yield to me, then you will have to fight me again, next time in front of all the others. You leave me no other choice. I waited for you here in order to preserve your honor. You don't need me to tell you that it doesn't look good to be beaten by someone as small as me, someone who does not yet bear the title of knight. And I assure you, if you insist on fighting, you will lose again. You have no hope of defeating me. If you can't do it with a wooden staff, what chance do you think you'll have with a sword?"

Straw paused to determine the effect of his words. Malvise had not moved from the spot. He looked up at Straw and his lips moved, but no sound came out.

"Malvise, you know that you cannot win. The others will see you defeated by a boy. Is that how you want to go? Beaten?"

Straw was praying that Malvise was hurting too badly to detect that he was bluffing. There was no way that Garth, let alone the king, would allow him to fight Malvise publicly. He was hoping that Malvise considered this normal procedure if the tournament should go against them.

Malvise's lips moved again. He spoke hoarsely, but with passion. "I'll burn your town and your compound to the ground." It was a terrifying threat, but at least it showed Straw that Malvise believed him.

"Who will follow you after they see you beaten by me? Is it worth losing everything you've already gained? You can go now with the honor that you defeated all the knights of the dragon compound. I will never reveal what happened here tonight. But first you must yield to me. Will you now yield?"

"Never!" the knight hissed. This brief conversation had rested him enough. He lunged once more to attack. Straw was prepared, and landed several harsh blows on the weakened knight, now intending to break bones, but not kill. A few moments later, Malvise lay unconscious in the straw.

The dragon boy took both staves and left the stall. It was now lantern lighting time, and workers were bustling here and there. But no one paid any special attention to Straw as he walked back to the carpenter's shop and replaced the staves.

Straw walked slowly towards his dormitory. Had he done the right thing? If the knight should go to the king and complain, the boy would be disgraced and Star would have to fight anyway. In the end he was certain that he had done what he could. He was at least content that he had left Malvise in no shape to fight a dragon. It would take him weeks to heal from his beating. Now he just had to wait and see what the next day would bring.

The next morning at breakfast, everyone was glum. A number of the barn boys, in particular Flek and his friends, were at least decently subdued in their glee over the coming battle. The unmistakable sounds of weeping came from the back rooms of the kitchen.

Loud trumpet blasts sounded before Straw had finished eating. Famished from the exertions of the evening before, he stuffed his mouth with bread before stepping outside with the others to see what was happening. Was it possible that Malvise was going to fight Star after all?

The trumpets were blaring from outside the compound wall. Straw was jostled as everyone filed through the open gates. What he saw made his heart beat faster. The whole of Malvise's army was mobilized and on their horses. At their head were the captains, surrounding Malvise. The captains had dark, severe looks on their faces. Malvise looked the darkest of all in his black armor. His face was frozen in a sneer. Were they mounted to attack the compound? Had he and all the people walked out to get slaughtered? He was about to dash back inside and alert the compound guard when he saw they were already standing in attendance. They were armed, but did not look alarmed.

It was then that he noticed for the first time that all of the tents and pavilions were gone from the fields. What could that mean?

Then he saw Garth and Keg standing side by side before the horses of Malvise and his guard. If Malvise attacked, the two of them would be the first to be struck down. For a long moment, Straw considered running to get Star from his barn. If he could get a sword and some armor, the two of them might be able to turn things if it came to a battle. He must act before it was too late.

The trumpets suddenly grew silent. Was this the sign to attack?

"Good people," Malvise called out. Straw was astonished how strong his voice was. He must be made of iron to have survived such a beating.

"We take our leave of you now," Malvise continued. Hope stirred in Straw's heart. "We have discovered that the air in your plains is unhealthy." Whatever is he talking about? "My knights are becoming ill." Suddenly, Malvise was taken by a fit of coughing. It caused him such pain that he doubled up over his horse. One of his guards moved over to hold the horse's reins steady. It was now obvious that he was in a great deal of pain. So the iron had some cracks in it. When he stopped coughing and caught his breath, Malvise continued.

"As you can see, I am also affected. I do not wonder that we were able to defeat you so easily, for you are weakened by an unhealthy climate. But it is not good for us to remain. We are going to leave this valley of sickness and return to our steppes where the air blows clean and is free of illness."

Malvise paused and looked around at the crowd gathered before him. His eyes found Straw and stopped. Their gazes locked and held for a moment. Straw expected hate, but was surprised to be met with respect. Malvise looked away and continued.

"I had come to fight with your dragon. I have found your knights to be worthy opponents, but weakened, no doubt the result of the dragon's foul breath over many years. It would be doing a blessing to this land to remove it from here. However, I must leave this work to you. I leave your lands victorious. If I hear that the pestilence the dragon brings is spreading to other lands, I will be compelled to return. At that time, I will not hesitate to free this land from its burden. Until then, you must endure the dragon's curse as best you can. Farewell!"

Thus speaking, Malvise wheeled his horse around and began riding through his ranks as they opened up before him. Once he was in their lead, the army departed, raising a great cloud of dust. The people of Nogardia stood there in a stunned silence. The only sound was the hoofbeats of many horses. Then they were all gone, and slowly the dust began to settle again.

The people looked at one another for the first time and suddenly broke out into a universal cheer. Hats were thrown into the air, many of the younger boys did cartwheels, and several of the women spontaneously grabbed one another by the elbow and began twirling around. The rumor circulated that they had just witnessed a miracle. Many voices were unanimous that their good fortune was due to Star. His very presence had averted disaster and brought peace. Star's praises were on everyone's lips.

Several voices announced it was finally time to celebrate the autumn procession. This year's Harvest Festival would be greater than ever before.

Straw took all of this in with great pleasure. He celebrated with Colin and Alis as heartily as the others. Star had told him that everything would turn out all right. How could he have known?

When the people began to make their way back to town and into the compound to go about their usual work, Straw headed for the barn. He found Star sitting serenely on his bedding.

"From the sound of things, we can get back to normal again," the dragon said calmly. "We'll continue our sparring tomorrow.

"Star, how could you have known?"

"I take it that you took my advice and had a chat with Malvise."

"I did as you recommended," Straw said simply. Star studied him for a moment, sniffed at him, and then sneezed. It came so suddenly that it made the dragon boy laugh.

"You don't look like it was very hard to persuade him," Star commented dryly. "Any bruises?"

"A couple, but nothing serious. You've given me far worse. I look forward to getting back to our practicing, you know." He stood a moment pondering what had happened. "Star, I didn't think that it would be that easy. After all, he defeated our best knights."

"That's simple to explain," Star said. "They weren't trained by a dragon."

Chapter Nineteen

The Witnesses

Straw hastily glanced down to check his leg. He knew he had only a moment to look and he hoped it would not be bad. His pants were torn, his leg bloodied, but he had seen worse. It would continue to hold him up, and he put all further thought of it out of his mind. His left arm was also badly scraped and bleeding, but he knew these were all surface injuries. It would take a broken bone to slow him down.

He steadied his breathing, knees slightly bent, ready to spring. His every sense was alert. He watched the great dragon before him as it paused in its attack and glared at him. The emerald eyes glowed with a vicious light. The horns along its head and running down its back were standing straight up in the air vibrating menacingly. Its immense mouth hung slightly open, revealing row upon row of razor-sharp teeth. It then lifted its long snout up to the clouds and bellowed. The roar was deafening.

It was the moment Straw had waited for. As the dragon roared, he leapt forward, sword raised. He fearlessly slipped under the dragon's head and came within reach of its neck. Holding his sword with both hands, he jammed it into the scales of the softer under-body. The roar was cut off mid-way with a snarl and the dragon threw itself on top of its attacker. Straw had anticipated this move and had already dived under its leg and rolled free. The dragon crashed down onto the bare ground but crushed nothing but the stones beneath it. Straw took advantage of the moment to once again jam his sword into the dragon, this time targeting the area underneath its leg which was lined with only a single layer of thinner, softer scales. He knew all of the dragon's weaknesses. Then he again leapt free.

The dragon roared its rage and whirled around to face its assailant, froth flying from its mouth in all directions. "You annoying, stinging fly," the dragon bellowed, thrusting its snout towards its attacker. "You can't escape me."

Straw did not bother to respond. He had reached into a small pouch that hung at his waist and pulled out a handful of fine sand. As the dragon's snout came menacingly closer, he threw it straight and hard in the dragon's nose. The reaction was immediate as the dragon's eyes shut for an instant and it sneezed hard.

The moment Straw had thrown the sand, he leapt forward swinging his sword with both hands and slapped it hard against the dragon's soft snout. Mid-sneeze, the dragon flinched backwards and reared up in pain.

Straw expected this reaction and dashed in again underneath the dragon's raised neck. As before, he jammed his sword into the dragon's thinner under-scales. The beast above him roared repeatedly and crashed to the ground, still hoping to crush its attacker. Yet again, Straw leapt underneath the dragon's leg and rolled out of harm's way.

This time, the dragon did not whirl around to face the swordsman. It kept its flank to him, curling its tail around on one side and its head on the other to enclose him in a large arc. Then it began to slowly edge sideways towards him. There was no escape to the right or left, and it forced him backwards.

Straw realized that the dragon was trying to drive him to the river which flowed serenely twenty yards behind him. Once the dragon had him on the sloping bank with nowhere to retreat, it would have a great advantage. He could not afford to let that happen. He knew that attacking the dragon's flank was useless. The scales there were too thick for him to inflict any pain or damage. He knew if he ran towards the head, the dragon would have a good chance to pick him off before he could dodge out of the way. He considered for a moment diving into the river, but he knew that dragons are as much at home in water as they are on land or in the air. He would never escape the dragon there. That left only one thing to do.

Straw jammed his sword into his belt and began running towards the dragon's immense tail. It was thrashing the ground and he timed his jump as the tail was moving towards him. As he landed on it, he grabbed hold of one of the protruding horns. It gave him just enough stability that he regained his balance and was immediately on the move.

Straw scrambled right up the dragon's back. He knew every handhold along the way, even though this dragon was bucking and twisting, trying to throw him off. Straw was too nimble to lose his balance, and he made quick progress along the raised horns, finding secure footholds among the scales.

When he reached the neck, he took his sword again in hand. The dragon was shaking its head and bellowing madly. It took every ounce of strength and balance for Straw to hold on and make his way along the dragon's snout. Several times he slipped to his knees, but was able each time to regain his footing. His single focus was to reach the nose, the dragon's softest part. He was totally alert, knowing that right below his feet was the dragon's mouth, and in the mouth were the dragon's immensely sharp teeth. He knew one snap of those jaws would break him in half. He had to hold tight.

The dragon paused a moment in its shaking and thrashing. Straw saw it close its eyes. He was certain the dragon was about to sneeze again. He realized this was his one chance to advance towards the nose. He let go of his handhold and dashed forward. This was the moment the dragon had been waiting for. There was no sneeze coming, and the dragon's eyes had not closed all the way. It was a trap laid by a clever dragon to finally defeat its assailant. With a quick toss of its head, Straw was thrown up into the air, his arms flailing, his legs askew. Then the dragon's snout batted against Straw's body as it flew mid-air, knocking him harshly down to the ground. Straw lay there unmoving in a crumpled tangle of limbs. With a fluid movement, the dragon stooped its head down and picked up the young man's body in its immense jaws.

Although this desperate battle transpired far from any habitation, out among rolling hills beside a broad river, it did not go unobserved. When it had begun, all the birds that lived, fed, watered and raised their young along that stretch of river had fled. The fox, deer, rabbit and squirrels that looked to the river for drink had also run off at the first blows. Still, two pairs of eyes watched this uneven battle.

Two young men crouched among the reeds and bushes on the opposite side of the river. They did everything they could to avoid detection, and they were successful, for neither Straw nor the dragon was aware of them. The young men kept themselves under cover out of sheer terror. They were convinced that if the dragon caught sight of them, they would be next. They never thought for a moment of offering Straw any help. How could they? They were unarmed and lacked any of the skills of agility, strength and courage which they saw in Straw, making it possible for him to resist the dragon for even a moment.

As it was, the first time the dragon bellowed, one of the young men was so shocked that he wet himself. So great was his terror, he was not even aware of it until later. They both lay there petrified, their eyes wide with horror, as they watched Straw in a battle he could not win.

They gasped when the dragon beat Straw down to the ground and moaned quietly when it caught him up in its jaws. The dragon was shaking the limp form in its mouth when one of them began urgently pushing the other one.

"We gotta go," he whispered hoarsely. "We gotta get out of here. Now, now, he's looking the other way. Go!"

The other youth was frozen to the spot. The speaker gave up on him and began to crawl away alone. His leaving gave his companion enough presence of mind to drag himself away as well. It was less terrifying to move than remain behind alone. They crawled from reeds to bushes to trees to bushes, repeatedly glancing back to see if they had been detected. They had no need for concern. The dragon was thoroughly occupied worrying its opponent to death. Or so it looked to the two who were fleeing.

After an agonizingly slow flight, they finally came to a place where they could put a low, rounded hill between them and the scene of horror behind them. They finally rose on shaky legs and began to stagger off down a well-trodden path. They were both weeping openly, their faces streaked with tears.

"We have to get back," one of them said between gasps. "We have to warn the others. We must tell them!" he paused to steady his breath.

"He's dead, Flek, he's dead," the other moaned. "Star ate him."

"I know, I know," Flek cried. "I don't understand. It's too early. We've got to get back. Warn the others. Before he attacks the compound. Star's gone wild."

"You said we'd catch them napping," the other wailed. "You said they'd just be lying in the grass."

"The whole town," Flek murmured. "He'll eat everyone in Nogardia. He'll destroy everything. My family. We've got to run. Got to run." And with these words, the two of them began to run erratically down the path.

Back at the scene of the battle, the dragon had come to rest. He had searched around until he found a small indentation in the ground. Into this dimple in the earth, he threw the defeated youth. Then he lay down on top of him, leaving only Straw's head and one arm exposed. He leaned heavily against the frail form beneath him and heard with satisfaction the air pressed out of his lungs. Then he lightened up his weight, not wanting to crush him all at once. Beneath him, Straw lay unconscious. Star looked up to the clouds and bellowed a roar of victory.

The shadows were beginning to grow long when Straw emerged from his troubled dreams to awaken crushed beneath the dragon. He coughed weakly and his body felt numb. Only one arm lay free from the paralyzing weight of the dragon. He raised it weakly and found that he still held tightly the pommel of the sword.

At least that, he thought to himself. *If I'm to be defeated by a dragon, at least I never lost my sword.* Small consolation.

He tossed the sword limply to the side and weakly lifted his hand. He reached up and touched the scales. He ran his hand over them and marveled at their smoothness, their perfection. It completely distracted him from the extremity of his position, and through half closed eyes he admired the rainbow sheen in them. He was jolted out of this reverie when the dragon above him pressed down harder and the little air in his lungs was forced out. *I must hurry,* he thought. He felt no panic, only an immediate need to keep searching.

The dragon left him enough space for very shallow breaths. The pressure on his ribs was intense, and he feared that if the dragon leaned any heavier, they would crack. Now with some urgency, he felt along the scales, searching their edges, confident that he would find what he sought. It did not take long before his fingers discovered the opening. He watched his hand disappear and felt a thrill penetrate the numbness that held his body. He pushed through the soft tissue, feeling its heat press upon his hand. He extended his arm as far as he could until he came against the pulsating membrane that separated him from the dragon's heart. He opened up his hand and placed his palm against it. He held it there a moment and felt how with every beat his hand was pushed away and once again pulled forward. He was filled with deep satisfaction and peace. Tears filled his eyes and rolled towards his ears.

"We be of one heart," his voice was hardly more than a hoarse whisper. "We be of one heart, thou and I, we be of one heart."

The great beast above him stirred. The weight on his chest lightened. "And we be of one mind, thou and I," a voice like chimes spoke. "One heart and one mind, we be one together. We are one."

Then the full weight was suddenly lifted, and Straw felt at first as if he were rising as well. And then he felt the pain. Through his blinking tears he saw Star lower his great snout and felt the dragon's breath upon his body.

"Is that you, boy? My, what a wild dream I've had."

It was like this every time. Nowadays, whenever he fought with Star, the battle would build to the point where the dragon forgot himself. Star had always warned him, but every time it took him by surprise. He knew that if he did not use the secret Star had taught him, he would lie beneath the dragon until all life was pressed out of him.

"I hope I haven't hurt you," Star said sounding concerned. He was nosing up and down Straw's body, prodding and poking.

"Nothing broken, I think," Straw said. "Although I'm glad to get you off my ribs. I've never felt you so heavy before." He was sitting up and stretching his limbs, testing wrists and ankles, knees, hips and shoulders. "That was quite an adventure we had," Straw chuckled. "You got really carried away with yourself."

"Well, what do you expect when you hit me on the nose like that? It's a good thing we still use wooden swords. If you had actually penetrated my scales…well, you have seen only a fraction of my fury."

"I've got to go wash this blood off," Straw said. "Would you give me a ride down to the river?"

"Hop on," Star said. Straw climbed up onto Star's nose and the dragon walked over to a place where the bank was gradual.

"You've become very good," Star commented as Straw washed his wounds. None was very serious. He was more worried about the tear in his clothing. Nowadays he kept a tunic and pants at the river for sparring so he could return to the compound with clothing that was not torn and dirtied.

"Well, not quite good enough, I'm afraid."

"If you're waiting for the day you can defeat me," Star said, "you're waiting in vain, you know."

"But I did give you some mighty whacks, you must admit."

"That was a good trick with the sand," Star commented. "You took me by surprise. But I warn you, it won't work again. I never forget a good move in battle and it will go differently next time."

"I thought you'd appreciate it," Straw said. "I got the idea at supper a couple of days ago when Mixer got some pepper up his nose and couldn't stop sneezing. I figured it would distract you enough to get past your guard."

"That it did. And as I said, if your sword had been sharp, the outcome of our sparring would have been quite different."

"How different?"

But Star did not answer. He was standing with his head raised, his nose catching the breeze.

"What is it Star? What do you smell?"

Star shook his head and snorted. "We haven't been alone," he said gravely. "It is very faint, but unmistakable. There were others here."

"Do you mean recently? Or was it just some traveler passing by, maybe having spent the night near to here?"

"I sense the distinct smell of stall boys," Star said. "We'd best get back as soon as we can."

When Straw was content that his wounds were already scabbing over, he changed into his clean set of clothes. He gathered together his pails and brushes and set himself onto Star's head.

"All right," he said. "Let's head home. Maybe you were mistaken. No one has ever come out here before, you know. Why now, after all these years?"

"Perhaps to let us know that our time is up," Star said solemnly. The dragon walked briskly, and the two were uncommonly quiet the whole way back.

When they arrived at the back gates to the compound, the gates through which the dragon boy had led Star in and out for countless days over the past years, they came upon a scene neither of them had ever been met with before.

There, before the gates, stood two lines of mounted knights fanned out, fully armed, lances lowered, ready to attack. When the dragon appeared, they had to rein in their nervous horses tightly to keep them in place. Behind the knights were massed the foot soldiers, twenty-five ranks deep, each one with a long lance from which a small pennant fluttered in the breeze. The knights and the soldiers stood there uncommonly quiet, as if waiting for Star to make the first move.

"I think you'd best do all the talking," Star commented softly.

"Hey," Straw called out from the dragon's head. "Hey, what's all the commotion?"

All eyes had been so focused on the dragon that no one had yet noticed Straw up on his head. He saw looks of astonishment when they located him up there.

"He's alive!" he heard one voice call out. Straw looked to see who had spoken. To one side, he found Flek standing beside Garth. Flek looked pale and his mouth hung open. He looked like he was seeing a ghost. "Not possible. I saw Star eat you. How are you alive? What sort of witchcraft is this?"

Straw was not sure what to say. He realized that the scent Star had detected was fateful. How could he pretend nothing had happened?

Garth stepped forward and placed himself between the line of knights and the dragon. He held up his hand, and spoke in a stern voice. "Stay your mounts until I've spoken with the dragon boy!"

Garth walked up to Star, looking at the dragon boy perched on his head. “Star, let the boy down,” he commanded.

Star lowered his head obediently. Straw slipped down to stand beside the Dragon Master. Garth said nothing, but took Straw’s arms and pulled up the sleeves. He looked at the fresh scrapes along his arms and hands.

“Lift up your pant legs,” he said tersely. Straw complied and revealed the bruising and scraping there as well.

“Is Star calm enough to put into the barn?” he asked.

“Star?” Straw asked. “Star is as tame as——”

“Silence!” Garth commanded. “I asked you only if he is calm enough to put in the barn. Yes or no.”

“Yes, Dragon Master,” Straw said meekly.

“Then put him away and we will follow after.”

Chapter Twenty

Exile

"You've betrayed my trust in you." The Dragon Master was frowning, his beard bristling. They stood beside the barn at the outskirts of the great open space where Straw had long ago first shown his command over the dragon. The mounted knights were now standing guard in this space, as a precaution against Star springing out at them. The ranks of foot soldiers stood at the ready behind the line of knights, tense and uncertain. Garth had led Straw away from this spectacle. They were surrounded by a crowd of workers from the compound.

Straw was miserable. He hung his head and although he wanted to speak, no words came to help him.

"But even worse," the Dragon Master continued, his voice edged with anger, "even worse, you have endangered the dragon's stay in our realm. You've encouraged him to grow wild and fight. And all for what?"

Straw desperately wanted to say that it had begun as Star's idea. He knew there was no way he could prove that. Everyone, including the Dragon Master would accuse him of inventing the story that the dragon could speak just to save himself. He had no choice but to accept full responsibility. He desperately wanted to explain that Star was unchanged, that Star had not grown wilder, but was actually more content. He wanted them to know that Star was enjoying their exercises.

"I just want you to know—" His voice was shaky.

"Silence!" the Dragon Master interrupted him immediately. "I do not care to hear any of your excuses. We all know that you have a special connection to the dragon. That is why you were given a unique responsibility. It's my own fault for thinking you could handle it alone. I should have sent someone with you. I've been warned before," and his eyes sought out Flek in the crowd. "Yet I did not listen. That was my mistake."

Straw stole a look around at the large semicircle of workers. So many familiar faces. He had known most of them for years. They had grown up together. He found Flek among the crowd. His malicious grin betrayed how much he was enjoying this. *If the dragon did not eat me*, Straw thought, *at least Flek can finally see me disgraced.* All of Flek's hatred for this commoner who had stolen into the compound to grab the highest honors was now coming down upon Straw with a vengeance. Straw wondered for the first time how many others might be feeling the same satisfaction as Flek.

"We can only hope that the damage is not too great. Star will need some very special treatment for awhile. I will oversee it myself," the Dragon Master said gravely.

Straw glanced over towards the barn. Star lay serenely in the middle as if nothing were out of the ordinary. He barely looked in their direction. He totally ignored the line of knights and ranks of soldiers that guarded him. It was as if nothing of importance had happened. Then he yawned, as if out of contentment or boredom. He had, after all, repeatedly warned the dragon boy that if what they were doing ever came out, he would be on his own to defend their activity.

"Garth, I assure you—"

"Silence!" the Dragon Master bellowed, cutting him off for the second time. "Your actions have spoken loudly enough. You are henceforth banished from the compound. You will leave in disgrace and never return. Your name will be erased from the records. Memory of your stay here will be obliterated. You will be forgotten, as if you had never lived. This is a black mark on our efforts here. When the king hears of it, he will be furious. And rightfully so."

Straw sensed the immensity of what he had done. He was beginning to understand that he must humbly accept whatever was dealt out to him. "I'll go," he said in a subdued voice. "I'll fetch my belongings."

"You will not step foot inside any of the buildings again," the Dragon Master said with a frown. "You will leave by a back gate and wait there until your things are brought to you. And precious little will you be allowed to take. The clothes on your back were given to you for working here. You may not leave here with anything bearing the crest of this compound. No one may know that you once lived here. That's as much for your own protection."

Straw looked puzzled.

"Once word gets out that you awoke the dragon's instincts to fight, people will be scared. They will become angry, mighty angry, unless I'm mistaken. There will be those who will make an attempt on your life."

Straw heaved a sigh. Had it all been worth it? Star wanted to teach him to become a warrior, and now he was forced to leave in disgrace. What good did all that training lead to? They were even taking the clothes off his back. "Can I at least go and say goodbye to Star?"

"Absolutely not!" was Garth's stern answer. "You've done enough damage already."

This stung, but what could he say? He glanced longingly in the direction of the barn, hoping to catch the dragon's eye. Star, though, was not in the least bit interested in looking in his direction. In fact, knowing Star so well, Straw realized that the dragon's full attention was focused on something or someone in the barn with him. This was odd, since Star aloofly ignored all the workers who tended him. He and Garth and Mali and even Keg were out here, the only people the dragon regularly showed interest in. He had the impression that this was not someone from the compound. Was it the commander of the knights? In the gloom of the barn he could make out only a long cloak topped by something white. A cloak ringed with white fur? The king, perhaps? Had King Pell already heard about this and come to see for himself that the dragon was safe?

He was not given any time to ponder further. He was being hustled towards the back of the compound. The crowd walked with him, ominously silent. The Dragon Master, accompanied by Keg, had walked off, his eyes aflame. Straw was now flanked by two of the gate guards, neither of whom he knew by name. He did not dare look for faces in the crowd. He was afraid he would know most of them and have to see their disappointment. He did not want to see Frog or Colin and not be able to explain that everything was really all right.

As they neared a single door built into the stone wall, something hard suddenly hit him in the side of his head. The blow was stinging and numbing all in one. He put his hand to his ear and instinctively ducked down.

"Stone him!" a harsh voice yelled from the crowd.

"He doesn't deserve to walk free," another voice cried and a second stone glanced off his shoulder. Straw felt the moisture on his ear and then saw his hand smeared with blood. He quickly searched his options, and there was only one. There was nowhere he could run, and there were too many of them to fight barehanded. He had grown taller since the day he had been locked outside the compound wall. He was sure that if he took a running leap, he would be able to scale the wall before being knocked senseless by a barrage of stones. He was still crouched down and about to bolt when a firm hand held him by the shoulder. He looked up to Mali's face. Mali's eyes were fierce, but they were looking at the crowd, not at him.

"You'll not stone him until you've stoned me first," he challenged the crowd. He placed himself between the group and Straw.

"He deserves to die for what he's done," cried one voice. Straw realized that it was Flek's.

"He's done wrong and is being justly punished. Garth has not asked for more. He will go as he came, with the clothes on his back."

"Get out of the way, Mali. We don't need to hurt you, too."

"You'll have to do worse than hurt me to get to him, Flek." He paused to let his words sink in. Then he continued with an even voice, showing no fear. "You're going to let him go without injury."

"And who's going to stop us?"

"I don't stand here alone," Mali bluffed.

"You look pretty alone to me," someone challenged with derision. It was true that the guards had stepped away and it was uncertain whether they would be protectors or join the assault if the whole crowd turned ugly.

That was when Colin stepped out to stand beside Mali. "He's not alone," he said quietly. Frog and Mixer stepped out with him. Mixer looked frightened, and Frog had tears in his eyes, but they stood their ground.

"So you want to go down with him?" someone sneered.

"There are more of us than you think," spoke another voice. It was Alis. She walked over to stand next to Frog, her face serious, resolute and calm.

When some of the men saw a woman step out, it was too much for them to pretend to stay out of it. Five others joined the group that was growing around Straw.

For a moment there was a tense silence. Mali was not going to give the crowd time to make up its mind. Leaving the others to block the way, he pulled Straw away and led him by the arm to the door in the wall. "Garth said you're to wait on the other side," he said tersely. "We'll make sure that no one follows to harm you. When your things have been brought, you're to leave. Best go to another town, far away from here. You're a hard worker, honest and trustworthy. You'll have no trouble finding a position."

By this time, he had drawn the iron bolt in the heavy wooden door and opened it. He began to push Straw through.

"Mali, I want you to know—"

"You don't owe me any explanations," Mali interrupted. "From first to last I've believed in you. Your friends feel the same. We could all tell the dragon was happy. But, whatever your reasons, what you did is forbidden. Now we've just got to deal with what we've got. Go, before they decide to stone us all."

Mali pushed him through the gateway. The last thing he heard as he passed through was Flek's sneering voice. "Back to the muck bins you came from, Dung Boy."

The gate closed at his back with a dull thunk. He heard the groaning of metal on metal as the bolt was drawn on the other side to bar the door. He turned and stared at the wooden planks out of which the door was constructed. A memory came flooding back. This was how it had all begun. Staring at the designs in the wood of the gate. Now he was outside again, facing a locked door. The gate blurred as tears filled his eyes.

What next? Where should he go? Should he just move on or wait until his few things were brought and tossed at him? He was so deeply embarrassed, he did not dare wait. There was nothing important in what he had left behind anyway. All that counted to him was his relationship with Star.

Star! Panic seized his heart that he might never see Star again. The tears now flowed freely down his face. He had to get out of there. It was too painful to sit around and wait.

He turned around to get his bearings. He looked out over open farmland. A flock of starlings fed restlessly on the leftovers from a harvested field. He heard the raspy cawing of crows from off around a bend in the wall. Nearby, a scarecrow left in the empty field mocked him.

A sudden snorting startled him. He quickly stepped around the bend in the wall to his left and saw to his amazement two horses tethered to a ring in the stonework. One was a large bay, well-formed in its limbs, standing calmly, nibbling at the grass that grew in the shade the wall provided, its tail flicking rhythmically. It was saddled and looked like it had seen hard traveling. Having spent so long tending to the dragon, Straw had developed a critical eye. The horse was quite handsome, but deserved a good grooming. Its withers and flanks were splattered and matted with more than one coat of dry mud. Obviously it had been some time since this horse had been pampered in the stables.

As impressive as the bay was, the second horse attracted his attention even more. It was a mare, young and not yet full grown, which he guessed by her size. Her coat was white, dappled with black and gray spots. She had a black blaze on her forehead in the most peculiar shape he had ever seen. It reminded him of something, but he was too distracted by his present situation to give it much thought. She did not show as many signs of the road as the bay, although she did look like she had traveled some distance to get there. She was no local horse.

The mare was restless and snorted again. She shook her head several times to dislodge the pesky flies. She pawed the ground hard with her foreleg and then shook her head once more. Straw had been around Star long enough to read her language. He did not need words to know that something was bothering her. Without thinking, he walked towards her, extending a hand to calm her. The mare shied and took a step backwards as he approached, pulling her line taut.

"Easy, girl," he spoke softly, as she raised up slightly on her back legs and came down hard on the ground, stomping with her forelegs.

"Easy, girl," he repeated, still moving steadily towards her. "Not so stormy." After working with a dragon, there was very little a horse could do to intimidate him. He took hold of her line and began to steady her. "It's all right, stormy girl. I'm not going to hurt you. I'm a friend."

The mare eyed him with caution, but his words were soothing and she had known kindness before and was willing to trust. She let him come closer. Before long he had his hand on her neck, soothing her and whispering quietly into her ear. Again she stomped with her right foreleg.

"I know, stormy girl," he explained patiently to her. "You've got something in that hoof. Let me have a look."

He worked his hands slowly down her neck. He slipped under her head and began caressing her right side. He slid his hands along her flank, and then moved them down her leg. She relaxed, sensing that his hands were knowing and kind. She steadied herself and let him lift her hoof. There it was. In the hollow below the fetlock sat a fat, nasty burr. It had worked itself up so deeply into the hair that it was pushing into the flesh. His fingers were callused enough from all the scrubbing on Star, not to mention his sword exercises, so the prickles could not penetrate into his skin. While he worked at loosening the burr, the mare reached around and pulled at his tunic with her teeth. At first he thought she was trying to bite him, but quickly he realized that she was encouraging him.

"That's right, stormy girl," he cooed as he worked. "It's coming out. You'll be fine in a moment."

The bay whinnied, but Straw was too busy to think whether it had any meaning. He had freed the burr and was about to flick it away. He realized too late that he had ignored a warning.

"Well, I see that you've already made friends," a gruff voice spoke from just a few feet away.

Straw was so startled that he dropped the hoof abruptly and the mare reared up with a cry. It was all he could do to calm her again. He flung both arms around her neck and spoke urgently into her ear. "Sorry, Stormy, it's all right. Settle down. Down, girl. It was my fault. It's all right, Stormy girl."

"And he's already given her a name," the gruff voice continued.

As soon as the mare had calmed down again, the boy could look at the man who had come upon him so suddenly. He was not alone, and, to his surprise, the other man was Garth, the Dragon Master. Where had they come from? Of course, as soon as he recovered from his surprise, he remembered that the wall had several well-barred gates at regular intervals. They must have come out from a gate further down the wall.

"So this is the young man you've been telling me about. The one who can talk to the dragon," the man said with a smile. "Of course, we all talk to the dragon, but this is the young man the dragon listens to."

He was an old man, by his looks, dressed in a long, dark, earth-colored robe. His beard and hair were long as well and nearly snow white. The boy suddenly realized that this was the figure he had seen in the gloom of the barn right before he was driven out the gate. It was not a fur collar around his robe he had seen, but flowing white hair and beard. *What an odd man*, he thought. Something about him stirred a memory. The man had the appearance of age, yet he stood straight and half a head taller than Garth. His eyes twinkled with such brilliance that it was hard to return his gaze. Unless Straw was vastly mistaken, there was strength and vigor hidden beneath that robe.

"Aye," answered Garth. The anger was gone from his eyes. He looked now only sad. "This is the boy who can talk to the dragon. He's been with us since he was hardly as tall as a broom handle."

The old man stood there considering something, lost in thought.

"Do I know you?" Straw asked. "You look so familiar, but I don't know why."

The old man looked up sharply at his question. "You've a good memory. The last time I saw you, you placed a mud pie in my hands. In your garden."

"In Galifalia's garden," the boy said, remembering the garden more than he remembered this old man. "You knew Galifalia."

"You were still quite young, boy." They were silent, both lost in their own memories. The old man was the first to shake himself out of his reverie.

"Let's get down to the business at hand. Garth, you've told me that this boy has trespassed upon the laws of keeping the dragon."

"That's right. He can't stay, much as I'd like to allow it. He has a fine understanding with the dragon. Far better than anyone, even myself."

"Well, that's to be expected, considering who he is."

"Wait," Straw interjected. "What do you mean, considering who I am? Who do you think I am?"

The old man ignored his question and continued. "And you're certain there's no way he can continue working with Star?"

Garth shook his head slowly. "He was discovered aggravating the dragon. They were fighting, the boy here had a sword. There's no way to cover that up. I can't lock down the compound. As we speak, it's probably being spread all over the town."

"You mean I could go back if no one knew about it?" Straw asked. Again he was ignored.

"Well, can't be helped," the old man said. "It was part of his training, after all. It's a pity that it had to end before he was fully grown."

"You mean you know what I was doing?" Straw asked excitedly. "Then you can vouch that I did Star no harm." Again, they acted as if he had not spoken.

"At least we can give him something to get him started on his journey."

"It's quite a mystery, Aga, that you would show up, of all days, today," Garth mused.

"It's my business to be at the right place when I am needed. And I fail doing that all too often. Considering that he leaves before the dragon, I'd say I arrived too late."

"Would one of you please tell me what's going on?" Straw asked, exasperated. Both men now turned their attention on him.

"First of all," Garth started, "I want you to know that I'd keep you here if I could. I believe you've done the dragon no harm. But I can't change the rules of the compound. You were given special privileges, and what you've done no one would understand. As it was, it took a lot of effort to keep your exercises a secret."

"You knew about them?" Straw asked incredulously.

"Now, boy," Garth said, standing to his full height and placing his hands on his hips. "You don't think that I sent you to the river alone, every day for the past five years, with the precious dragon just so you could have a picnic, now do you? Did it never seem strange to you that until you began taking him, I had always sent a crew of five to work on Star?"

"Well," Straw stammered. "I did wonder, but I was just too happy to question it much."

"Or that I'm so mean-spirited that I would force you daily, for years, to scrub a whole blessed dragon all alone?" Garth continued. "Of course I knew what you were up to!"

Straw was confused to hear that Garth shared his secret. He needed to know something, and finally found the right question. "Well, if you know about it, why can't I stay?"

Garth heaved a sigh. "Because others know now as well. And if you stay, they'll cause trouble. Probably already causing trouble."

"You mean Flek," the boy said bitterly.

"Doesn't matter who I mean. And it's bigger than Flek. It's about the people having confidence that we're caring for the dragon to assure that he never goes wild. When you taught the dragon to fight, you challenged that relationship. You simply can't stay longer."

"I didn't teach him to fight," Straw protested. "He was teaching me."

"But can't you see that no one will ever believe that. Star's not likely to make an announcement."

Straw knew that Garth was right. Star had warned him of this many times already.

"But where am I to go?" he asked, full of desperation.

"Away from here, first of all," the old man called Aga said solemnly.

"But I have nothing but the clothes I wear," Straw protested.

"Wandering knights rarely have much more," Aga said pointedly.

"What?" He wasn't sure that he had heard right. "Wandering knight?" A glimmer of hope flared up in his heart.

"That's what Star was training you to be, wasn't it? Why match yourself up against a beast as big as a mountain unless you were training? Wasn't that the agreement you made with him?"

"I guess so," Straw said slowly. "I mean, when we first started, that's what we agreed to do. I stopped thinking about it a long time ago. We just did it because we both enjoyed it."

"Well, you are one of those rare young men who has been apprenticed to a dragon," the old man said crisply. "And your apprenticeship has come to an abrupt end. But that's just the way it is with dragons. Expect the unexpected. It's time for you to do what you've been trained for."

"But I still don't understand. I've got nothing to my name, not even a change of clothing."

"Well, then, let's do something about that," Garth said with a slight smile.

Aga looked up and his gaze fell on the horses.

"You know, I've got two horses. Silly of an old man to own two horses. Lucky if I can stay in the saddle of one of them. Which one do you want?"

Straw's mouth fell open.

"Close it, close it," Garth laughed. "Flies, you know. They've got no manners. Go on, boy, choose a horse before he changes his mind."

Straw looked from one man to the other to see if they were mocking him. They gazed at him steadily, waiting for his reply. "Uh, uh, the white one, I guess. No, yes, I want the white horse, if I may, I mean." He was so confused, he could barely find the right words.

Aga looked displeased. "She's a fine horse, and I'm sorry to let her go. She needs some training still, since she's yet young. She hasn't finished growing. But then the same goes for you. And seeing you've already given her a name, I guess I can't go back on my offer."

"I gave her a name?" he said bewildered.

"I heard you myself call her Storm. It's a fitting name, considering who she's bred from. Well, good choice, young squire," Aga said with a broad smile. "She's a mare, as you've no doubt already noticed. She comes from a long line of war horses. She'll be a steady mount in travel and in battle. She's not bred for speed as much as for endurance, agility and cleverness. Aye, mighty clever that one. Pay attention and she'll teach you a thing or two. But then, you're good at taking lessons from dumb beasts." The old man looked at the boy intensely, as if he dared him to share that the dragon could speak.

Straw could only stand there and stare. Were they really just giving him a horse?

"Now that we've got your transportation arranged," Aga continued, as if there were nothing out of the ordinary happening, "it's time to get you properly dressed."

"Aye," muttered Garth. "I hope it fits."

"I'm sure he'll grow into it," Aga commented without concern. The two men turned to a pile of things lying on the ground next to the wall. With all of the excitement since leaving the compound, Straw had not even noticed the tumbled mass of clothing, armor and weapons lying there. Garth was already rummaging through it, pulling out an item and tossing it to the boy.

"Try that on," he said curtly. "Then that."

Straw stood there staring at the leather clothing he'd been tossed. There were so many straps and laces it confused him. Garth looked up and noticed his hesitation.

"Oh, of course. No way you'd know how to put all that on. That's one thing the dragon couldn't coach you on."

So saying he stepped over to the boy and had him pile his clothes on the ground. One stray piece of material caught Aga's attention.

"Let me see that," he said. It was an old and faded piece of cloth. It had once been dark blue and was embroidered with equally faded golden stars. He turned it over and over in his hands. Then he looked up and peered at the boy.

"This was from her, wasn't it?" he inquired.

Straw nicked his head.

"You've kept it all these years," Aga mused.

"It's all I have of her," Straw murmured.

Aga stretched out his hand and gave it back to him.

"Then guard it well, as you have until now." And then he said something puzzling. "You never know when you may find another piece to match it." Then he looked up at Garth. "Go on, get him dressed."

As Straw put on the new clothes, Garth laced them up. Aga stood watching, and yet not watching. He was lost in some far away memory.

Before long, Garth stood back to admire his work. Straw stood there, dressed all in leather, and Garth nodded his approval.

"These are your traveling clothes, particularly if you're uncertain about your reception. It won't stop a sword blow or an arrow, but it'll give you much more protection than your regular linen tunic."

"Feels big," Straw commented.

"That's all right. You're not finished growing. You can still swing your arms, can't you?"

Straw tested out rotating and raising and lowering his arms. He could get used to it. In the meantime, Garth was at the pile again, picking up chain mail and armored plates.

"All right, get the leathers off. We'll put this right over your tunic. Now pay attention so you can do all this on your own later. You've got simplified armoring that won't require a page to truss you up."

This took longer, and once Straw was dressed, Garth had him take it all off again and redress himself a second time. When he was finished, Garth stood back and turned to the old man.

"What do you think, Aga? Not so bad as it could be, I'd say."

"He'll do." Then he laughed. "He has no choice. He'll make do if all this is not to come to naught."

Straw walked around, feeling clumsy and out of touch covered by so much armor. "I prefer the leathers," he commented dryly. "I'm used to fighting in just my tunic, you know."

"That's when you're dueling with a dragon that would never really harm you," Aga explained. "When you're facing men with swords, you'll be grateful for the steel skin. Garth, it's getting late. Give him the rest."

Straw did not know what else was missing until he saw Garth reach for the shield and the sword that lay propped against the wall. Of course! Shield and sword, a knight's greatest treasures.

First Garth buckled the sword around Straw's waist. "Go ahead," he encouraged the boy. "Pull it out and get a feel for its weight. I think you'll be pleased with its balance."

The sword came singing out of its sheath. It felt light and powerful in his hand. He swung it and cut the air with a tearing sound.

"It's sharp, so have a care."

The pommel fit his hand as if he had molded it himself.

"The king's own armorer forged it," Garth commented.

"Whose is it?" he asked, staring at the intricate engraving of a dragon etched into the blade close to the pommel.

"It's yours, boy," Garth answered.

"I mean, who was it made for?" he persisted.

Aga stepped in. "It was made for you, boy. No one else."

"But how?" he asked perplexed. "How could anyone know?"

"I guess I owe you some explanation," Garth began. "Soon after you came to the compound, Aga passed through. In his usual manner, he kept things mysterious, but he did make clear that I should keep a special eye on you. He indicated that a time would come when you would show a remarkable relationship to the dragon. He instructed me to support you in whatever way I could."

"I came from time to time to check up on you," Aga added.

"So that was you," Straw interrupted excitedly. "I knew I'd seen someone in the barn with the dragon. More than once. But Star always avoided answering my questions."

Straw suddenly realized what he had just said and clapped his hands over his mouth, wishing he could pull the words he had spoken back in.

"So, there it is," Garth said dryly. "Aga, you told me that he could talk with the dragon, but I never wanted to believe you. Guess I was just too jealous to want it to be true."

"It's not personal, Garth," Straw blurted out. "Star is very fond of you and wishes you could understand him. It's not his choice who he can talk to. I don't know why I can."

"That's a whole mystery in itself," Aga interjected. "We'll not be figuring it out this afternoon."

"Who are you?" Straw stared at Aga with wonder.

"For now, let it suffice to say that Star and I have known each other for a long time. There was no reason to confuse you or distract you from your training. I was always content with the progress of things, so I kept myself hidden from you, and from what you say, Star was willing to go along with it."

"All these things were made for you, knowing this day would come," Garth added.

"Only we hoped it wouldn't come quite so soon," Aga pointed out, raising his eyebrows as if disapproving.

"Can't be helped," said Garth. "I'm surprised we kept it quiet this long."

"Give him the shield and let it be done," Aga said dryly.

Garth went one last time to the wall and picked up the shield that was facing away from him. When he turned, the boy saw the shield's emblem, and he took a sharp breath. It was a red dragon rampant on a field of white.

"Stormy's blaze!" he suddenly blurted out. That's what had been so familiar about the blaze on the white mare's forehead. He could not believe that he hadn't immediately recognized it. The black blaze resembled a dragon rearing up.

"That's right," the old man said, nodding his head. "Until I saw her, I had been certain that her race had died out. You can't imagine the trouble I went to in finding her."

"She's a dragon fighter's horse," the boy gasped.

"Well, let's just say for now that she's a knight's horse. And a fine horse she is. She's courageous. You'll never see the day that anything spooks her in battle." He paused for a moment before continuing. "Not even a dragon. It's in her blood. As it is in yours, from all the signs of it. I'd say the two of you are well matched."

"Well, then," said Garth promptly, "are we finished?"

"Not quite," the old wizard said with a warm smile barely hidden beneath his beard. "This young man deserves a name."

Straw was startled when Aga said this. He only ever knew himself referred to as 'Boy,' and later in the compound as 'Straw.' Star had never even taken up his nickname, satisfied with calling him 'boy.' Even Galifalia had never called him anything different. All these years, he had not thought of himself as anyone else.

"It's time," Aga began, "for you to grow up and take on a man's task and a man's name, even if you are still only a pup with fuzz on your chin."

Aga came and stood directly in front of him. His eyes glistened. "All these years, you've not known your true name. It has been kept hidden and safe, just as you have been kept hidden and safe. It is time to return it to you. Hand me your sword and kneel."

The boy still had the sword in his hand, and he carefully turned it, offering it to Aga by the pommel. The old wizard took it and placed the blade on the boy's shoulder.

"I hereby dub thee Knight, Dragon Keeper and Dragon Tamer. Knight in the ancient Order of the Dragon, descendant from the line of Soran the Great. Be ye known, from this day forward, before God and man, as Knight Michael." He pronounced it My-kah-el. A thrill ran through the young knight's whole body when he heard his name spoken, his hair standing on end.

"Thou shalt wander over the face of the earth, calling no place thy home. Thou shalt bring goodness and aid wherever thou goest. Thou shalt be an enemy to greed, hate, cruelty and deceit. Thou shalt be a friend to the needy, the poor, the oppressed and the downtrodden. Bring hope and courage to the hearts of those you help. Serve in rightful causes and never for thine own profit. Good fortune shall follow thee. A stalwart shield arm, a skilled sword arm and a clever, courageous horse are thy companions."

So speaking, he handed the young knight his sword.

"Rise, Knight Michael," Aga spoke seriously. "We have done for you all that we can. You've had the best training a knight can wish for. We've horsed you, clothed you and given you a name. The rest is left up to what you do with it."

Knight Michael's head was still swimming. It had all happened so quickly. "What do I do now?" he asked innocently.

"You ride off and seek adventure. You are dragon-trained. Any adversary you meet will always be less skilled, less intelligent and remarkably smaller than a dragon. I seriously doubt you will ever know fear in battle. Go and seek adventure."

Seek adventure? It all sounded so vague. "But where will I find adventure?"

Aga laughed deeply and filled the air with his merriment. "I doubt that you will actually have to."

"What does that mean?" Michael asked, bewildered and innocent in the ways of the world.

Garth answered for him. "What he means is that adventure will come looking for you. The world is filled with fellows like Flek who prey on those who are weaker. As much as you wanted to avoid it, Flek also provided you with some training. Now that you know what Flek is like, you'll have no problem finding others like him."

"Never turn down a sincere call for help. You need only to make yourself seen, and you will be kept busier than..." the wizard paused, choosing his words, "busier than a dragon's personal scrub boy." All three laughed at this.

Thus Michael's new life began. Garth helped him change back into his leathers and stow his gear behind his saddle on the white mare. Once he had hoisted himself into the saddle, Aga handed him a small leather bag. When he took it, Michael realized there were coins inside. "That's to tide you over for the time being."

The young knight stared for a moment at the gate. On the other side lay his old life, everything he had known and loved.

"If only I could..." he stopped himself from asking again. Still, the pain was great and he could not prevent the feelings pulling at his heart.

As if the old wizard knew what was troubling him, Aga said, "It's not what you think. Pray that you never meet him again. One day you might understand why I say this."

"But he was all I had. He was for me what family is to others."

"Consider how lucky you've been. Galifalia saw you from babe to boyhood. Star took you from boy to nearly man. They both bestowed upon you gifts of spirit, courage and goodness. Go now and use those gifts. Go on your way and pray that you never see another dragon in your life."

"But why?"

"Because if you do, you will have to fight it. That's really what you've been trained for. In the meantime, help those who need a strong arm to defend themselves against injustice." Aga suddenly whistled shrilly. The mare's ears went straight up, and, reeling on her hind legs, she turned towards the open fields. Aga gave her a hard slap on her hindquarters and she bolted away.

"Ride, boy!" the wizard cried after him. "Ride to the corners of the earth!" And then he muttered under his breath as the mare streaked off, carrying the newly-dubbed knight on her back. "And may all your skills serve you well should you ever meet a dragon again. It will likely be the last battle you ever fight."

Chapter Twenty-One

The Beginning of Adventure

Knight Michael discovered very soon that his mare had remarkable stamina. He rode without stopping the rest of that day until nightfall prevented their continuing any further. While Storm grazed on the grass of the fields, Michael found in his pack a sack of dried rations that would keep on the road and nourish him. He discovered a bedroll as well and realized that the two men had sent him off with everything he would need for his first days. But where was he going?

He wanted some distance between himself and the compound. He would ride until adventure found him, just as he was promised. He liked the sound of that, and on his first night fell peacefully asleep beneath a canopy of stars.

The next morning, after a spare but satisfying breakfast, he resumed his journey. He had never traveled before, never needed to, and now he was fascinated by the prospect of seeing lands and people he did not know. His journey alternated between cultivated fields and wild lands blanketed with dark, forbidding forests. He realized how difficult it would be to find his way through a trackless forest and so he skirted around them.

On his second day, whenever he came near a village, he gave it a wide berth. He was not ready to encounter people who would stare at this wandering knight and ask uncomfortable questions. He was not quite sure who he was yet. How could he explain it to others?

In the open, uncultivated land he occasionally encountered a shepherd standing at the edge of his flock of grazing sheep. The knight would wave and receive a nod in return, the shepherd's eyes following him as he rode past. Near villages, at the edges of the forest, he would often encounter a young boy with a stick playing among the bushes, tending a small herd of goats that scrambled over roots and stood up on their hind legs to snag low hanging leaves off the branches. These boys were much more expressive than the silent shepherds, often running after his horse, waving their arms in the air and shouting at him some combination of greeting and boyish challenge.

Storm was tireless. On she rode, as far and as long as her mount wished. The knight realized that he needed rest more often than she did. No matter. There was nowhere to hurry to, no one expecting him, only adventure waiting to find him.

By the third day, he was beginning to hunger for conversation. He was not used to going this long without having someone to share his thoughts with. Star had loved to talk and they often spent the whole afternoon in conversation. Storm was a remarkable horse, but speech failed her. The young knight had spoken directly to her on several occasions, but she responded with nothing more than perking her ears, a toss of the head or the stomp of a hoof. As eager as he was for spoken companionship, he still was not ready to enter a town, or even brave a village. Finally, he decided that he would try spending an evening with a shepherd.

It turned into everything he did not want. The glow of the sun had diminished and darkness would soon dominate the land. He saw a flock in a tight knot on a meadow, the shepherd to one side busying himself with a small fire. Michael rode over and asked if he could share the fire and companionship.

At first, he was delighted that the shepherd welcomed him. He was ready to share his food, but the shepherd made it clear that his own provisions were plentiful, more than enough for both of them.

They shared a small feast of cheese and olives. There was even some bread, although it was on the hard side.

All went well until the shepherd began to ask questions. Where was he from? Where was he going? Whom did he serve? What adventures had he seen? All very innocent questions, but the young knight was not ready for them. He could not divulge where he was coming from, he had no idea where he was going, he served the call of the road and he had not yet had any adventures. He was very embarrassed, and feigning exhaustion, he turned in early to avoid being plied with any more questions for which he had no answers.

The next morning he rose early, and although the shepherd offered to break bread with him again, he made his excuses and rode off. The shepherd watched him with a look of immense curiosity, perhaps mixed with some suspicion. Young Michael realized that he had a few things to figure out before he could spend time with others. For the time being, he would have to content himself with Storm as his sole companion.

Adventure did finally catch up with him on the afternoon of the fifth day. In spite of his self-imposed isolation, Michael was enjoying his new life, his freedom, the open road, a swift horse and a promising future full of interesting encounters. He was inventing a few fanciful adventures in preparation for the next time that someone would ask him. He was not paying enough attention, though, to his surroundings.

He had once again left cultivated fields behind. The land was rocky, bushy with sparse grasses. Good enough to graze goats, perhaps, but not the kind of land to grow crops or raise good cattle on, and even sheep might remain lean. He was passing along the edge of another forest which looked as dark and tangled as all the others.

Suddenly his attention was caught by a young woman, hardly more than a girl, waving frantically at him from up ahead. As he rode closer, he could hear bits and pieces of what she was yelling.

"...quick...my father...help!"

When he reached her and pulled Storm to a stop, she grabbed hold of the reins. She appeared out of breath and upset. "Please help," she panted. "My father. Brigands have my father. Stolen away. You must help."

She was in great distress. He hardly noticed her clothes, which might have given him a clue, had he been attentive. All he could think was that adventure had finally found him, and he was ready to do whatever was needed.

"Where?" he asked earnestly. "Where will I find them? I'll help. I'll get him back for you. Just tell me where."

"In there," she screeched, pointing into the forest. "Quick!" She pointed to a gap in the trees. He spurred Storm on and galloped right into that opening.

He never saw the rope slung between the branches of two trees and then pulled tight. It had been cunningly placed among the first shadows cast from the towering limbs where his eyes had not yet adjusted from the brightness of the sun-drenched fields. He hit it at a gallop and it swept him right off Storm's back. He slammed against the ground, and that was the last thing he remembered.

The first thing he perceived again was voices. The memory of what had happened came flooding back to him. He had enough sense to keep his eyes closed and not move, hoping to hear what they were saying and maybe pick up some clue as to what he should do next.

"I don't know why you don't just give him the big smile," someone was saying. It was a man's voice, and it was whiny. "It's enough we have his horse and gear. He's only trouble now."

"You never know about these things," another answered. It was also a man's voice, stronger, more grounded, maybe the leader. "It won't hurt to ask a few questions. I say we take him with us to the others. Maybe he can be ransomed. If not, he can always smile later." What was all this talk about smiling?

"It's a fine piece of horse flesh," a woman's voice said. She sounded closer. "'Twould be a pity just to eat it. Maybe we could sell it somewhere. The money would be nice to have."

"In truth," said the whiny voice. "And the moment the likes of us show up with a horse like this, we'd be clapped in irons for horse theft. I say we eat it and be done."

"There'll be no eating of the horse." It was the other man's voice again. "At least, for now. It's much more than the four of us can manage. We'll just take it with us. It can walk, you know. And carry things. No more decisions now until he wakes and we see if he was alone or not."

"We can figure that out well enough by watching the pathways," the other man grumbled.

Making small movements, Michael discovered two useful things. The first was that he did not seem to have broken any bones in his fall, even though it had stunned him. The second was that his hands were tied together. Fortunately, he thought, they were tied in front of him, rather than behind his back. That gave him some mobility. He did not know about his feet, though. He had not tried moving them yet.

"I think he's kinda cute," said another voice, this one very nearby. He was certain it was the young woman who had lured him into the trap. How stupid he'd been. If he had taken a moment to wonder what she was doing out here in the wilderness, he would have proceeded with more caution. He suspected that she was now watching him closely.

"He's not very big, for a knight." It was the other woman's voice again, still nearby. "And he seems young. Not much older than you."

"Aw," exclaimed the young woman with joy. "Can I marry him, then? Please, Mum. I think he's really cute." She sounded close enough to be leaning over him. He could now smell the reek of garlic in her breath. He was certain she was watching him when she said, "And I also think he's awake."

He felt a sudden sharp dig in his ribs, and he involuntarily jumped and grunted. His eyes also flew open.

"He's awake," she announced. Her broad smile grinned down at him. "Not nice," she continued, speaking now to him, leaning over from above, her stringy hair hanging down and tickling his cheeks. "Not nice to listen in while other peoples are talking." She wagged her finger in his face. "Not nice at all. And I thought you was a gentleman."

"You see," said the whiny voice, "he's already causing trouble." Michael took a look at him. He was a thin fellow with a scraggly beard and a tangled mop of curly hair on his head.

"What's your name?" the young woman who was leaning over him asked. She had a pretty face, although her hair was rather a mess, and she was dressed in an unusual fashion. She wore a man's doublet over her blouse and her skirt was patched over in many places. How could he have missed so many signs of trouble? When he had still lived on the streets, he had seen plenty of her kind.

He was about to answer her question and then caught himself. He had almost responded, Straw. He cleared his voice and steadied himself before replying, "Michael. What's your name?"

"Time for introductions, is it?" she said with a naughty smile. "My name is Maisy," and she curtsied.

"Maisy, you lied to me," he said.

"I did?" She acted astonished. "What did I lie to you?"

"You told me that brigands had your father."

"I did?" she asked, scratching her head and crinkling her nose. "I must have got that backwards, I must. What I meant to say is that my father *is* a brigand. I never could get it straight, you know. Is, had, had, is. Sorry." She looked down at him and shrugged her shoulders, as if she couldn't help herself. "I'm not so bright, you know." And at this the others laughed.

"For the last time," said the man with the scraggly beard, "I say we give him the smiley and eat the horse."

"Well, I duly note your say, if it makes you any happier," a second man said, taking him to the side. He was a powerful looking fellow, hair just beginning to gray. The two began a heated argument that Michael was not interested in following until he had some answers. He turned his attention to Maisy.

"Maisy, tell me something."

"What is it, sweets?" she asked with a coquettish wink.

"What's the smiley? What is he talking about?"

"Aw," she said and made a face as if she had eaten something nasty tasting. "You don't want to know about that."

"Tell me what it means," he persisted.

The other woman Maisy had addressed before as 'Mum' looked at Michael with a serious face and made a gesture with her extended thumb across her throat. "No matter what you think about it, you can't help but smilin'," she added with a blank expression. Now he knew. They were debating when they were going to slit his throat.

He had to find a way to escape, but he had no clue how to go about doing it. With his sword, he could take on the two men, but his hands were tied. He felt at his waist for his knife, but the sheath was empty.

"Now, now," Maisy said patting him on the head. "You don't think we'd've left you with anything you could hurt yourself with, do you? You just rest there quietly, my sweets. You've had a bad fall."

She turned her attention to the older woman who had gone to crouch at a pot over the fire. "Now, Mum, why can't I marry him? If only for awhile."

The young knight took this chance to get his bearings. He first looked for Storm, but could not see her from where he lay. He was certain she was nearby. His eyes scanned their camp quickly. It was a disorganized mess of gear strewn here and there. If they were that sloppy, then maybe they were careless with his things as well. Then he saw what he was looking for. His sword was propped up against a tree not more than ten feet away. There was the key to his escape. He just had to get to it before they got to him. As he lay there, he worked the rope that tied his hands together, to give them as much movement as possible. What he needed was a diversion. How was he to create it, though? He could not wait until they broke camp and took him to the others they had mentioned. He had to act now.

The diversion he was looking for came a moment later. From behind him he heard some grunting, and then the whiny voice called out angrily. "Ow! The beast bit me! Man-eater!"

The ground thudded twice, the man cursed, and then Michael heard Storm's shrill cry. There was a thud again, and he realized that Storm was rearing up. The man cursed again and called for help. That's when Michael whistled and pandemonium broke loose.

There was another cry of pain, and Storm came galloping into the camp, neighing loudly and shaking her head. Her eyes flashed furiously. The older man ran over to catch her reins and she reared up, nearly hitting him with her hooves. The two women who had been by the pot scattered as it toppled from the fire and spilled half its contents.

Michael was up in an instant and leapt for his sword. Although his hands were bound together, he was able to get both of them around the pommel. It was awkward, and two-hand swinging did not give him the same reach as one-handed, but it would do.

The older man was now caught between a raging Storm and a furious knight. It took him but a moment to assess his situation, and he ran for the trees, diving between the bushes. The women had already disappeared. Michael looked around for the other man, but he had obviously seen the way of things and made his escape. The young knight cautiously surveyed the trees in the direction the man had fled, expecting a counterattack. None came.

The moment they were alone, Storm grew quiet. She came over and sniffed at her master's neck and then gently nudged his shoulder.

“Thank you, girl,” he said grinning. “You’ve saved us both. Keep watch now, while I cut this rope.”

Confident that Storm would warn him if they tried to return, he sat down on the exposed root at the base of a tree. He wedged his sword between his legs and proceeded to cut his bonds. As Aga had warned him, the edge of the blade was indeed quite sharp. Once free, sword in hand, he walked around the camp. It was a pitiful collection of odds and ends, probably pilfered from the edges of villages.

He wondered if he would have to give up finding his knife when he came to the spilled pot, and there it was stuck in the plank the women had been using to cut up roots. The stew they had prepared suddenly smelled good. There was still a portion of it left in the pot. He tasted it with the spoon that they had used for stirring. He took the pot and settled with his back against a tree and ate his fill.

“Aw, he’s eating our dinner, he is,” he heard Maisy’s muffled outrage coming from the cover of the bushes. So they were not far away and they were watching him. He had to stay on guard for any further treachery. At least he would come away from his first adventure with a full stomach. And his life.

Storm had all of his gear still strapped behind the saddle. Maybe that’s how all the commotion had begun, when one of the men had wanted to remove his things and go through them. The young knight looked around to see if there was anything from their camp he needed. He took their axe in hand and mounted Storm. He picked his way back through the trees towards the edge of the forest.

On his way out, he came to the rope that had snagged him. It was still tied between two trees. A good length of rope could come in handy. Using the axe, he cut it free and left the axe embedded in the branch. He looped the rope and added it to his pack. He continued to ride away from his first adventure and had just left the line of trees when he heard Maisy’s voice calling to him, “Don’t go, young fellow. I still want to marry you!”

He smiled at the persistence of her sentiment and looked in the direction of her voice. What he saw caused him to rein Storm in and freeze. Standing in a break between trees amid waist high bushes, Maisy was next to the man with the scraggly beard. He held a drawn bow, the arrow pointed at the knight.

"Come on back," she called with a saucy smile. "It's too soon to go. I promise, no one's going to hurt you. Anyway, I think you're too cute to hurt."

The knight just sat on his horse and stared back. He rued how mistaken and over-confident he had been. His adventure had not yet ended, nor was his life secure. He panicked for a brief moment at the thought of becoming their prisoner again. Then Star came vividly to mind. The dragon had always encouraged him, "The courageous act is the one least expected. When you're at a loss what to do, be courageous and outrageous. The combination is nearly undefeatable."

With this in mind, he made a decision. Little did he realize in the moment how often he would have to do this over and over again in the years to come.

"You'd best be a sure shot," he called out.There was a moment's hesitation, but then the man called back, "Why's that?"

"Because unless you kill me outright with your first arrow, you'll never get another one strung. I'll slaughter the lot of you. Which is better than you deserve."

He was betting that this man was no more than a common thief, skilled enough to hit his target only if it were large enough, but not able to place his shot. To make his threat believable, Michael drew his sword. This was no bluff. If shot, he thoroughly intended to attack. He was far enough away to dodge the arrow, even though it might wound him. That would be better than the certain death if he became their prisoner again. He was willing to gamble that if he spurred Storm just at the moment the arrow was released, he could avoid injury altogether. He subtly raised his feet, heels aimed at Storm's sides. He noticed Storm's ears pulled back, listening for his softest murmur.

The man with the bow pulled the taut string further back as if preparing to let it fly when the knight heard someone from the cover of the trees hiss, "Mack, don't be such a fool!"

There was a tense moment, and then the man loosened the arrow and put the bow down. He and the girl slipped in between the trees and Michael was once again alone.

He kept his sword in his hand and rode on. He listened intensely for the twang of the bow, for the ambush that never came. It was not long before he was out of bowshot.

His new life opened up before him like the beckoning road. His first adventure. Although he came away with nothing worse than a sore back and a bump on his head from the fall, he had learned a lot about what he might encounter on his way. Expect the unexpected. Be wary of deceit and treachery. His journey had only just begun. Where would it lead him next? Would he ever meet Star again?

He reined Storm in and looked off towards the horizon where the sun had set, back in the direction from which he had come. A single star hovered in the sky, sparkling fiercely in the sun's afterglow. He gazed at its beauty and his thoughts settled on his beloved Star. He heaved a deep sigh.

Storm grew impatient, snorted and shook her head. It was as if she could read his heart. She seemed to be saying, *Enough mourning for the past and worrying about what might come. The one is gone and there's no way to tell about the other. Let's do our best right here where we are.*

Knight Michael leaned over and patted her neck and spoke softly into her ear. "My sweet stormy girl, I owe you my life. I have a feeling it won't be the last time. I'm with you here. Let's go meet whatever is waiting for us."

He no longer feared meeting with others. A story was forming in his head, a story that would satisfy curiosity until he had a truer one to tell. And besides, if anyone asked him about his adventures, he already had a pretty good yarn to spin. And there would be more. Of this he was now certain. He and Storm rode on.

That night he lay under his cover and gazed up at the starry heavens revealing their splendor to him, luminescent dust scattered on the broad tapestry of the night sky. He could not keep from thinking about Star. They had been separated so suddenly and the hurt was still new. "Will we ever see one another again?" he wondered to the stars above him. "Will I ever have the chance to gaze again upon your magnificent beauty? Hear the music of your voice? My beloved, Star, I will carry you with me always," he promised. "All that I am I owe to you."

Nearby, Storm whickered. Knight Michael could sleep peacefully this night. Though heavy with pain and loss, his heart rejoiced at the coming day, the coming adventures. He rejoiced for the gift of the life that had been given him.

"Ah, Star," he whispered into the night. "We be of one heart, thou and I. We be of one heart."

Thus ends Book One of

The Star Trilogy

About the Author

Raised in Los Angeles, Donald Samson spent the first twelve years of his adult life respectively in a Greek fishing village, a small German border town and finally in the mountains of Switzerland, healing from a mega-urban childhood.

Upon returning to the States, he took up the art of teaching children. He was a Waldorf class teacher for nineteen years. His teaching experience spans grades 1–12. He lives with his family along the Front Range of the Rocky Mountains.

Mr. Samson has written the concluding books of the *Star Trilogy*: *The Dragon of Two Hearts* and *The Dragon, the Blade and the Thread.* In addition, he has written a classroom reader for fifth graders, *At the Hot Gates: An Account of the Battle of Thermopylae.* His published works include two translations of Jakob Streit's biblical stories, *Journey to the Promised Land* and *We Will Build a Temple,* and he was a contributing author to *Gazing into the Eyes of the Future, the Enactment of Saint Nicholas in the Waldorf School.* All these titles are available from AWSNA Publications.

Read the acclaimed concluding books of
The Star Trilogy.

The Dragon of Two Hearts and
The Dragon, the Blade
and the Thread
are available from:

AWSNA Publications
publications@awsna.org
518-634-2222

or on order from your favorite bookseller.

For more information on these books
as well as upcoming titles, visit

www.thedragonboy.com

The Star Trilogy

by Donald Samson

The Dragon Boy

Gold Medal:
Moonbeam Children's Book
Awards: Best First Book

Mom's Choice Award for
Fantasy, Myth and Legend

Finalist: Young Adult Fiction
Eric Hoffer Book Award

The Dragon of Two Hearts

Silver Medal:
Moonbeam Children's Book
Awards for Young Adult Fantasy

Mom's Choice Award for
Fantasy, Myth and Legend

The Dragon, the Blade and the Thread

Bronze Medal:
Moonbeam Children's Book
Awards for Young Adult Fantasy

Finalist: Ben Franklin Award for
Young Readers

Finalist: Colorado Book Award
for Young Adult Literature

Mom's Choice Award for
Fantasy, Myth and Legend